Fifteenth Summer

ALSO BY MICHELLE DALTON

Sixteenth Summer

Fifteenth Summer

MICHELLE DALTON

Simon Pulse

New York London Toronto Sydney New Delhi

SIMON PULSE

An imprint of Simon & Schuster Children's Publishing Division
1230 Avenue of the Americas, New York, NY 10020
First Simon Pulse edition May 2013
Copyright © 2013 by Simon & Schuster, Inc.
All rights reserved, including the right of reproduction
in whole or in part in any form.
SIMON PULSE and colophon are registered trademarks of
Simon & Schuster, Inc.
For information about special discounts for bulk purchases,
please contact Simon & Schuster Special Sales at
1-866-506-1949 or business@simonandschuster.com.
The Simon & Schuster Speakers Bureau can bring authors to your live
event. For more information or to book an event, contact the
Simon & Schuster Speakers Bureau at 1-866-248-3049 or visit
our website at www.simonspeakers.com.
The text of this book was set in Berling.
Manufactured in the United States of America
2 4 6 8 10 9 7 5 3 1
Library of Congress Cataloging-in-Publication Data
Dalton, Michelle.
Fifteenth summer / by Michelle Dalton. — 1st Simon Pulse ed.
p. cm.
Summary: Fifteen-year-old Chelsea and her family are spending the summer
at a cottage on the shore of Lake Michigan, where Chelsea meets and falls for
Josh—the cute and shy employee at the new bookstore in town.
[1. Dating (Social customs)—Fiction. 2. Sisters—Fiction. 3. Books and
reading—Fiction. 4. Family life—Fiction. 5. Michigan—Fiction.] I. Title.
PZ7.D16942Fif 2013   [Fic]—dc23   2012029540
ISBN 978-1-4424-7267-9 (hc)
ISBN 978-1-4424-7266-2 (pbk)
ISBN 978-1-4424-7268-6 (eBook)

For Paul, Mira, and Tali, for all seasons

With special thanks to Elizabeth Lenhard

June

When you're stuck in the backseat of your parents' car—on hour twenty-five of the drive from Los Angeles to Bluepointe, Michigan—the last thing you're thinking about is love.

But somehow that's what my two sisters were discussing. They chatted over my head as if I was no more than an armrest between them.

Actually, it's a stretch to say they were talking about *love*. They were really talking about boys. The boys of Bluepointe. Two of them in particular.

"Liam," Hannah breathed. She propped her feet on the hump in the middle of the backseat, even though that was clearly *my* personal space. "That was my guy's name, remember? We saw him at the beach at least four times, and the last two, he definitely noticed me. Now, which one was yours?"

"You know," Abbie said impatiently. She did most things impatiently. "The guy who worked at the market. That boy could *shelve*."

I snorted while Hannah said, "Well, did you ever talk to him? Was he interested? What was his name?"

Hannah always liked to have all her facts straight.

"John," Abbie answered, nodding firmly as she stared out the car window. Then she frowned and clicked one of her short,

unpainted fingernails against her front teeth. "Or . . . James? It
was definitely John or James or . . . Jason? Ugh, I can't remember."

"If you were a boy," my dad chimed from the front seat,
where he had the car on cruise control at exactly sixty-five miles
per hour, "we were going to name you Horatio. No one *ever* for-
gets the name Horatio."

My dad thinks he's hilarious. And because he works from
home, doing other people's taxes, he's around a *lot* to subject us
to all his one-liners. My mom is the only one who doesn't roll her
eyes at every joke. She even laughs at some of them. Dad always
says that's why they're still married. That and the fact that my
mom is super-practical with money, which is very romantic to an
accountant. All it meant to me was that I had to babysit to earn
every paltry dollar of my spending money.

I sighed and glanced at the novel in my lap. That book—the
latest dystopian bestseller—was torturing me. I was dying to read
it, but every time I did, I got carsick. I was still feeling a little
green after reading two irresistible pages (two words: "prison
break") twenty minutes earlier.

Texting with my best friend, Emma, made me feel slightly
less queasy.

*Ugh. Today is the shortest drive of our trip but it's the most soul-
killing. I feel like it will NEVER. END. And why do I always get the
middle seat?*

BECAUSE YOU'RE THE YOUNGEST. BE GLAD THEY DIDN'T PUT YOU IN
THE TRUNK.

Don't gloat cuz you're an only child.

. . .

Are you texting with Ethan right now?!?

HOW'D YOU KNOW?

I can tell your palms are sweaty. Plus there are the long delays.

HAR-HAR. YOU KNOW BALLERINAS DON'T SWEAT.

Uh-huh. Even when they're sending mash notes to their boyfriends?

. . .

Hello?

GOT TO GO TO CLASS. LUV U! AND ETHAN SAYS HI. ;-)

Ethan was Emma's boyfriend of two weeks. And class was at "the Intensive," which is this hard-core, fast-track-to-prima-ballerina summer program at the LA Ballet. All spring Emma had talked about nothing else. She'd angsted about her floppy fouettés and worried that she'd be too tall for the boys to partner. She'd wondered if the *mesdames* would be harsh and beautiful, like the ballet teachers on *Fame*, and she'd considered cutting off all her hair to make herself stand out.

But then Ethan Mack asked Emma to fast dance at our spring semiformal, and everything changed.

When it happened, I was already out on the dance floor (which was just our school gym floor covered with a puckery layer of black vinyl) with Dave Sugarman.

Dave was nice enough. He had a round, smooth face and one of those nondescript bodies that always seemed to be hidden inside clothes a size or two too big. He was in a couple of honors classes with me, so he was smart. I guessed. He never really spoke much in class.

He was, I thought, a tennis player. Either that or he did track and field.

5

Dave was perfectly nice.

But here's what Dave wasn't. He wasn't Mr. Darcy. Or Peeta Mellark. He wasn't even Michael Moscovitz.

And *they* were the boys I was searching for.

I don't mean I wanted an actual revolutionary hero or a guy with an English accent and ascot. (Okay, I wouldn't turn down the English accent.)

I didn't want the perfect boy either. We all know Mr. Darcy could be a total grump.

What I wanted was to *feel* like Lizzy and Katniss and Mia felt. And not because my boy was tall and broad-shouldered and blue-eyed. That wasn't how I pictured him. He wouldn't be everybody else's version of gorgeous. He would have a funny extra bounce in his walk or a cowlick in his hair. He would be super-shy. Or he'd have a too-loud laugh.

He would make me swoon for reasons that were mine alone. I just didn't know what those reasons were yet.

Dave Sugarman?

There was no swoon there. The most I could manage for him was an uncomfortable smile while we raised our arms over our heads and swished our hips around, throwing in the occasional clap or semi-grindy deep knee bend. When I glanced at the other couples nearby, I took comfort in the fact that they almost all looked as awkward and goofy as I felt.

There was one exception, though. Emma and Ethan. They seemed to fit together as neatly as their names.

Ethan was definitely tall enough to partner Emma. He put his hands on her waist and swung her around in graceful circles.

He held her hand over her head, and she improvised a triple pirouette before landing lightly on his chest. She turned and leaned back against him, and they shimmied from side to side as if they'd rehearsed it.

Do you even have to ask if their dance ended in a dip?

After the song ended, Dave gave me a little pat on the arm, then hustled back to his friends, who were pelting each other with M&M's.

But Ethan left the dance floor with Emma.

They headed directly outside, where, according to Emma, they leaned against the school and kissed for a full twenty minutes without coming up for air. That twenty minutes was all she needed to fall deeply, *deeply* in love.

Dancers are like that. One good dip, and they are *yours*.

After that, Emma stopped obsessing about the Intensive and started obsessing about her new boyfriend.

"Kissing Ethan," she told me one night after a long make-out session on Ethan's patio, "it's like ballet. My head disappears and I'm just a body."

"Wow," I said. I couldn't relate at all. Most of the time I felt like I was just the opposite—no body, all head.

"I mean, he kisses me and I just *melt*," Emma went on. "It's like our bodies *fuse*."

"Whoa," I said this time.

"Oh my God, not like *that*," Emma said, reading my mind. "I'm just saying there's something about being mouth to mouth with someone for forty minutes . . ."

"You beat your record," I muttered.

"Yeah," Emma giggled. She hadn't caught the tiny touch of weariness in my voice. "Anyway, it's almost like you're touching each other's souls."

"Really?" I said. "Your souls? *Really?*"

"Really," she said with the utmost confidence.

I knew nothing of this soul-touching kind of kiss. The few kisses I'd had had been brief. And awkward. And, to tell the truth, kind of gross. I'd clearly been doing it wrong.

I was happy for Emma. But it felt weird to watch her join this club that I was *so* not a member of.

Before you became a member of this been-in-love club, life was murky, mysterious, and, most of all, small.

Post-love, I imagined, your world expanded with all the things you suddenly knew. You knew what it felt like to see a boy's name on your caller ID and suddenly feel like you were floating. You knew a boy's dreams and fears and memories. You knew what it was like to open the front door and feel a burst of elation because your boy was standing there.

You'd kissed that boy and felt like you were touching his soul.

I didn't know if Abbie had ever felt that way. She had a string of two-month relationships behind her. Almost every time, she'd been the one to break things off when the boy had gotten too attached.

But Hannah had definitely been there. She'd dated an older boy, Elias, for a year. Then he'd enrolled at UC Berkeley and had broken up with her to "focus on studying." Which Hannah had sort of understood, being a studious type herself. It was when Elias immediately hooked up with a girl from his dorm that he'd broken her heart.

She seemed to be completely recovered now, though.

"When's that sailboat race they have every year?" she was asking Abbie. She grabbed her sleek, white smart phone out of her bag. She'd gotten it for her eighteenth birthday in March. Abbie and I were bitterly jealous of it.

"It's probably sometime next week, right?" Hannah muttered, tapping away at the phone screen. "I'm sure we'll see them there. . . ."

"Hannah, honey," my mom said a little too brightly, "don't completely fill up your schedule. You know we want to spend some quality time with you this summer. I know you. Once you start classes in the fall, you'll work so hard, we'll never hear from you!"

"I know, Mom," Hannah said with the tiniest of sighs.

"I think my guy is a runner," Abbie said. "I could tell by his legs. So maybe he'll just *happen* to go running on the beach while *I* just happen to do my two miles in the lake, and one thing'll lead to another—"

"Abbie," I broke in, "do you really think hauling yourself out of Lake Michigan after swimming two miles is the best way to meet a boy? Who knows what you'll look like. You could have dune grass or seagull feathers in your hair. Yuck."

"Plus, there's the issue of your Speedo," Hannah pointed out. Like all competitive swimmers, Abbie snapped herself into a high-necked, long-legged black bodysuit for her distance swims. It made her look like a slick-skinned seal. A cute little bikini it was not.

Abbie put on her cocky Supergirl face.

"You know I look hot in my Speedo," she said.

Hannah and I glanced at each other, silently agreeing. Abbie's arms and legs were long and lean. She had a perma-tan that made her limbs almost glow. Her waist had been whittled down by eight million strokes of the Australian crawl. And while pool chlorine turned some swimmers' hair into yellow straw, Abbie's long, straight hair was dark brown and silky.

Clearly just the thought of swimming made Abbie antsy. She flung her perfect legs over mine and planted her feet in Hannah's lap.

"Hey!" Hannah and I protested together.

"I can't help it. I've gotta stretch. I'm dying in here!" Abbie groaned. She flopped her arm into the front seat and tapped my dad on the shoulder. "You guys, remind me why we got rid of the minivan again?"

"Other than the fact that it was a giant, ugly egg, you mean?" I asked. I had a dream of someday having a vintage car with giant tail fins, a pastel paint job, and wide, white leather seats.

Mom twisted in her seat to look at us with wistful eyes that she quickly whitewashed with one of her forcefully perky smiles.

"Abbie and Hannah, you're both driving now, and Chelsea will be next year too," she said, her voice sounding tinny and cheerful. "You girls don't need us to carpool you anymore. It was time for a grown-up car."

"Plus, this little guy gets fifty-one miles to the gallon," Dad said, giving the putty-colored dashboard a pat.

"'Little' is the operative word," I grumbled. "There's barely room for us, not to mention certain essential items."

"Are you still pouting that you couldn't bring that ridiculous box of books?" Abbie sighed.

"*No,*" I said defensively.

By which, of course, I meant *yes.* Ever since my e-reader had been tragically destroyed, I'd had to revert to paper books. I'd spent *weeks* collecting enough of them to last me through the long Bluepointe summer, but at the last minute my mom had nixed my entire stash.

"We just don't have room in the car," she'd said as we were packing up. "Pick a few to throw into your backpack."

"A few? A *few* won't get me through Colorado," I'd complained.

"Well, maybe next time you try to prop your e-reader on the soap dish while you're showering," Mom had responded, "you'll think twice about it."

Which had caused Abbie to laugh so hard, she'd dropped a suitcase on her foot.

Hannah had been slightly more sympathetic. Probably because *she* got to bring all her books with her. She was starting her freshman year at the University of Chicago in September and had given herself a huge stack of summer reading to prepare.

Even now, as she gazed out the car window, Hannah was being scholarly.

"Dad, don't forget," she warned, "we've got to get off at exit forty-eight if we're going to the Ojibwa history museum."

"Ooh, arrowheads and pottery bowls," Abbie said. "Thrilling."

"Well, if you know how to look at them," Hannah said haughtily, "they are."

Now it was Abbie and I who sent each other a silent message in a glance: *Our sister is a super-nerd.* She'd already mapped out her future of a BA in biology and anthropology, followed by an MD-PhD. Then she was going to get the CDC to send her to some third world country where she'd cure malaria. Simple, right?

It didn't seem fair that, in addition to being ridiculously smart, Hannah was just as pretty as Abbie. She had the same coloring and same long willowy limbs, though her skin was less tan, her figure softer, and her shiny hair chopped into a chin-length bob.

Whenever anybody saw the three of us together, they assumed I was some distant cousin, because my skin was freckled and anything but golden, and my hair was red. *Bright* red. It was also very thick and *very* curly, just like my grandmother's. Until I was born, she was the only member of the family who had this crazy hair. . . .

As I thought about this now, with endless, flat Iowa skimming by outside the car window, I inhaled sharply. Something had just occurred to me for the first time.

Now *I* was the only one in the family with this crazy red hair.

$\mathcal{M}$y grandmother had a stroke early one morning in January.

I'd just woken up and had been walking down the hall to the bathroom. My dad had blocked my way to tell me the news.

"Granly's in a coma, sweetie," he told me. His eyes were red-rimmed, and his face looked pale and clammy beneath his early-morning scruff. "Her friend, Mrs. Berke, went to the cottage after she didn't show up for their breakfast date. You know Granly never locks the door. Mrs. Berke found her still in bed and called 911."

There was no sit-down, no soften-the-blow discussion about the circle of life. Dad just blurted it out.

I stared at him, completely baffled.

Through the open door of my parents' bedroom, I could see my mom frantically packing a suitcase. Hannah was in the bathroom, issuing updates: "Mom, I'm packing your toothbrush and your moisturizer, okay?"

And Abbie was curled up in my parents' bed, hugging a pillow.

"But she's gonna be okay, right?" Abbie cried. "She'll wake up, *right?*"

So that was why my poor dad had broken the news to me so bluntly. He'd already had to tell Hannah and Abbie.

My brain refused to register what had happened. The only thing I remember thinking at that moment was that I really had to pee.

After that I remember thinking I should call Granly to clear up this ridiculous rumor.

"I'm *fine*, Chelsea," she'd say with a laugh. "You know Mrs. Berke. She's an alarmist. She's the one who always used to wake her husband up in the middle of the night because she was sure that he was dead. And of course, he never *was*. Well, except for that last time . . ."

Then she'd laugh wickedly, and I'd say, "Granly!" and pretend to be shocked.

But of course that phone call never happened.

After Mrs. Berke called the ambulance, Granly was taken from Bluepointe to South Bend, Indiana, which was the closest city with a big hospital. My mom took the first flight out and spent an entire day and night at Granly's bedside, holding her hand. Then Granly's doctor told my mom that Granly *wasn't* going to wake up. My mom had followed Granly's living will and allowed her to die, which she did "peacefully" two days later.

Through it all, none of it felt real to me. Granly's number was still in my phone. I still had e-mails from her in my inbox. She was in at least half of the Silver family portraits that hung on our dining room wall. And in all those photos she was surrounded by the still-living. The irony was, she looked more alive than any of us in the pictures. She always seemed to be laughing, while the rest of us merely smiled.

Depending on the year the photo was taken, Granly's hair was either closely cropped or sproinging out wildly, but it was always the exact same glinting-penny red as mine. That's because when I was little, Granly snipped a lock of my hair and took it to her hairdresser.

"*Nobody* could get the color right until you came along," she told me after one of her triumphant trips to her salon. "Now I have the same hair I had when *I* was a girl. You should save some of your hair for you to use when you're old and gray like me. Red hair is really difficult, Chels."

"It *is* difficult," I agreed with a sigh. Of course, I'd meant it in a different way. I hated that my hair was as bright as a stoplight. I cringed when people assumed I had a fiery temper or was as hilarious as an *I Love Lucy* episode. And I resented Granly's *Anne of Green Gables* law (that law being that a redhead in pink was an abomination and completely undeserving of gentleman suitors).

So I kept my hair long, the better to pull it back into a tight, low ponytail or bun. And if I fell for a coral shift dress or peppermint-colored circle skirt at one of my favorite vintage shops, I bought it—Anne Shirley be damned.

Before Granly died, my hair had felt simply like an inconvenience, like being short or needing glasses. But now it seemed like this precious legacy, one I wasn't worthy of.

Thinking about this in the backseat of the car made me feel short of breath—not from carsickness but from panic.

To put it as bluntly as my dad had that morning in January, Granly's death had freaked me out. I knew that she was gone. I knew she was never again going to call me just to tell me some random, funny three-minute story. I knew that we'd never again pick her and her enormous, bright green suitcase up at the airport.

I *knew* this, but I couldn't quite bring myself to *believe* it. It just didn't feel possible that someone could exist and then— poof—not.

That was why I hadn't wanted to look at Granly in her casket before her graveside funeral service.

And it was why I really didn't want to spend this summer in Bluepointe.

We'd never stayed at Granly's cottage without her. The cottage *was* Granly.

When I was little, Granly had also had an apartment in Chicago.

That's where my mother grew up, spending weekends and summers at the cottage.

Granly's apartment had been filled with masculine mementos of my grandfather, who'd died before I was born. There'd been a big leather desk chair and serious Persian rugs and a half-empty armoire that had smelled like wood and citrus, like men's aftershave.

But Granly had decorated the cottage all for herself, and eventually she'd decided to live there full-time. The walls were butter yellow and pale blue, and the floorboards were bleached and pickled, as if they'd been made of driftwood. Every wall was a gallery of picture frames. She'd hung the same family portraits that we had in our house in LA, plus oil paintings, nudes drawn with breathy wisps of red Conté crayon, arty black-and-white photos, and, in the breakfast room, paint-blobbed kindergarten artwork by Hannah, Abbie, and me. She'd picked the fanciest frames of all for our "masterpieces." It was a gesture that had seemed kind of goofy when Granly was alive. Now that she wasn't, I cried every time I thought about her framing those sloppy paintings.

But apparently I was the only one who felt that way. My parents spent most of the drive through Nebraska debating whether to keep or sell the cottage, as if the decision should be made purely on the basis of property taxes and the cost of a new roof.

And when we were deep in Iowa, Hannah gazed out at the wall of cornstalks that edged the highway, and laughed suddenly.

"Remember Granly's garden?" she said.

"You mean the petting zoo?" Abbie replied with a laugh of her own. "Oh my God, it was like Granly sent engraved invitations to every deer and rabbit within a five-mile radius. 'Come eat my heirloom radishes!' They loved it."

"Well, it was her own fault," my dad said from the front seat. "She refused to build a fence or use any of those deer deterrents."

"Coyote pee!" Abbie snorted. "I mean, can you imagine Granly out there in her Audrey Hepburn sunglasses, spraying the stepping stones with coyote pee?"

"She wouldn't admit it, but you know she loved watching those deer walk by her window every morning. They were so pretty," Hannah said. "She didn't even *like* radishes. She just liked the idea of pulling them up and putting them in a pretty basket."

My mom shook her head and laughed a little. "That was *so* Granly."

"Wait a minute," I said quietly. "I didn't know Granly hated radishes. How did I not know that?"

Hannah shrugged lightly, then closed her eyes and flopped her head back. Clearly the subject of Granly's radishes didn't make her the slightest bit sad.

Meanwhile I was biting my lip to keep myself from bursting into tears.

I knew this was what we were supposed to do. We were supposed to talk about Granly and "keep her memory alive." Mrs. Berke had said that to me after Granly's funeral, before giving me an uncomfortable, hairspray-scented hug.

I didn't want to forget Granly, but I didn't really want to think about her either. Every time I did, I felt claustrophobic, the same way I feel every time I get on an elevator.

It's a well-known fact in my family that I'm a mess on an

elevator. My ears fill with static. I clench my fists, take shallow breaths, and stare intently at the doors until they open. When they do, I'm always the first one off. Then I have to inhale deeply for a few seconds before resuming normal human functioning.

I wondered if this whole summer in Bluepointe would feel like that. Without Granly there, would I ever be able to take that deep breath and move on?

We spent most of Illinois in silence because we were so hot. And cranky. And completely sick of each other. Hannah had even consented to skipping the Ojibwa museum in favor of just getting to Bluepointe—and out of the car—as soon as possible.

Just when I started contemplating something seriously drastic—like borrowing my mother's needlepoint—we began to follow the long, lazy curve around Lake Michigan. We couldn't see the lake from the expressway, but we could *feel* it there, waiting to welcome us back.

I'd always preferred Lake Michigan to the ocean. I liked that it was a moody, murky green. I liked that it was so big that the moon mistook it for an ocean, which meant it had waves. But not loud, show-offy Pacific Ocean–type waves. Just steady, soothing, unassuming undulations that you could float in for hours without feeling oversalted and beaten. Lake Michigan was like the ocean's underdog.

As we drove through Gary, Indiana, which riddled with paper mills that spewed sulfurous plumes of smoke, I daydreamed about jumping into the lake. It would wash away the ickiness of too many fast-food french fries and too many gas station restrooms.

I pulled a pen and a little notepad out of my backpack. Lethargically I flipped past page after scribbled-on page until I found a blank one.

Gary, Indiana, I wrote in green ballpoint. *Our motto is, "The Smell of Rotten Eggs Is Character-Building!"*

What's it like to live with that smell in your pores, your tears, your breath? What's it like to smell a smell so much that you don't smell it anymore? But then you take a trip. You go to Chicago for the weekend. You go camping in the woods. You go to summer camp in Iowa, where the air smells like fresh corn. And you come back and realize that your hair, your clothes, the sheets on your bed, you, *smell like Gary, Indiana.*

I flipped my notebook closed and tossed it back into my pack. Then I breathed through my mouth until we reached Michigan.

Finally we pulled up in front of Granly's squat, shingled house on Sparrow Road and all limped out of the car. As my sisters groaned and stretched, I was stunned by the sudden wave of happiness that washed over me. The air smelled distinctly Bluepointe-ish—heavy and sweet with flowers, and pine needles, and the clean aftertaste of the two-blocks-away lake.

I tromped up the pea gravel drive to the screened-in front porch, where everything looked just the same as it always had. It was neatly furnished with deep-seated wicker rockers and a couch, lots of glass lanterns, and a big bowl full of shells from the lake.

My mom, already in to-do mode, bounced a big roller suitcase up the steps and joined me in the screened porch. She gave me a big grin before turning the knob of the front door.

It didn't turn.

It was locked.

Of course it was. My parents had probably locked the house up after the funeral. It made sense.

Mom shook her head and grinned at me again, but this time her smile was tight and her eyes looked a little shiny. She fumbled with her key chain for a moment before finding the right key.

Even though part of me didn't want to go into the cottage, I took a deep breath and went to stand next to my mom at the door. I pressed the side of my arm lightly against hers as she unlocked it.

Maybe it's mean to say, but it kind of helped me to realize that my mom might be in even more agony than I was at that moment, that she needed my support as much as I needed hers.

Mom opened the door, and I followed her in.

The air in the cottage felt still and stale, so my mom briskly started opening windows. I rolled her suitcase to the tiny bedroom my parents always used, then wandered back to the living room up front. I let my eyes skim over the framed watercolors of beach scenes and cozy cabins. I peered at the crowd of family photos on the mantel. I kicked off my flip-flops and padded across the nubbly braided rag rug and . . . continued to feel surprisingly okay!

Outside, Hannah was struggling to pull a big bag of shoes out of the back of the car, while Abbie lurched toward the house, dragging another suitcase behind her.

She spotted me through the open door and scowled.

"Why are *we* doing all the unpacking while you just stand there?" she said. "You're not allowed to crack one book until you've helped us unload."

I stomped to the screen door and said, "You're not the boss of me." Which made me feel about ten years old. But it was true! I couldn't *not* say it.

I also couldn't get away without helping, so I shuffled my feet back into my flip-flops and began hauling stuff from the car to the cottage.

I think we were all glad for the distracting bustle of unpacking. While Mom organized dry goods in the kitchen and Dad lined our beach shoes up on the screened porch, Abbie, Hannah, and I crammed into our room. Abbie and I were in the bunk beds, and Hannah had the twin bed near the window, with the slightly faded flower curtains Granly had bought at a local antiques shop.

"It's nice to be here," Hannah said, sounding as surprised as I felt.

"Well, yeah!" Abbie said. "*Thirty* hours in that car plus two nights in icky motels. It's cruel and inhumane, if you ask me."

"That's not what she meant," I said, frowning at Abbie.

Abbie looked down at her feet.

"I know what she meant," she said quietly.

That also made me feel better. So I *hadn't* been the only one freaking out about coming to the cottage. And I wasn't the only one feeling half-guilty, half-happy to be here.

I headed to the kitchen to see if Mom had unpacked the

bread and peanut butter yet. As I passed through the breakfast room, my gaze fell on the shelves holding Granly's egg cup collection.

Some people collect silver spoons or snow globes. Granly collected egg cups. Egg cups in graduated sizes painted like Matryoshka dolls. Egg cups shaped like rabbits, guinea pigs, and a mama kangaroo. (The egg sat in her pouch.) Egg cups made out of jade-colored glass and crackle-glazed ceramic and whittled wood.

Granly and I had had a breakfast ritual. She would boil water and put white bread in the toaster while I pondered the hundred or so egg cups. I would agonize over the choices. Did I want the shiny blue striped cup or the minimalist white one with the funny mustache? The cup bedazzled with pink jewels (always a popular choice, especially during my tween years) or the one made of hammered pewter?

By the time I'd made my decision, Granly would have fished our eggs out of the water and cut our buttered toast into narrow strips.

Then, pretending we were in a Jane Austen novel, we'd carefully *tap, tap, tap* the caps off our shells with tiny teaspoons and scoop the egg out in tiny bites, occasionally dipping our buttery toast strips into the yolk.

The secret I never told anyone was this: I did not like soft-boiled eggs. They were jiggly and runny in a way that made my stomach turn just a little bit. But I ate them with Granly (and with lots and lots of toast) because I loved the ritual of it. And I loved the just-us-ness of it. (Abbie and Hannah had made no secret of their loathing for soft-boiled eggs, so they never joined us.)

And, of course, I loved those egg cups, just as much as Granly did.

Looking at them now, I tried to remember which one Granly had bought on her trip to Moscow, and which was from Norway. Had Grandpa given her the *Make Way for Ducklings* cups for their anniversary or her birthday? Which had been her favorite?

My answer to each of these questions was, *I don't know.*

And now, I realized as tears began to roll down my cheeks, I never would.

I turned abruptly and headed for the back door. I slammed through it, swiping the tears from my face.

Out of the corner of my eye, I saw Granly's vegetable garden. It looked awful—so overgrown with weeds that I could barely see the neat brick border. The laminated signs Granly had made—TOMATOES, CUKES, SQUASH—had faded and tipped over.

I quickly turned away from the garden. That put me on the stepping stones, which led me to the road. A left turn would take me to the lake—a right, to town. And even though diving into the lake might have felt delicious, at that moment there was something else I needed even more.

I turned to the right.

"Uh, Chels?" my dad called from the screened porch. "Going somewhere?"

"I'm going to the library," I announced, hoping he couldn't hear the choke in my voice. "You didn't let me bring my books, and . . . and I need some."

My dad cocked his head and gave me a long look. I saw him lean toward the front steps, on the verge of coming over. If he did, he'd be close enough to see my pink-rimmed eyes and to say those dreaded words: "Want to talk about it?"

But here's the thing about my dad.

He may not get that his bad puns are really, *really* bad.

He may not understand that showing up somewhere in the right outfit is much more important than showing up on time.

But the guy lives with four women, and he knows when one of them needs to be left alone.

So he waved me off and said, "Be back before six. I'm cooking tonight."

I felt myself choke up again, partly because I was grateful to my dad and partly because I'd just pictured Granly's chair in the dining room.

How could I possibly eat next to Granly's empty chair?

At the moment it didn't seem to be an important question. Thinking about those soft-boiled eggs had killed my appetite.

A mile later I stood in front of the Bluepointe Public Library, sighing wearily.

I'd been coming to this library since I was a kid, but every summer it was freshly disappointing.

I wanted all libraries to be made of ivy-covered stone bricks, with tall, arched windows and creaky wooden floorboards. I wanted quiet, romantic staircases and window seats where you could read all day.

Bluepointe's library had none of these things. It was a squat single story, and it was made of sand-colored concrete that left scratches on your skin if you brushed up against it. The floors were covered in forest-green carpeting.

But the worst part about this library was its hours, in that there were hardly any of them. The place seemed to be open about four hours each morning. This being the afternoon, it was locked up tight.

I shoved my hands into the pockets of my cutoffs and found a couple scraps of paper I'd scribbled on in the car, as well as a wad of crumpled dollar bills that I'd forgotten about. I'd stuffed the money into my pocket that morning, thinking I'd want it for snacks on the road. But there are only so many stale corn nuts a girl can take, so I'd never used it.

I decided that if I couldn't get myself a book, at least I could get something cold to drink. The wooded road that led from the cottage to town had been shady and breezy, but now the sun felt scorchingly strong.

I headed for Main Street.

This was the one part of Bluepointe that looked just like it should. The storefronts all had big plate-glass windows and striped awnings, and above them were loft apartments owned by artists who hung burlap curtains in the windows and made sure everyone had a good view of their easels.

The first shop I passed was Ben Franklin, a this-and-that store that sold dusty stuff that wasn't supposed to exist anymore, like quilting supplies and shower caps and rainbow-colored glue that you could blow into balloons with a little red straw.

I smiled at the inflatable rafts, buckets, and shovels in the window. The store had the exact same display every summer. Each year it just grew more yellowed and saggy.

I also loved Estelle's, the art gallery a few doors down.

All the artists in town sold their stuff at Estelle's, *except* for the rotating roster of people that Estelle had decided to feud with. That was her thing. She loved to throw people out of the gallery, shaking her fist at them and making a big scene.

Today on the sidewalk in front of Estelle's, I spotted the Pop Guy and his gleaming silver freezer on wheels, complete with a rainbow-striped beach umbrella.

Unlike the Bluepointe librarians, the Pop Guy was *always* around. His frozen pops were famous for sounding weird but turning out to be delicious.

Perfect. By then I was parched.

But when I alighted in front of the Pop Guy's chalkboard menu, my heart sank a little bit.

BALSAMIC STRAWBERRY, GRAPEFRUIT MINT, AND LEMON ROSEMARY.

What was with all the herbs? I'm sure my parents would have swooned over these flavors, but to me they sounded like the names on bars of soap. I steeled myself for another bummer, until I came to the last item on the menu. Then I grinned.

"Raspberry Limeade," I said with relief. I handed him a few bills and said, "I'll have one of those, please."

"Nice safe choice there," the Pop Guy muttered as he dug into his steamy freezer. I would have been stung, but the Pop Guy was also famous for being a cranky food snob, so I just ducked my head to pull off the cellophane wrapper, and headed off.

Before I could get very far, though, the Pop Guy called after me, completely ignoring a cozy-looking couple who looked like they'd been just about to order.

"Hey, I've seen you here before, yeah?" he said. "I recognize that hair of yours. Been a while."

I nodded.

"Been a year," I said.

I thought back to the fourteen-year-old me the Pop Guy remembered.

That version of myself wouldn't have even caught the Pop Guy's dis. The insult would have skimmed over her head—most stuff that adults said did. The fourteen-year-old me had also been wearing her first underwire bra. She'd worn way too much frosty lip gloss, and she'd wanted nothing more than to have a sleepover with Emma every Saturday night.

And it had never occurred to her that her grandmother wouldn't be around forever, or at least until she was very old herself.

To the fifteen-year-old me, that fourteen-year-old seemed really, really young.

I did still like her taste in frozen treats, though. My herb-free pop was fabulous—almost as good as a dunk in Lake Michigan.

I strolled slowly up the sidewalk, pausing to peek into each familiar shop.

But then, on the corner of Main and Althorp, I spotted something that almost made me drop my pop in the gutter. Across the street, next door to Mel & Mel's Coffee Shop, where I'd been eating pie since I was a toddler, was something *new*.

There was *never* anything new in Bluepointe.

The sign over the door said DOG EAR in a funky typewriter font. Next to the name was a cartoon of a floppy-eared Labrador retriever. The dog was resting its chin on its front paws while it gazed at—

This was the part where I really did drop my pop, right onto my flip-flopped toes.

The dog was reading a book.

Which meant not only was there a new shop in Bluepointe, but it was my favorite kind of shop ever—the kind that sold books.

As I race-walked across the street, pausing only to shake the sticky raspberry juice from my feet, I tried to lower my expectations.

It could be a new age bookstore, I told myself. *All crystals and tarot cards and self-help books.*

Or worse, *I bet it's a pet store, with an entire* Dog Whisperer *book section and toy poodle outfits and liver-flavored cupcakes.*

I arrived at the bookstore and plunged through the door with so much breathless drama that the little bell on the door *clanged.* I could feel a dozen heads turn toward me.

"Welcome to Dog Ear!" said a woman behind the counter. She had long, gray-streaked hair that looked soft and pretty instead of scraggly and old. She looked small behind the stacks of books on the corner of the L-shaped counter. Propped against these stacks were little cards with paragraphs written in pink, orange, and lime-green ink.

"Grab something to read and a cookie," the woman told me with a warm, deeply dimpled smile. "We've got vanilla wafers today."

She gestured toward a lounge in the back corner of the shop.

Two people were already there, tucked into a faded blue couch, absorbed in books. At their feet was a huge black Labrador retriever. It must have been the dog on the sign. One of the readers, a woman in cuffed denim cutoffs just like mine, had her bare feet propped on the dog's ample back as if he were no more than a furry ottoman. She popped one vanilla wafer into her mouth and tossed another to the dog, who gulped it down with a loud smack.

On the lemon-yellow wall overlooking this little lounge was a gallery of amazingly detailed posters, each advertising a book signing and featuring a mash note from the author.

To the best little bookstore in town! And I'm not just saying that because you're the only bookstore in town. . . .

Tell E.B. he owes me my sandwich back. XOXO . . .

On the opposite side of the store, tucked behind a few rows of turquoise bookshelves, was a children's area enclosed by a tiny white picket fence. It had a fluffy green shag rug and beanbag chairs, plus a bright-red train engine, the perfect size for a toddler to climb into.

String after string of fairy lights swagged from the ceiling. Between the light strands dangled random stuff like a cardboard moon, a Chinese lantern, and a disco ball.

Normally I would have fallen on the bookshelves like a bear just out of hibernation. But I found that I couldn't quite move. Because when you walk into the bookstore you've always fantasized about but never thought could exist in real life, it kind of throws you. Some irrational part of me thought if I went any farther, or touched anything, it would all vaporize and I'd wake up from a dream.

When the woman at the counter started to look concerned, I did take a few stumbling steps forward.

I picked up one of the index cards propped against the books on the counter. Next to the book's title, someone had written: *A-minus. As you know, I rarely give out such a high grade. I read this book when I was recovering from a breakup. Yes, I know all of you were rooting for the breakup. Don't gloat, people. Anyway, next time somebody stomps on your heart, you should read this book. You'll hate the lead character for being much prettier than you, but you'll forgive her when she fails to make tenure at her hoity-toity liberal arts college.*

"Everyone who works here writes up little book reviews," the woman at the counter said, interrupting me. "That one's by Isobel. She's not here right now, so I can tell you . . ."

She shifted to a stage whisper.

"She's a bit of an oversharer."

I laughed.

"Good books will do that to you," I said.

"Oh, honey," the woman said, "Isobel doesn't need a good book to tell us the most appalling things about her personal life. She'll read the *weather report* and start spilling her guts."

This woman was talking to me in that frank way that middle-aged people only talked to other middle-aged people. Which made me feel both proud and paranoid. This couldn't all be for real, could it?

"Who *are* you?" I blurted. "I mean, um, when did this store open? It wasn't here the last time I was in Bluepointe."

"Do you like it?" the woman said with a conspiratorial grin.

"Good, 'cause it's mine! Well, my husband's and mine, but I do more of the day-to-day because he's a professor in Chicago. We're nearing our one-year birthday."

"I like it," I said as I continued to take it all in. Outside the kids' picket fence was a tall refrigerator box painted purple and labeled THE PHANTOM TOLLBOOTH. And next to the couch, where you'd think there'd be an end table or something, there was a basket of yo-yos. Not shrink-wrapped yo-yos for sale. Just loose, mismatched yo-yos, their strings trailing over the basket's edge. Clearly the Dog Ear owners believed that shopping for books just naturally led to the urge to yo-yo.

"I like it a lot," I breathed.

"Well, go get you some cookies, then, before E.B. eats them all," the woman said. "Yesterday we had Fig Newtons, and he did not like *those* at all, so he's playing catch-up."

She craned her neck to address the dog, who was still sprawled beneath the feet of the reader.

"Aren't you, ya big fatty?" the owner cooed.

The reader with her feet on E.B. gasped.

"Don't you listen to Stella," she told the dog, feeding him another cookie. "There's just more of you to love."

Stella rolled her eyes and said to me, "He looks more like Wilbur the pig than a dog. That's why we named him after E. B. White."

While I laughed, Stella turned to the girl on the couch. "Darby, are you going to buy that book ever, or just come here every day to read it?"

The woman grinned and said, "I'll take option B."

Stella laughed and shrugged, as if to say, *Fine with me.*

Best. Bookstore. Ever.

I finally found the strength to drift over to the YA section. Refreshingly, it was placed smack-dab in the middle of the store, instead of tucked into some shadowy corner in the back. I rounded the aqua bookcase, almost licking my lips in anticipation of all the pretty book jackets arrayed on the shelves like candy.

I stopped short when I saw that somebody else was in the aisle.

Not just any somebody. A boy. A boy so tall and long-limbed that his slouch against the bookshelf make him look like the letter C. A boy with fair skin, and a perfect nose and neatly shorn brown hair.

A very cute boy.

He was squinting at the cover of a paperback, but when I took a few steps down the aisle, he looked up at me. I saw a flash in his eyes. They were brown—the exact same brown of my favorite velvet chair at Granly's cottage. They had long lashes and thick brows the same wet-sand color as his buzz-cut hair.

The pretty brown eyes glanced back at his book for a moment, then quickly snapped right back to me. Now they were widened in an expression that seemed a little stunned.

This, of course, caused me to catch my breath and spin around to face the bookshelf.

That was a double take, I thought. *It was* definitely *a real-live double take! For . . . me? For me!*

A feeling of both giddiness and panic bubbled inside me. Hoping my face wasn't turning bright red, I bent toward the bookshelf and pretended to search for a particular title. Meanwhile, I could feel the boy staring at me.

My hand floated up to my ponytail, which felt like it had frizzed into a giant puffball in the heat. I twirled a lock of hair nervously around my finger.

He was still looking, I could tell.

For maybe the first time in my life, I wished I *were* a stereotypical redhead, all sassy and impulsive. I'd swing myself around and stare right back at him. My dark blue eyes would crackle impishly, and my smile would be twisty and mischievous, just like the redheads I'd read about in books but had never actually met in real life.

Of course, even those redheads might have hesitated if they'd just emerged from a three-day road trip, plus a crying jag, with barely a glance in the mirror. My sleeveless red-checked shirt, which had surely been cutely crisp and picnicky when it was first made in the 1970s, was now faded and wrinkly and had a permanent ballpoint pen stain near one of the buttons. The Revlon Red polish on my toenails was chipped, and for all I knew I had a raspberry limeade drip on my face.

I skimmed my fingertips across my chin, feeling for stickiness. Then I tapped at the corners of my mouth to make sure there were no raspberry remnants there.

Since I seemed to be drip-free, I shot the boy a sidelong glance.

He was still looking at me.

And now he was *saying* something to me.

"There's nothing on your face, you know," the boy said in a low, somewhat raspy voice.

It took a second for me to realize what he'd said and what it meant. Clearly my attempt at a subtle chin check had been anything but subtle.

"What?" I blurted.

"It looked like you were wondering if you had something on your face," he said. "Maybe mayonnaise. You know, from the coffee shop? I just thought I'd let you know, there's not."

"Oh," I said. "Um, thanks. I wasn't at the coffee shop."

"Oh, okay," he said.

We looked at each other blankly for a moment before I blurted, "Besides, I'm not so into mayo. I'm more of a mustard girl."

I cringed. *What was that? Please tell me I'm not talking to this boy about condiments!*

But the boy nodded as if this were a perfectly normal thing to say to a cute person of the opposite sex. Who knew? Maybe it was. Maybe I should ask him what kind of stuff he put on *his* ham sandwiches.

Then I imagined those words coming out of my mouth, and I clamped my lips shut to make certain that they didn't.

The boy returned to his book, which gave me the chance to stare at *him*. He looked so different from most of the boys I knew. They were always swinging their hair out of their eyes with swoops of their heads, something that I hadn't realized I found annoying until just now. This boy's hair was sleek and neat and allowed a view of his very nice forehead.

Wait a minute, I thought. *There's no such thing as a nice forehead. Foreheads aren't nice or not-nice. They're just . . . foreheads.*

What kind of weirdo admires a guy's forehead *of all things? What does* that *mean?*

But I think I already knew.

It meant that I had been struck with an instantaneous crush—a crush that was possibly mutual (there'd been that double take, after all) but just as possibly not.

I tried to think of something to say. Something breezy and bright that had nothing to do with ham sandwiches. Of course, my mind was blank—except for the part that was consumed with this boy's long fingers and his stylish Euro sneakers and (still!) his forehead.

So I just watched in silence as he turned to a wheeled cart behind him. It was stacked neatly with paperbacks. I assumed that Stella, the store owner, had left them there so she could shelve them later.

The boy took a silver pen off the cart.

It hovered over the front cover of his book.

I felt myself tense. What was he doing? Was he going to *write* something on the book cover?

Only when I heard the sound of paper tearing did I realize that he was doing something even worse. He was *slicing the cover off the book!* The pen was not a pen. It was an X-Acto knife!

Maybe Stella didn't mind if customers read her books without buying them or got vanilla wafer crumbs in the bindings. But even she wouldn't stand for this, would she?

"What are you doing!" I cried, grabbing the boy's wrist.

Now it was his turn to be shocked.

"I'm doing my job," he said. "What are *you* doing?"

I realized I was still clutching his wrist. It felt satiny smooth and warm. I dropped his arm like it had burned me.

"What kind of job involves slashing a book cover?" I demanded. "What did that book ever to do you?"

That's when something weird happened.

Weird in a wonderful way.

The boy smiled.

His teeth were very white and straight, except for one crooked eyetooth. Each of his cheeks had a dimple in it.

"It's nothing personal against the book," he said. "It's just being remaindered. These all are."

The boy gestured at the cart full of paperbacks.

"Remaindered?" I asked. "What's that?"

"They're not selling," he explained. "So we return them to the publisher. But it's too expensive to ship back the whole book, so we just send them the cover and recycle the rest of the book."

"Oh," I said, feeling stupid and sad all at once. I eyed the cart full of books.

"You're going to slice up *all* those books?" I said. "How can you stand it?"

"They're not selling," the boy repeated with a shrug. "If we don't get rid of the ones that won't sell, we won't have room for the books that will."

I plucked a tomato-red paperback off the cart.

"Waiter, There's Soup in My Fly," I read.

"Fly-fishing humor," the boy said with a sorrowful shake of his head.

"Well, I don't know why *that's* not selling," I said sarcastically. I reached for another book.

"My Life as a Cat Lady," I read with a shudder.

"I'm telling you," the boy said. With one hand he reached out to take the book from me. With the other he held up his X-Acto knife.

"No," I protested, plunking the book back onto the cart. "How can you kill off all those innocent cats?"

"Well, we *are* dog people here," the boy said, glancing toward the lounge, where E.B. was wetly gobbling another vanilla wafer. The boy rolled his eyes and shook his head.

But he also smiled, and those dimples showed up again.

My stomach fluttered. I hoped he couldn't tell. Quickly I bent down so I could peer more closely at the books on the cart—and hide my face from him.

One paperback was sunset orange. I pulled it out.

"Coconut Dreams by Veronica Gardner," I said. "That sounds beachy to me. I'll take it."

The boy laughed.

"You're not actually buying that," he declared.

"I'm *rescuing* it," I said, hugging the book to my chest. "This book does not deserve to die."

"Do you even know what it's about?" he said.

I glanced at the back of the book.

"It's a dollar ninety-nine on clearance," I said, eyeing the red sale sticker. "Ooh, and it's YA! That's a good start. Let's see . . ."

I began to read the description on the back cover aloud.

"'Nicole can't believe her parents have shipped her off to

camp for the summer. Even if the camp is on a tropical island—'"

I paused to snort.

"Sounds deep," the boy said, prompting me to read on.

"'Nicole is *super*-mad about it. What about hanging out at the mall with her friends? What about her job at the frozen yogurt shop? She'll miss all the parties and all the fun, which is just what Nicole's parents want! At first Camp Coconut is awful—early wake-up calls, catch-your-own-fish breakfasts, a monsoon—'"

"A monsoon!" the boy and I blurted out together.

"Okay, safe to say that's a stretch," I said with a giggle.

"'But then,'" I read on, "'everything changes. Nicole meets a local boy named Kai. Their summer love blooms like a coconut flower, but like the tide, Nicole knows it can never last.'"

This was the part where I was supposed to groan and make a joke about two bad similes in one sentence.

But instead my throat seemed to close up as I realized something—

I was reading to my new crush from a *summer romance novel.* It was about as subtle as my sticky-chin check.

Okay, I told myself. I tried to take a deep breath without *appearing* to take a deep breath. *Maybe he's not making the connection. He's a boy, and lots of boys are clueless. Or maybe he* isn't *clueless but he just doesn't associate* me *with a summer romance* at all.

How could I figure out which one it was? And how could I *also* find out his name, his age, and whether he'd been on Team Peeta or Team Gale? (Either one was fine, as long as he'd never been on Team Edward or Team Jacob.)

When you were in a bookstore, those were perfectly legitimate things to ask, right? So why was I still speechless?

We were just verging on an awkward silence when Stella's voice rang out from the front of the store.

"Josh, honey? You back there?"

The boy looked up at the ceiling and sighed quietly before calling out, "Yeah?"

I felt that little flutter in my stomach again.

His name is Josh.

Then the boy spoke again. "What is it, Mom?"

This time my eyebrows shot up.

His name is Josh and his parents *own the bookstore of my dreams.*

It seemed so perfect that I couldn't help but grin. My smile was unguarded, uncomplicated, and delighted. I did not have this sort of smile very often. It felt a lot like the smile that had been on Josh's face a moment ago.

Luckily, Josh was listening to his mother and not looking at me while I grinned like a big goofball. I only half-heard the question she asked him—something I didn't understand about a packing slip and a ship date.

Whatever it was, it seemed to bring Josh back to the serious worker-bee place he'd been before we'd started talking.

"It's in the office file cabinet, third drawer down in the back," Josh called. Then he added, in a mumble, "Where it was the last time you asked."

He stared at the X-Acto knife in his hand for a moment. I could tell he wasn't seeing it, though. His eyes were foggy and distant, and they were definitely not too happy.

Then he seemed to remember I was there and looked at me. He pointed at the book in my hand.

"So, are you buying that or not?" he asked gruffly. He was suddenly impatient to get rid of me so he could get back to his book destruction.

And just as suddenly my rescue of *Coconut Dreams* didn't seem cute, clever, and boy-impressing. It was silly, a waste of Josh's apparently very valuable time.

I wondered if I'd been mistaken about his double take. And maybe we *hadn't* just had an amazingly easy and fun conversation about his cart full of doomed books. Maybe I'd imagined all that, and in fact I was just another annoying customer at Josh's annoying summer job.

So now what was I supposed to do? Put the book back and skulk away? If I did, I'd have to sidle past Josh in the narrow aisle. Twice. It'd be much quicker to just make a dash for the front desk.

So I nodded at Josh.

"I'll take the book," I said quietly.

"Fine," he said, looking stony. "I'll ring it up for you."

"That's okay," I said. "Your mom can do it."

Josh shrugged—looking a little sulky—and turned back to his cart.

I headed back up the aisle toward the front desk. Just before I emerged from the stacks, I heard the awful sound—*rrriiiiip*—of another book cover getting slashed.

I couldn't meet Stella's eyes as I handed her *Coconut Dreams*.

"Well!" she said brightly. I nodded sympathetically. What else *could* you say to such a pathetic purchase? I could have told her the book was supposed to have been a joke between me and her son, but now the joke had fizzled and it was just a cheesy book on clearance that I was buying before I made a quick getaway. But that seemed like a *lot* to explain, so I just stayed silent.

Why, I asked myself mournfully for the hundredth time, *did I take my e-reader into the shower?*

"So that's a dollar ninety-nine," Stella said. I handed over two of my precious dollar bills, then dug into my pocket for the tax.

"No tax, sweetie," Stella said. "After all, that book was headed for the shredder. You rescued it!"

"That's what *I* said," I said. She grinned at me, and I half-smiled back, feeling a little less mortified.

"Okay," I sighed. "Well . . ."

I cast a glance back toward the stacks, where Josh was still hidden. Suddenly I felt a rush of tears swell behind my eyes.

How had this gone so wrong? I wanted to linger in Dog Ear. I wanted to slowly browse the stacks, then take a tall bundle of books over to the lounge. I'd flop into that cracked-leather chair, where I'd skim through six different first chapters while nibbling vanilla wafers. Then I'd buy myself a *good* book and take it straight to the beach.

But instead I'd met Josh, and somehow we'd gone from flirting to flame-out in less than five minutes. I was too mortified to stay. I had to slink out of Dog Ear, with a lame book, to boot.

It just wasn't fair.

I turned back to Stella to thank her for ringing me up, but she was peering with concern into the lounge.

"E.B.," she said with a warning tone.

The dog lifted one eyebrow at her and whimpered.

"Oh, no," Stella cried. "E.B., hold on, boy!"

She swooped down to reach for something under the counter. When she came up, she was holding a leash.

Now the dog let out a loud, rumbling groan.

"Noooo, E.B.!" Stella cried. She raced over and grabbed the dog by the collar. She clicked on the leash and hustled E.B. to the door.

"You *know* you shouldn't eat so many cookies," she scolded.

I clapped a hand over my mouth to keep from laughing out loud as Stella hustled her rotund black Lab through the door.

But a moment later I felt a presence behind me, and my urge to laugh faded.

It was him. I just *knew* it.

I paused for a moment before turning around. I inhaled sharply.

You know how some people's looks change once you get to know them? Unattractive people become better-looking when you find out how funny and smart they are. And gorgeous people can turn ugly if you find out they're evil inside.

Well, now that I'd seen Josh's surly, sullen side . . . that didn't happen at all. He was somehow cuter than ever. Which is really annoying in a boy who's made you feel like an ass (even if he did make me feel pretty amazing first).

"E.B. has a touch of irritable bowel syndrome," Josh explained.

"Am I supposed to laugh at that?" I asked.

"No," Josh said simply. "It's not a joke. It's really gross, actually."

That, of course, made me *want* to laugh. So now Josh was making me feel like an *immature* ass.

"Well, I hope he feels better. See ya," I said. Of course, I *didn't* plan to see Josh. I was already wondering how I could find out his work schedule—so I could be sure to avoid him.

"Look at this," Josh said, thrusting a book toward me. It sounded a lot like an order.

"Excuse me?" I said. I raised one eyebrow, which was a skill I'd learned recently. I'd had a lot of time to practice it during the drive from California.

It worked. Josh looked quite squirmy.

"I mean, well, I think you might like this book," he said more quietly. When I didn't take it from him, he put it on the counter next to me. I glanced at it only long enough to see that the cover was still intact. It had a photo that looked blue and watery.

"Listen, *Coconut Dreams* is not my usual kind of book," I said. "If this is *anything* like that, I think I'll pass."

"It's not, I swear," Josh said. "Look, it's not even on clearance."

I gave him a look that I hoped was deeply skeptical, and picked up the book.

I loved the look of the cover. It was an undulating underwater photo. In the turquoise water you could just make out a glimmer of fish scales, a shadowy, slender arm, and one swishy coil of red hair.

Beyond the Beneath, the book was called, and *oh*, did I want to flip through it and find out if the words were as flowy and beautiful as that cover. But I wasn't about to tell Josh that. He'd already gotten me all confused with his mixed signals and his cuteness. Plus, I only had five bucks left in my pocket, so I couldn't afford the book anyway. I was going to make my escape while I could.

"I don't think so," I said, trying to sound breezy. I tossed the book back onto the counter. "But thanks."

"Oh, okay," Josh said. He dug his hands into his pockets and looked away, the way I always did when I was disappointed.

I'm sure that's not it, I told myself. *That's probably just where he keeps his extra X-Acto knife blades.*

Josh seemed to have spotted something behind the counter. I followed his gaze to the receipt paper trailing out of the cash register. It had a bright pink stripe running along it.

"Oh, man," he muttered. "She never remembers to change the tape."

He ducked around the end of the counter and started extracting the paper roll from the register, scowling as the thing seemed to evade his grasp.

"Weird," I said.

Josh stopped fiddling with the receipt tape and looked at me.

"What's weird?" he demanded.

"I think it would be a dream to work in a bookstore," I said, "and you don't seem to like it at all."

"I like it—" Josh started to say, sounding super-defensive. He stopped himself and frowned in thought. "It's not that I don't like it. It's just that, when people open a bookstore, they think it's going to be all, you know, *books*."

"Isn't it?" I asked.

"Well, yeah," Josh said, "but it's also receipt tape. And packing slips and book orders and remembering to pay the air-conditioning bill."

"But *you* don't have to worry about that," I scoffed. "I mean, you're . . ."

"Fifteen?" Josh said. "Yeah, well, you don't have to have a

driver's license to pay the air-conditioning bill. You just have to have a tolerance for really boring chores."

At that moment he looked a lot older than a boy my age.

Even though, I couldn't help noting, he *was* a boy my age. Not college age or even my sisters' age.

I don't know why that mattered to me, though. Who cared if he was age-appropriate? Yes, he was really, really good-looking. And mature. And for about three minutes it had seemed like he thought I was pretty intriguing too.

But now I didn't know *what* to think about this boy. How could I have anything in common with someone who found a bookstore—*this* bookstore—as uninspiring as receipt tape?

And how, I wondered as I walked out the door, could I possibly feel worse leaving Dog Ear than I had before entering it?

*T*hat night my dad grilled corn and salmon, and my mom tossed an arugula salad with hazelnuts and lemon juice. Abbie and I collaborated on wildly uneven biscuits. Mine looked like shaggy little haystacks, while hers were perfectly round but as flat as pancakes. Hannah made a fruit salad, then muddled raspberries and frothed them into a pitcher of lemonade.

But instead of setting the table like usual, we piled all the food into boxes and baskets and toted them down the two blocks to the lake.

Sparrow Road was narrow and sharply curved. Though the road was paved with used-to-be-black pavement, walking it meant wending your way around various large cracks and potholes. Before you knew it, you were usually in the middle of the road. Which was fine because there were hardly ever any cars. There was no reason to drive on Sparrow unless you lived in one of the twenty-or-so houses on it.

I always loved our first shadowy walk to the lake. It was so thickly overhung with trees that by August you felt like you were in a tunnel. Of course, by August you also had to spend most of that walk slapping away mosquitoes and horseflies. But even that—after doing it my whole life—felt like a ritual.

I think we all exhaled as we rounded the last bend in the road that led to our "stop." This was a little wooden deck with a bike rack (not that anybody bothered to lock their bikes here) and a rusty spigot for hosing the sand off your feet. A little gate on the far end of the deck led to the rickety, narrow boardwalk that led to the beach.

None of us spoke as we kicked off our shoes, then walked down the boardwalk single file.

Tonight the silence seemed heavy with meaning and mourning. But actually we were always pretty quiet during our first visit to the lake. After the Pacific, so violent and crashy, the lake seemed so quiet that it always made us go quiet too. As a little kid I imagined that this water kept people's secrets. Whatever you whispered here was safe. The lake would never tell.

As we stepped—one after another—from the boardwalk onto the sand, I realized that maybe I hadn't completely outgrown that notion.

After we'd settled onto the sand (nobody had had the extra arm for a picnic blanket) my mother declared, "Dinner on the beach on our first night in Bluepointe. It's a new tradition."

Even though her voice caught on the last syllable and her eyes looked glassy in the light of the setting sun, she smiled.

I gave her my own damp-eyed smile back. It felt weird to be simultaneously so sad without Granly and so happy to be there in that moment. The smoky, charred corn was dripping with butter and the sand was still warm from the sun, which had become a painfully beautiful pink-orange. The gentle waves were making the *whooshing* sound that I loved.

When I'd finished my salmon and licked the lemony salad dressing from my fingers, I got to my feet. I scuffed through the sand, tiptoed over the strip of rocks and shells that edged the lake, and finally plunged my feet into the water. It was very, very cold.

I gasped, but forced my feet to stay submerged. The cold of the water felt important to endure for some reason. Like a cleansing of this very long day.

I glanced back at my family. Abbie was sitting with her legs splayed out while she gnawed on her cob of corn. Hannah was lying on her stomach gazing past me to the sunset. My parents were sitting side by side, both with their legs outstretched and crossed at the ankles, my mom's head resting on my dad's shoulder.

There was only one person missing.

My mind swooped to an image of Granly. If she were here right now, she'd be sitting in a folding beach chair. Maybe she'd sip a glass of wine while she searched the sky for the first stars of the night. Or she'd be efficiently packing the dishes up while she gossiped with my mom about old Chicago friends.

But then something surprising happened. Just as quickly as my mind had swooped to Granly, it swooped away again and landed on—the boy from the bookstore.

I wondered what it would be like if *he* were here on the beach with me. He didn't seem like the goofy splashing-around-in-the-water type. But I could definitely picture him taking a long, contemplative walk along the lake. Or building a sand castle with me, with all the turrets carefully lined up according to size.

I wondered if he knew the constellations and would point them out as the night sky grew darker. Or maybe he didn't like to talk much. Maybe he was more of a listener.

I tried to imagine what it might feel like to lean my head against his shoulder or snuggle into those lanky arms. And I remembered the way his face had lit up when he'd smiled at me for the first time.

But after his mom had brought him back down to earth, his face had tightened. His mouth had become a straight, serious line as he'd struggled with the receipt tape and perhaps reviewed a long to-do list of chores in his head.

It had not looked like a kissable mouth.

And those broad shoulders? It seemed there was enough leaning on them already. There was no room for my head there.

Even if there was, was Josh thinking about me in the same way?

Was he thinking about me at all? He didn't even know my name!

I couldn't stop repeating *his* name in my head. *Josh*. I loved the one-syllable simplicity of it. I loved the way it ended with a *shhhh* that you could draw out, like the soft sizzle of a Lake Michigan wave.

But I stopped myself from whispering the name out loud. If I did, I felt sure that I wouldn't be able to get it—to get *him* and my does-he-like-me? angst—out of my head.

So instead I tromped back to my family, who looked blurry and ghostly now that the sun had set.

"Isn't it time for frozen custard?" I asked.

*I*t was funny that we had so many rituals in Bluepointe, when we had hardly any in LA.

At home we went to whatever brunch spot had the shortest line. Here we might wait for ninety minutes to get Dutch baby pancakes (and only Dutch baby pancakes) at Francie's Pancake & Waffles.

In LA my mom marked our heights on the laundry room wall whenever she remembered. Not on birthdays or New Years or anything that organized.

But in Bluepointe we always took the exact same photo on the exact same day, which was the last day of our visit. Hannah would kneel in the sand, Abbie would sit next to her, and I would lie on my stomach, my chin on my fists, at the end of the line. We even took that shot in the rain once, because there was no leaving Bluepointe without the "stack of sisters" shot.

Yet another tradition here was frozen custard on our first night in town. We always went to the Blue Moon Custard Stand.

As we drove there Hannah said, "I wonder what color it's going to be this year."

The Blue Moon got a new paint job every summer, going from bubble-gum pink to neon yellow to lime green—anything as long as it was ridiculously bright. I guess it was easy to paint, because the stand was no bigger than a backyard shed. There was barely enough room inside for two (small) people to work, and even that looked like a struggle. They always seemed to be elbowing each other away as they took orders, exchanged money, and handed cones through the stand's one tiny window.

This meant the line was always long and slow-moving, which was part of the fun of the Blue Moon.

Sure enough, when we pulled up to the stand (purple!) just outside of town, there was a crowd milling around it. But as usual nobody seemed to mind the wait. The evening air was cool and breezy, and the air was so lit up with fireflies, it made the weedy gravel lot feel like a fairy ring. Nobody was in a rush, and you didn't even have to expend mental energy mulling your custard order, because the Blue Moon had exactly two flavors: chocolate and vanilla.

We always ordered the same thing anyway. Dad and Hannah got hot fudge sundaes, hers with sprinkles, his with nuts. I got chocolate custard in a cake cone. Mom had a cup of vanilla drizzled with chopped maraschino cherries, and Abbie got a butterscotch-dipped sugar cone. We all got huge servings, even though frozen custard is about as bad for you as a bacon-topped donut, as distant from the calorie-free, pomegranate-flavored frozen yogurt of our hometown as you could get. That was exactly the point. This first-night ritual was our way of saying good-bye to California for the summer, and hello to Bluepointe, where things—until now—had always been as sweet and easy as frozen custard.

I took a giant bite of my cone as soon as the kid behind the counter handed it to me.

"Oh!" I groaned through a messy mouthful of chocolate. "Thish ish shooo good! How do I always forget the perfection that is frozen custard?"

"If you remembered," my dad said, wiping hot fudge off his chin with his napkin, "you'd never need to go back for more. And what fun would that be?"

I grinned and took another huge bite. As I swallowed, though, I felt a wave of cold surge though my head.

"Owwwwww, brain freeze!" I groaned. I turned away, squeezed my eyes shut, and slapped a hand to my forehead.

In a few seconds the yucky feeling in my frontal lobe passed, and I opened my eyes—to find myself looking right at—Josh! He was just walking away from the Blue Moon window, holding a simple vanilla cone. Behind him was his mom, digging into a sundae with about half a dozen colorful toppings on it.

Also just like me—he seemed stunned. After what felt like a *long* moment, during which we just stared at each other, he gave me a little wave.

I gave him a little smile.

And then Stella spotted me. Waving at me with her fudgy spoon, she said, "You were in Dog Ear today, weren't you, honey? How do you like that book?"

"Oh," I said, trying to sound breezy and comfortable even though I *completely* wasn't, "I haven't had a chance to start it yet."

"Well, you let me know, okay?" she said.

I nodded as, out of the corner of my eye, I saw Josh's gaze drop to the ground. He ate his frozen custard in giant, hurried bites until his mom wandered off to chat with someone else. Then he took a few steps toward me.

"You should," he said seriously.

"I should . . . what?" I asked him. I wondered how this was going to go. Was he going to be flirty Josh or surly Josh?

"You should come back to Dog Ear," he said.

I raised my eyebrows. That definitely didn't sound surly.

"I finished the remainders," Josh went on. "I promise, all the books are safe for the next few months. And . . ."

Now Josh looked a little embarrassed. "I can also promise you the staffers will be more polite."

"Oh," I said. "That sounds sort of like an apology."

"It sort of is," Josh replied.

Which might have been sweet in a different tone of voice. But Josh said it in such a somber, almost curt way, I didn't know quite *how* to take it. Was this just him doing the right thing, clearing his conscience? Or did he want me to come back to Dog Ear . . . to see him?

I didn't know what to say. What's more, my melting tower of frozen custard was beginning to tilt dangerously in my cone. And my family was not two feet behind me. I knew it wouldn't be long before they emerged from their custard hazes and noticed me talking to a boy. That would mean awkward introductions, followed by a sisterly interrogation for which I would have absolutely no answers.

What could I tell them? *This is Josh. We totally hit it off this afternoon. And then we didn't. And now I don't know what's going on, except that I still find him painfully cute.*

It would have made no sense to any of them. It barely made sense to me!

So I simply said to Josh, "Well, I guess I'll see you then."

As I turned back to my family, I realized I'd said pretty much the same thing when I'd left Josh at Dog Ear that afternoon. Of course, I'd been completely lying then.

Now? I hoped what I said would actually come true.

I barely tasted the rest of my frozen custard. In fact, I threw my cone away when it was only half-eaten. This was unheard of.

But, of course, everything was different this summer.

My parents hammered *that* point home as we walked back to the car, doing our best to wipe our sticky hands with flimsy paper napkins.

"Your dad and I have decided that we're going to move into Granly's room," my mom announced. "Hannah, you can have our old room so that you can have a quiet place to study. Abbie and Chelsea, we can split up the bunk beds for you if you want."

"But—" Abbie began. It was pure reflex for her to protest the injustice of Hannah getting her own room. But then it all must have sunk in, because Abbie clapped her mouth shut.

Mom and Dad were moving into Granly's room—her *empty* room.

It made sense. After all, the house was small and it was silly to leave an entire bedroom empty all summer.

But it was also incredibly depressing.

After we'd loaded ourselves soberly into the car, I pressed my knuckles to my lips.

Part of me wondered, why had we even bothered with this first-night outing? *All* our Bluepointe rituals were shattered now that the person at their center was gone.

But another (guilty) part of me was glad that we'd gone and I'd gotten another glimpse of Josh.

After we got home, I flopped into the rocker on the front porch. I didn't want to go in and watch my parents move their stuff into Granly's room. Instead I rocked slowly while the crickets sawed away outside the window screens. After a few minutes I picked up my purse from the floor where I'd tossed it and fished out my wrinkled memo pad and a pen.

What if? What if Granly was still here? What if I hadn't run to town this afternoon? What if the library had been open? That whole "butterfly causing a tsunami with one beat of its wings" thing has always made me crazy. It makes it seem like there's an either/or between everything—your grandmother living or dying. A summer spent in humongous Los Angeles or a tiny town in Michigan.

Why can't you have both sides of the either/or? If my grandma was here, maybe I wouldn't have met a cute boy today. Now I've met the cute boy, but I can't tell my grandma about him. See? Either/or. I guess that's just how life works.

I scratched out my exhausted thoughts until the pen almost fell out of my hand. Then I stumbled to my room and flopped into bed in my checkered shirt. I hadn't unpacked yet and couldn't find any of my pajamas.

In the middle of the night, I was awakened by the muffled (but still unbearable) sound of my mother crying from Granly's room on the other side of the wall.

It didn't wake Abbie up, because *nothing* ever woke Abbie up.

But just to test the theory, I grabbed the little flashlight that was always in the nightstand drawer. I flicked it on and aimed it at Abbie's face—her utterly placid, sleeping face. I wiggled the light back and forth over her eyes, but they remained stubbornly closed. Then she made a cooing noise and flipped over so she faced the wall.

It didn't seem fair that Abbie was not only sound asleep but was having a good dream.

Now in the next room I heard the low grumble of my dad's voice. He must have said the exact right thing, because my mom gave a sniffly laugh, then quieted down. Gratefully I smushed my head deeper into my pillow and resolved to laugh at my dad's next joke, no matter how corny it was.

I aimed the flashlight at the wall. It was papered instead of painted because Granly thought wallpaper was warm and cozy. The paper was barely pink and dotted with tiny impressionistic butterflies—each one just a few swipes of ink and a couple blobs of watercolor. They were the pale greens, blues, pinks, and tans of birds' eggs.

This wallpaper was in one of my earliest memories. I don't

know how old I was—young enough that I was put to bed before the sun had fully set. I was also young enough that I couldn't yet read myself to sleep. So instead I tried to follow the pattern in the wallpaper. I found the gray-blue butterfly that seemed to be dancing with the coral one, then I searched for the spot where the pair repeated. I pointed at the blue and coral butterflies over and over, working my way around the room, until my eyes became the butterfly wings and fluttered shut.

Now, at three a.m., searching out my favorite butterflies with a flashlight felt more like a hunting expedition than a relaxing way to drift off to sleep. So I groped for the nightstand and grabbed the first thing I found there.

I squinted at the book through half-closed eyes. Oh. *Coconut Dreams.*

Stella wanted to know what I thought of it. So did Josh. At least it had *seemed* that way.

So, even though I was already pretty sure what I would think of *Coconut Dreams*, I smiled as I cracked it open and started reading.

The best thing I could say about the story of Nicole's exile on the Island of Bad Similes was that it put me to sleep within three pages. The last thing I thought as my flashlight slipped out of my fingers and I fell back asleep was, *This is better than a sleeping pill. I wonder if I could stretch* Coconut Dreams *out to last two and a half months.*

With all the *what ifs* I had to think about—not to mention the *what nows*—I had a feeling I was going to need it.

*M*aybe it was because my dad was taking some time off work. Maybe it was because my mom was a fourth-grade teacher who thought every moment of every day should be educational.

Whatever the reason, our first weeks in Bluepointe became all about family outings.

Normally my sisters and I would have protested. Our time in Bluepointe was supposed to be lazy, so lazy that moving from the couch to the kitchen required serious consideration. So lazy that you could spend two hours in the lake, just bobbing around and counting clouds. So lazy that you'd subsist on chips and salsa for lunch *and* dinner if it would get you out of having to think about or help prepare a real meal.

But this summer, of course, was different. None of us wanted to be in the cottage much, especially me. Being home made me ache for Granly. It also gave me time to talk myself in circles about Josh. One moment, I felt certain that he liked me, and I would make *definite* (okay, definite-ish) plans to put on my cutest vintage sundress and head to Dog Ear.

The next minute, I would talk myself out of it. I wondered if I'd misread what he'd said. I pictured myself showing up at Dog Ear, clutching my long to-read list like a total dork, only to have Josh be all casual and brush-offy.

Or maybe, I thought, I'd show up and he wouldn't even be there. Then I'd have to go *back*. It might take multiple attempts to pin him down. The next thing you know, I'm a stalker.

The idea that it could all go well—that was the scenario I couldn't quite envision. I knew that kind of thing happened all the time. It had been the easiest thing in the world for Emma and Ethan. But it had never happened to me, and I just couldn't bring myself to believe that it ever would.

If I just put off going to Dog Ear, I told myself, I could delay the inevitable disappointment.

So that was how I ended up joining my family for an endless series of day trips. We went wild mushroom hunting in the Michigan woods. My parents had read about it in some foodie magazine, and they would not be deterred by the fact that choosing the *wrong* mushrooms could kill us all. (Somehow we survived. And the mushrooms actually weren't bad, if you could get past the lingering taste of dirt.)

After that we spent an afternoon churning butter at a living history museum a few towns over.

We rode inner tubes down the South Branch Galien River.

We cooked massive breakfasts and elaborate dinners, each involving new and difficult recipes that my parents had squirreled away over the course of the year.

And, oh, the antiquing. I knew we'd gone overboard with that when I found myself having a serious internal debate about which kind of quilt pattern I liked best, Double Wedding Ring or Log Cabin.

But toward the end of June it all fell apart. Abbie slipped out one morning for a "quick dunk" in the lake and never came back, so I was sent to look for her.

When I got there, she was still in the water. And even though she was just bobbing around in a bikini instead of seriously training in her Speedo, I decided I'd better not disturb her. I had no choice but to flop onto the sand and start texting with Emma. I'd just happened to stash my phone in my bag on my way out the door, along with a giant tube of sunscreen, Granly's old copy of *Sense and Sensibility*, and my bathing suit and cover-up.

You know, just in case.

One by one the rest of my family arrived. First came my dad with a soft cooler full of soft drinks. Then Hannah, who had a beach blanket and a mesh bag of clementines. And finally my mom, wearing her purse and a confused expression.

"But we're going to that artists' colony to watch them make fused glass," she complained. She was decked out in touristy clothes: capri pants, walking sandals, floppy-brimmed hat—the works.

"That sounds fascinating," Hannah said, shielding her eyes with her hand and squinting up at Mom. "But you know what would be an even *more* interesting way to spend the day?"

"What?" Mom asked.

"Lying on this beach doing absolutely nothing," Hannah said.

Without looking up from my phone—where Emma had just finished a long, dramatic story about getting caught making out with Ethan in the parking lot of the LA Ballet—I raised my fist in silent solidarity.

"There's not another glass demonstration until August," my mom protested feebly. I couldn't help but notice, though, that she kicked off her sandals as she said it.

"Maybe Hannah's right, hon," my dad said. "It's been a long few weeks. It's been a long *year.* Maybe it's time for a breather. We can go see them blow glass next time."

"*Fuse* glass . . . ," my mom said. But her teacherly voice trailed off as she gazed out at the blue-green, sun-dappled lake.

She sat down gingerly on the blanket.

"Cold Fresca?" Hannah asked, digging into the cooler for my mom's favorite drink.

Mom shrugged as she took the can and popped it open. She took a sip. It turned into a deep swig. Then she dug her toes into the sand, flopped back onto the blanket, and said to the sky, "Oh. My. Gawd."

"See?" Hannah said to her. "Nice, huh?"

I held up my hand so Hannah could high-five me, then returned to my cell phone.

That's when Abbie emerged from the lake, shaking the water out of her hair like a wet puppy.

"Uh-oh," she said, eyeing Mom. "Well, I guess it was too good to last. So what's on the agenda today? Making our own soap? Tracing Johnny Appleseed's steps through Michigan?"

"Here," Mom said as she reached into the cooler. "Have a Coke. We're not going anywhere."

"Oh. My. Gawd," Abbie said, gaping at our mother.

"She's crossed over to the dark side," Hannah said happily. Then she flopped onto her back next to my mom and closed her eyes for a nap.

At some point we got hungry. So we threw on our flip-flops and shuffled up to town.

Perhaps because it was the first café we hit on Main Street, we wandered into Dis and Dat. A little hole in the wall with mustard-yellow walls, Dis and Dat sold two things and two things only: hot dogs and french fries. Both the food and the thick-necked guys behind the counter had south-side-of-"Chicawgo" accents. They clapped their serving tongs like castanets and pointed them at you as they interrogated you about your hot dog toppings.

"You want some of dese pickles?" they'd demand. "How about some of dose peppers?"

They'd shake celery salt on your dog and announce, "A little of dis."

Then they'd squirt on some mustard and say, "And a little of dat."

I couldn't help but feel a little insider pride when Hannah marched up to the counter and barked, "Five of 'em with everything."

She knew not to say "please" and she *definitely* knew not to ask for ketchup. Chicagoans have this weird thing about ketchup on a hot dog. Ask for it, and they'll act like you said something disgusting about their mother.

"That's what I like to heah!" the guy behind the counter said to Hannah. He started tossing butterflied buns onto an orange plastic tray. Hannah couldn't have been more pleased if she'd gotten an A-plus on an exam. My dad laughed and gave her a squeeze.

"Think she'll do all right at U of C?" he asked the counterman.

"Don't you worry 'bout *her*," the counter guy said, pointing his tongs at my dad now. "A U of C girl. She's a sharpie."

"She's a genius!" my dad agreed.

"Daaaaaad," Hannah said. Her grin faded fast.

But at least the hot dogs were amazing. We sat down at one of the cramped sidewalk tables to devour them. In addition to the celery salt, peppers, pickles, and mustard, each dog was piled with chopped onions, tomatoes, and pickle relish dyed an unnatural emerald green. I sat with my back to the plate-glass window so the Dis and Dat guys wouldn't see me picking off the onions.

"Yummmm," Abbie said as she wolfed down her dog. "I'm *so* getting something from the Pop Guy for dessert."

As she peered down the street to see if the rainbow umbrella was there (it was, of course), she suddenly clutched at Hannah's arm.

"Hey," Hannah said, dropping her french fry. "That hurts."

"It's him!" Abbie hissed. She released Hannah's arm to gesture wildly at the other side of Main Street.

"Oh my God," Hannah said, covering her face with both hands. "You're such a spaz. He'll see you!"

"It's not yours," Abbie almost shouted. "It's *mine*. You know— James. Or John . . . Wait a minute—Jim? Jim! I think it's almost definitely Jim."

She crammed her last bit of hot dog into her mouth as she stood up.

"What are you doing?" Hannah asked.

"Catching up to him," Abbie declared. "Hello. We have it all planned, or did you forget?"

"Didn't the plan involve you looking hot in your swimsuit?" I said as I crammed a fry into my mouth.

"What?" Abbie said. She glanced down at the wrinkled shorts and baggy T-shirt she'd thrown over her bikini. She shrugged and whipped off her shirt, revealing her tan, muscly abs and her skimpy swimsuit top.

"*No,*" both my parents said at the exact same time.

"You guys are so hung up," Abbie sighed as she shimmied back into her T-shirt. "It's just a body. What's the big deal?"

"Don't answer that," my mom said to my dad with a wry smile. "It's a trap."

Hannah and I rolled our eyes at each other. My parents loved it when they got to join forces and tease us. Which, if you asked me, was kind of mean. It's not like we could help being teenagers any more than they could choose not to be old and wrinkly.

Abbie knotted her T-shirt at the waist and wove her disheveled hair into two sleek braids, which rendered her instantly adorable.

The she crossed her arms over her chest and glared at me and Hannah.

"Hurry up!" she said.

"What?" I squawked. "I'm not going with you!"

I glanced over my shoulder to look at myself in the Dis and Dat window. My outfit was okay—I was wearing a gauzy vintage swim cover-up that looked better the more it wrinkled, which was a good thing, because it was *very* wrinkled. But from the neck up my look was . . . problematic. Even in the dim reflection of the window, I could see that a bunch of new freckles had popped out on my face in the morning sun. My hair was so lake-tangled that a neat braid like Abbie's was out of the question. Even my usual ponytail could barely contain it. Spiral curls sproinged out along my hairline, pointing in all different directions.

"A, yes you are going with me. Both of you," Abbie said to me and Hannah. "And B, it doesn't matter how *you* look."

Hannah looked at me and bit her lip.

"It matters a *little* bit," she said before reaching over and snatching the rubber band out of my hair. I felt my wild ringlets bounce off my shoulders.

"Hey!" I said.

"I've been wanting to do that for the past hour," my mom said with a grin. Turning in her seat next to mine, she scrunched my hair a little bit and then smiled. "I love it. It's just like Granly's."

Then her eyes went glassy.

And I really didn't want to go down that road—not after the perfect morning we'd just had. So I grabbed my beach bag and jumped up to follow Abbie, who was already halfway down the block. Hannah huffed into place behind me a moment later.

The Silver sisters began to stalk their prey.

Jim or John or James was sauntering slowly about a block ahead of us. He was totally Abbie's type. Super-tan, super-muscly, and happily aware of both. It turned out he was moving at that turtlelike pace so he could check himself out in every store window he passed. He also had to shake his long, blond-tipped bangs out of his eyes every few steps.

Hannah and I rolled our eyes at each other.

"Perfect summer fling material," she whispered to me.

"Ugh," I said. "I know where *I'd* fling him."

Abbie was so fixated on sneaking up on him, she didn't hear us. When she turned to whisper to us, her face was alight.

"I think he's heading to the Pop Guy," she whispered. "Score! I can get the boy *and* dessert!"

"If I hadn't just seen her in a bikini," I said to Hannah, "I'd swear *she* was a boy."

"'It's just a body,'" Hannah mimicked. She put her hands on her hips and swished them back and forth. "'What's the big deal?'"

I laughed so loud that Abbie turned around and glared at me. I tried, not very hard, to quiet down. Not that it mattered. Jim (or John or whoever) was completely oblivious to us.

He also didn't seem to be in the mood for a pop. Just before he reached the rainbow umbrella, he jaywalked across the street, heading for the corner.

And on the corner was—

"Oh, no," I breathed, skidding to a halt.

"What! What is it?" Abbie asked as she and Hannah hopped off the curb in pursuit.

When I didn't answer, Abbie huffed with impatience and grabbed my hand. She dragged me across the street, almost getting us hit by a pickup truck while she was at it.

Before I knew it, we were pushing through the jangly front door of Dog Ear. Immediately after feeling a rush of best-bookstore-ever happiness, I was seized with panic.

Josh couldn't see me like this! I was supposed to be wearing my favorite yellow sundress with the bell-shaped skirt. I should have on mascara and lip gloss. My nose should *not* be bright red after a morning in the sun, and my hair . . . Well, there was nothing that could be done about my hair, but a big hat would have been nice.

I froze in my tracks. Abbie, still clutching my hand, tried to get me to follow her to the lounge, where her boy was headed (probably just to snap up some free snacks without even making the pretense of reading something). But I wouldn't budge. My eyes darted around the bookstore. Behind the half-dozen stacks of books on the corner of the L-shaped counter, there was a girl with cherry-red streaks in her hair. She was sitting on a stool, reading a book and scratching her head with a neon pink pencil. A gray-haired man was unpacking a box in the kids' section, and a half-dozen people were browsing the stacks. But I didn't see Josh.

I breathed a little easier, but I wasn't in the clear yet. I decided that if he didn't surface in three minutes, he probably wasn't there and I was safe.

Until then I was staying put. I pretended to study the table full of bestsellers just inside the door.

"Oh, fine!" Abbie whispered. "I should have known I couldn't count on you in a bookstore. Come on, Hannah."

Hannah followed her to the lounge. I watched as Abbie smoothly grabbed a random book off a shelf, then flopped herself onto the couch next to her boy. She kicked off her flip-flops and plunked her feet onto the coffee table, the better for J-boy to check out her legs.

It took, oh, about thirty seconds for him to recognize Abbie and start chatting with her. Hannah perched easily on the couch arm and joined in on the banter. How did my sisters make it look so effortless?

I pulled my ragged little notepad out of my bag. I jotted down all the things that would have been going through my mind if I were Abbie:

Okay, so he remembers me, I wrote, channeling my sister, *but that doesn't mean he* likes *me. What if he doesn't?*

What if he does?

What if he does but he has a girlfriend?

What if I become *his girlfriend and then find out he kisses like a fish?*

I stopped scribbling and looked at Abbie's face. It was as open and sunny as the mason jar full of daisies on the coffee table. Clearly she was thinking *none* of these ridiculous things. I bet the only loop running through her head was: *I look awesome! This hottie is the perfect match for me. Until I dump him to head back home.*

I sighed as I flipped my notepad closed and tossed it back into my bag. When Abbie was born, she hogged all the badass genes, leaving none for me when I came along.

On the bright side, I realized, three minutes had passed and Josh hadn't emerged from a back room or from behind a bookshelf. He clearly wasn't there. Which meant I was free to dig into Dog Ear without worrying about how horrid I looked.

I glanced at Abbie and Hannah. Hannah had found a book and sunk into the leather chair to read it. Abbie was laughing with J-boy. She flicked one of her braids over her shoulder and propped her chin on her fist. She was laying it on thick! I had time.

I wondered if that book Josh had showed me, *Beyond the Beneath*, was still in stock. I started for the YA section.

But as soon as I passed the stacks of books on the corner of the counter, I realized I'd made a grave miscalculation.

The only person I'd *seen* behind the counter was the girl with the red streaks. But behind that barricade of books, there was plenty more room for another person. Especially if that person was sitting in a low chair and bent over a desk tucked below the counter.

I stifled a gasp as Josh came into my sight line. He was doing his letter C slouch again, so hunched over that you could almost see the knobby curve of his spine through the thin, white fabric of his T-shirt.

And in case you were wondering whether I thought his spine was as cute as his forehead, the answer, pathetically, is yes.

I froze in place, debating whether I should tiptoe back to the front door, where Josh couldn't see me, or dart into the stacks to hide among the books. Before I could do either, though, I got distracted by the thing on Josh's desk.

It was a huge poster. It had a blown-up image of a book cover in one corner. I couldn't read the name of the book, but I could see that it was an image of blue sky filled with perfect fluffy clouds.

Josh was inking in a sketch above the cover. It was a beautiful girl's face, gazing down at the book. She looked hazy and transparent—like she was one with the sky.

It was really, *really* good.

In another corner of the poster, Josh had made block letters in a funky, slanty font. I recognized it from the Dog Ear sign.

I glanced around at some of the other posters on the walls, each advertising an author reading or book launch party. Josh's same leaning font was on every one.

Other than that, they were all wildly different. One poster—

for a book about a London punk—featured E.B. the dog with a Mohawk, black eyeliner, and safety pins in his floppy ears. Another, for a campy zombie book, had a funny portrait of a zombie gnawing on a human arm like it was a cob of corn. Still another, for a children's picture book, had a pigeon pitching a fit from all different angles, like a police mug shot.

Clearly Josh had made all of these.

With my mouth hanging open in surprise, I glanced back at him. That's when I saw that he was staring at me!

As our eyes met I snapped my mouth shut with such force, I felt my teeth jangle a bit.

Josh did the exact same thing.

I didn't know whether to burst out laughing or to duck my disheveled head and run out of Dog Ear. Given my lack of makeup, I kind of wanted to do the latter.

But given Josh's adorable face?

I stayed.

"You finally came," he said.

He had a nervous/sweet half smile on his face. And his smooth cap of hair was kind of flattened in the one part where I guessed he'd been propping it on his hand while he drew. His shoulders were angular and adorable inside his thin T-shirt.

"Um, yeah," I said. "I've been meaning to, but things have been kind of family-intensive. I'm with my sisters right now, in fact . . ."

My voice trailed off as I gestured at them in the lounge.

What I didn't say was, "My sisters dragged me in here because I was too terrified to come by myself."

"Oh," he said. Which made me wonder what *he* wasn't saying.

"So you made all these?" I said, pointing at the framed posters lining the wall.

"Well . . ." Josh glanced at the half-finished poster on the desk, and then I *could* tell what he was thinking. He was wishing he could do a full-body dive on top of it, covering it up so I wouldn't know his secret.

"So . . . it's not all receipt tape?" I broached.

He looked squirmy again. But a sheepish smile snuck through. And even though he was trying to fight it off, it lit up his face.

"Did you ever start that book?" he said, changing the subject. "The one with the monsoon?"

"No monsoon yet," I said with a laugh. "But she did compare the rising tropical sun to a hothouse hyacinth."

"Ooh, that's bad," he said, and cringed.

"Oh, *wretched*," I said happily. "Which, you know, can sometimes be a good thing. Like Lifetime movies of the week? My sisters and I love them."

"Because you can laugh at them—"

"Not with, but at," I interjected.

"Right," Josh said. "But the point is, you do it together. Can't do that with a book."

Then his eyes lit up.

"Wait a minute," he said.

He disappeared beneath the counter. I heard a shuffling sound, and the *slap, slap, slap* of paperbacks hitting the floor. I glanced nervously at Abbie and Hannah. Hannah was completely immersed in a book that just reeked of important subject matter.

And Abbie was giving J-Boy a flirty punch in the arm. She practically batted her eyelashes at him.

Suddenly Josh reemerged. His flattened hair had popped back up. And he was holding a coverless paperback book. I pointed at it.

"Is that—"

"*Coconut Dreams*," Josh said. "We had two copies. This one was in the recycle box. My parents are supposed to drive the stuff over to the office supply place to get them shredded, but of course that hasn't happened yet."

This time, though, Josh seemed kind of delighted to have parents who neglected the boring bookstore chores.

"So . . . what?" I said. "You're gonna read that?"

"*We* could read it," he said. "You know, at the same time."

"Like a book club?" I said. That sounded, um, wholesome, in a middle-aged kind of way.

"Naw," Josh said. "It's like an *anti*–book club. We could both read it and make fun of it."

"So you *do* hate books," I joked.

"No, I don't!" Josh said. "There are a lot—well, some—that I think are amazing."

He dropped *Coconut Dreams* onto the desk and grabbed another book off it. It had the same cover as the book on Josh's in-progress poster. It was called *Photo Negative*.

"*This* one is amazing," Josh said, showing me the new book. "You haven't read it because it's not out yet. But when it does come out, you've got to get it."

"And the writer's coming here?" I said, nodding at his poster.

"Yeah," he said, clutching the book a little more tightly. "He is."

He looked so cutely vulnerable that I smiled. I couldn't help it. It was like I had no control over my face.

Josh smiled too—tentatively, like he'd dodged a bullet. He glanced back at his desk and seemed about to say something, when I felt Abbie *tap-tap-tap* my shoulder. I jumped.

"Hey," I said, turning to give her an irritated look. Hannah was behind her, looking amused.

Abbie whispered gleefully, "I've got good news and bad news."

She pulled me over to a display case that blocked our view of the J-boy in the lounge. It was also conveniently out of earshot of Josh.

"The bad news is," Abbie breathed, "I still don't know his name."

I looked over at Josh. His smile had faded, but it hadn't completely disappeared. He turned back to the desk.

I turned back to Abbie. She was so giddy with her impending good news that she didn't even seem to notice me making eye contact with Josh.

It probably doesn't occur to her that I could have a J-boy of my own, I thought ruefully.

"The good news is," Abbie said, "he's invited us to a party on Sunday. It's called a lantern party. I guess they do it every summer on the last day of June."

"That's weird," I said. "Why that day?"

"Oh, I don't know," Abbie said, waving her hand dismissively. "He explained it, but I didn't get the whole story. It's some small-town private joke."

"Huh," I said. I shot Hannah a dubious looks. "So he invited all of us?"

"Yeah, essentially," Hannah said. "I bet Liam will be there."

"Oh, great," I said. "So you can both go off with your boys and leave me with a bunch of strangers."

"A bunch of *potential*," Abbie declared. "We're going to be here the rest of the summer. Don't you want to make some friends? Don't tell me you want to stay home with Mom and Dad every night."

I glanced over my shoulder at Josh. He was sitting back at his desk, scribbling intensely on his poster.

I crossed my arms over my chest and faced my sisters again.

"What's a lantern party?" I asked.

"It's at the big dock at the marina," Abbie said with a shrug. "I assume they're lighting it all up with lanterns. You'll love it."

I cocked my head.

"I might like it," I said slowly.

"She's in!" Abbie blurted. She thrust her hand toward Hannah, and Hannah high-fived her. Abbie started for the door.

Perfect. If she and Hannah went outside, I could finish talking to Josh.

"Oh, no!" Abbie said. She pointed at the Pop Guy's stand across the street. He was pulling down his giant umbrella, which meant he was closing up shop. "We've gotta catch him!"

She trotted to the door, then looked back and gestured wildly at us.

"Come *on*," she said. "It's so hot out, if I don't get something cold in me, I'll pass out."

"Okay, okay!" Hannah said with a laugh. She headed for the door.

"I'm going to . . . ," I began.

Hannah turned and looked at me impatiently.

"What?" she said. "Aren't you coming?"

I glanced again at Josh. His head was still down and he was frowning in concentration. Clearly he was back in work mode. I shrugged unhappily and headed for the door. Before I let it close behind me, I snuck a last peek over my shoulder—and saw *Josh* peeking around the book stacks at me! My stomach swooped. I managed a little wave before the jingly door slammed behind me.

I considered going back in to say good-bye in a less awkward way, but going back in seemed more awkward still.

And besides, he hadn't waved back.

I left so fast, he didn't have time to, I told myself as I trotted across the street after my sisters. *Right? It's not because he realized I'm a spaz with even spazzier siblings. Right? Right?*

I was lost in these neurotic thoughts as my sisters bought up the dregs of the Pop Guy's wares. As we headed down the street toward home, Hannah handed me a napkin and a creamy white frozen pop.

"What flavor is this?" I asked. I held it up. It looked like there were *raisins* in it.

"Rice pudding," Hannah said.

"Oh, yuck!" I said, curling my lip.

"Hey, at least it doesn't have tarragon or sage in it," Abbie said. "We know you hate those."

"What'd you guys get?" I said, tentatively taking a lick of

my pop. It was actually cinnamony and delicious, if I could just ignore the nubbly texture of the rice.

"Coconut jalapeño," Abbie said, hanging her tongue out. "Spicy!"

"Cherry vanilla," Hannah said. "Mmmm."

"Ooh," I said. "Let's go halvesies."

"Nope!" Hannah said. "Abbie said I could have the good one. Wingman's honor."

I grumbled as I nibbled at my pop, trying to avoid the bits of rice.

It was only when we turned off Main Street and Abbie and Hannah started debating outfits for the lantern party that my thoughts drifted back to Dog Ear. Suddenly I remembered something Josh had said.

"We could both read it."

My eyes widened. I froze mid-lick.

He asked me to form an anti–book club with him, I realized. *That's definitely more meaningful than just saying, "You should come into Dog Ear sometime," right?*

I started to get a little short of breath. I trailed behind my sisters as I debated with myself.

Okay, hold on, I told myself. *It's not like he was asking me out on a date. He just wants to goof on a bad book. It's not a big deal. Or is it?*

"We could both read it and make fun of it." That's what he said. So where would this fun-making take place? Over coffee? On the beach? On a picnic blanket on the beach on which he has laid out a spread of all my favorite herb-free foods?

The itchy feeling of melted ice pop dripping down my arm pulled me out of my daydream, which had been veering into the truly ridiculous anyway. As I mopped the melted milk off my wrist, I shook my head.

He just means we could have a laugh the next time I wander into Dog Ear, I admonished myself. *That's all. I bet he won't even bother to actually read it.*

But that night in bed, as I flicked on my reading light and regarded the two books on my nightstand—*Coconut Dreams* and *Sense and Sensibility*—I couldn't stop myself from grabbing the tropical romance.

As I read it, every florid paragraph seemed to have a footnote filled with the banter I could have with Josh.

And suddenly *Coconut Dreams* became a book that I really didn't want to put down.

*B*y the day of the lantern party, we'd been in Bluepointe for almost three weeks. We'd gotten used to having nothing to do—no jobs or sports practices to rush to, no exams to study for, no friends to meet up with. Everything had slowed down. And what little we had to accomplish could be stretched out for *hours*.

Which was why, after a morning at the beach and a protracted, piecemeal lunch on the screened porch, my sisters and I spent almost the entire afternoon getting ready for our evening.

This was not our usual thing. Abbie was strictly a wash-and-wear kind of girl, and Hannah could blow-dry her hair into a perfect, sleek 'do in about three minutes. My routine mostly involved working copious amounts of product into my hair to make it go corkscrewy instead of turning into a giant poof of frizz.

But this afternoon we were a veritable movie montage of primping, perfuming, and outfit sampling.

But that was the thing about having sisters. We fought and made fun of each other and stole each other's clothes, but we also kept each other's secrets. Abbie and I, for instance, never reminded Hannah about the time she threw up in the mall food court in front of about a hundred people. And whenever Abbie lost at a swim meet, Hannah and I knew that she wanted us to be near, but silent. So we'd sit with her on the couch, turn on a dumb reality show, and hand her a big bowl of Lay's potato chips. By the time she made it to the bottom of the bowl, she was ready to talk about the meet, and we were there to listen.

So today, when all three of us turned into total girly-girls, which we definitely *weren't* in our "real" lives, we knew that nobody outside that room would ever hear about it. We could be as ridiculously giggly as we wanted.

"I can't decide!" Abbie groaned. She was looking at three outfits arranged on the big bed in Hannah's room. "I can't wear the dress, can I? That's just trying too hard."

"So you wear the white capris and the tank top," I said. I was on the floor painting my toenails a buttery yellow color. "That's more you anyway."

"Yeah, but white means I have to be careful not to get dirty," Abbie complained.

"What are you going to do?" Hannah demanded. "Roll around in the dirt with What's His Name?"

Abbie tapped a fist on her head.

"Argh," she groaned. "What *is* J-boy's name? It's too late to ask now!"

"Somebody will say it at the party," Hannah said. "You just have to keep your ears open."

"Or you could just skip right to 'honey,'" I posed. "That wouldn't freak him out at all!"

"I would *never*," Abbie gasped. "Now, 'Pooh Bear' on the other hand is completely acceptable."

"Totally," Hannah said. "You know what's even better? 'Sweet Cheeks.'"

"Love Muffin!" I yelled.

"Come here, Love Muffin," Abbie cried, grabbing a pillow and kissing it passionately.

"Ew, I sleep on that," Hannah said. She snatched the pillow away from Abbie and tossed it back onto the bed. Then she spotted my pedicure and gasped.

"Oh, *no*!" she said. She grabbed the bottle of polish remover from the dresser and plopped down in front of me. "*So* wrong."

"What?" I said. "I love this color."

"Me too," Hannah said, "but not on your feet. You're too pale. You need contrast."

She held up two bottles of polish—one shimmery hot pink, the other a bright turquoise.

"All right," I grumbled, pointing at the blue-green bottle. "But you do it. I hate painting my toes."

While Hannah polished, Abbie got busy on my hair.

"You can't keep yanking it back like you do," she said, fluffing up my hair. "You're gonna get a bald spot."

"What!" I cried, clutching at my scalp. "Is that even possible with this much hair?"

Abbie didn't answer as she rifled through her cosmetics bag. She came up with a wide elastic headband with a cute blue and green flower pattern on it. She snapped it around my head and arranged my curls behind it, with a couple tendrils popping out at the temples.

"Really?" I said skeptically. "There's just so *much* of it."

"Wear a tank top," Abbie said decisively. "Then your hair isn't competing with your sleeves."

Hannah finished my toes, and I leaned over to fan them dry with one of Hannah's *National Geographic*s.

"How come *I'm* getting all the makeover attention?" I said. "You're the ones trying to bag the love muffins."

Abbie and Hannah glanced at each other.

"What?" I demanded.

"We're just trying to help you, Chels," Hannah said.

"Why?" I demanded. "What's wrong with me?"

"Nothing, except you're a little . . . stuck," Hannah said carefully. "Uncomfortable in your skin. You need to be more confident and own who you are."

"'Own who I am'?" I said mockingly. "Who are you, Oprah?"

"Okay, smart-mouth," Abbie said. "Let's put it this way. You are standing in the way of your own hotness with this shy, bookwormy I-hate-my-hair routine. You need to lose the ponytail and stop hunching over just because you have boobs."

I could almost feel my eyebrows meet my hairline. I was literally speechless. We were always blunt with each other, but this was new terrain.

When I got over my shock, I scowled.

"I'm not shy," I said. "Just because I don't want to be the center of attention like some people I could name"—I looked pointedly at Abbie—"doesn't mean I'm an introverted freak."

"Look," Hannah said. "You're lucky. You've got two sisters who've just been through all this. We're trying to help you."

I frowned at my turquoise toenails. I hated to admit it—and I sure *wasn't* going to admit it to them—but deep down I knew Abbie and Hannah were right. Not about the hot part. Even if I did have boobs, I still couldn't fathom a version of hot that included bright red hair and freckly skin.

But it was true that I didn't exactly exude confidence. And I knew you didn't have to be gorgeous or super-popular to have it. Look at Emma. Sure, she had that graceful ballerina bod, but she also had oily skin and a hawkish nose. But it didn't matter, because Emma knew she was talented—special—and she carried herself that way. Sure enough, Ethan had fallen so hard for her that he was practically asphyxiating himself with all the kissing.

But how do you just suddenly decide you're special? Emma got on that track when she took her first baby ballet class at age four. Hannah had studied her way to brilliance, and Abbie had just been born with all that personality.

Me? I had nothin'. Reading about extraordinary people in books didn't make you extraordinary.

Of course, if I chose to believe my sisters (and that was a big *if*), I wasn't a total untouchable.

Own who you are, Hannah had said.

It would have sounded great on a greeting card, but in real life? I had no idea how to do that. I wondered if being "comfortable in my skin" was just another area in which I was doomed to fall short of my sisters.

*T*he moment we showed up at the dock that night, just after sunset, we knew we'd wasted all that time primping.

Not that we didn't look kind of fabulous, with our fresh, color-correct mani-pedis, our summery makeup, and our bare shoulders dusted with shimmery powder. (Hannah had read about that in a magazine that was *not*, for the record, *National Geographic*.)

As Abbie had directed, I'd chosen a white sundress with skinny straps. It also had a tight bodice and a flared, knee-length skirt. The salesgirl at the vintage store where I'd bought it had told me it was made in the early 1960s.

To match my headband I'd borrowed Hannah's flat, royal blue sandals. Between those and my turquoise toes, my feet had never been so colorful. I hoped they would draw attention away from my voluminous hair.

But as it turned out, looking good at a lantern party didn't seem to be the point. At all. Most of the kids milling around the dock—which was a big square wood plank platform surrounded by anchored speedboats—looked happily disheveled in shorts and T-shirts. They had paint smears on their arms and arts-and-crafts glitter in their hair. And every one of them held an elaborate homemade lantern. Even though they weren't lit yet, presumably because there was still a bit of dusky light left, the lanterns were dazzlingly creative. There was a lantern that looked like a Japanese temple and one that looked like a fairy-tale mush-room, the kind with the white-dotted red cap. One lantern was an elaborate geometric shape that even Hannah might not have been able to identify. And there were side-by-side lanterns that looked like Fred and Wilma Flintstone.

Hannah walked over to a nearby girl who was bobbing her head to the music. Her lantern dangled from the end of a long stick. It was a cylinder made of flowery paper. Cut into the lan-tern was a window of waxed paper, which contained a funny silhouette of a dog.

"Love your lantern!" Hannah said as Abbie and I stood behind her. "Did you make it yourself?"

"Thanks!" the girl said, crinkling her nose happily at her lan-tern. "It was a hard one. It took me the whole pre-party. I guess you guys weren't there?"

"Pre-party?" Abbie said, closing in on the girl. "When was that?"

"Oh, it started around noon," the girl said. "We do it every year—get together and make our lanterns. We order in fried chicken and get all gluey. It's pretty goofy, but we've all been doing it since, like, middle school, so you know—it's a tradition now. At the end of the night there's a lantern contest."

"Wow, that sounds awesome," Abbie said flatly. If there was

anything she hated more than being left out of the loop, it was losing a contest. "Where was this pre-party?"

"It was at Jason's house," the girl said, cheerfully pointing to a far corner of the dock. There stood Abbie's J-boy, flanked by two laughing girls. He was holding up his lantern like it was a trophy. It was a very lumpy papier-mâché sculpture of Darth Vader's head. Presumably, once it was lit up, the eyes would glow.

Abbie's face darkened, but she kept her voice light as she answered, "Oh, it was at *Jason's* house. That's cool. Well, good luck in the contest."

"Thanks!" the girl chirped as Abbie drifted away.

Hannah and I gave each other a look.

"Let's see if there are any potato chips on the refreshment table," I whispered.

"She's already on her way," she said, pointing at Abbie as she made a beeline for the junk-food-laden table. Luckily, it was on the opposite side of the dock from Jason.

I arrived at Abbie's side just as she scooped a handful of chips out of a big bowl and stuffed at least four of them into her mouth.

"Well," I said brightly. I sounded just like our mom, who always got annoyingly chipper when the going got rough. "The good news is, now we know your guy's name! J-boy is Jason."

"The bad news," Abbie said grimly, "is he blew me off for someone else—*two* someone elses—before I even got here."

"Wait a minute," Hannah said as she poured soda into plastic cups for us. "You don't know that. You heard what that girl said. These people have all known each other forever. Those girls are probably just friends of his."

"Well, how do you explain the fact that he didn't invite me to the main event?" Abbie said, jabbing her thumb in the direction of a passing lantern that was about six feet tall and made to look like a tree, complete with a robin's nest and a squirrel scampering up the trunk.

"You're all confident and stuff," I said. I couldn't help but get that dig in. "Go and ask him!"

I gave her a little shove in Jason's direction. Abbie glared at me, but then she slapped her remaining chips into my palm with a crunch and headed over.

Hannah and I grinned at each other.

"Okay," she said. "One boy found. One to . . ."

Her voice trailed off as she spotted something—or rather, someone—at the other end of the refreshment table.

I followed her gaze to a boy pouring himself a big cup of sparkling water. He was dressed in khakis and a golf shirt, both of which were neat enough to give him a cute, preppy look but not so crisp as to make him look uptight.

His hair was blond and tidy. His face was sun-burnished and all-American, and he had earnest-looking blue eyes.

In other words he was *exactly* Hannah's type.

"Is that—" I started to say. "Is he—"

Hannah didn't answer me. She just pressed her cup into my hand and floated over to the boy.

"Liam?" she asked. Her tone of voice was perfect—mildly surprised and casually pleased to see him. You'd *never* guess that she'd been hoping for this moment for the past three weeks.

I tensed up as I watched the boy make eye contact with my

sister. I squinted as his face went from blank confusion to recognition to . . . delight.

Delight!

"Hannah, right?" he said. He gave her a quick hug, then stepped back to look at her admiringly. "You're back!"

Hannah shrugged. I couldn't see her face, but I didn't have to. I knew what was flashing in her eyes: triumphant relief, hopeful swooning, and just a hint of fear.

After the Elias breakup, Hannah had been single all year. She'd said it was because she was cramming for all her AP courses and applying to colleges, but Abbie and I knew that had been a convenient excuse. The truth was, she'd been truly heartbroken and afraid of being hurt again.

But now Hannah was in the lovely limbo that was Bluepointe. She'd left LA—the scene of her romance with Elias—and she hadn't yet arrived at U of C, where she'd be with the same people for the next four years.

This was her moment to have a romance that was lighthearted and fun.

I knew that if I'd come to this conclusion, Hannah would have arrived at it also. For all I knew, she'd made a whole PowerPoint presentation about it. My sister really *was* that analytical, even when it came to love. *Especially* when it came to love.

As I looked at Liam's sweet, open face, I felt hopeful for Hannah too. He looked like the perfect summer fling—cute and uncomplicated. What's more, after hugging her, Liam had let his hand linger on Hannah's arm. It looked like he was definitely interested.

I wonder what that's like? I thought a little wistfully. *To have a boy just grab you and hug you, instead of being all shy and proposing cryptic things like an anti-book club?*

I popped one of Abbie's chips into my mouth, took a swig of Hannah's drink, and turned to face the party. Nobody seemed to take much notice of me. Clearly being lanternless at a lantern party immediately consigned you to the lowest social order.

I shoved the rest of the chips into my mouth, wondering how many minutes of this party I'd have to endure before I could drag Abbie and Hannah away.

I cast a sidelong glance at Hannah and Liam. His hand was no longer on her arm, but he was standing close to her—quite close—as they chatted. He poured her some sparkling water. He let his fingers linger on hers when he handed it to her.

I grimaced and grabbed another handful of chips. It was going to be a long night.

*I*f I was a good and loyal sister, I wouldn't have felt elated when I saw Abbie stalking toward me a few minutes later. She was so angry, you could practically see a cartoon scribble of smoke over her head.

Apparently Jason had turned out to be as jerky as he looked.

And I felt bad about that. I really did. But not as bad as I'd *been* feeling a moment earlier, when I'd been alone on the party's sidelines, glaring at all the local kids with their ridiculously clever lanterns and annoying lifelong friendships.

It was also maddening watching Hannah and Liam as they visibly swooned over each other. Hannah was doing everything right—chatting easily, laughing adorably, blushing at all the right moments. And she was clearly melting every time Liam touched her arm. Or her waist. Or her hand. (Come to think of it, Liam was a pretty handsy guy.)

It had all been very, very depressing.

So when Abbie flopped into a folding chair next to the one that I had miserably occupied for the past fifteen lonely minutes, I admit that I responded a little inappropriately.

"What happened?" I asked eagerly. "Was it really bad?"

Abbie glared at me.

"Of course it was bad!" she said. "Do I look like it was good? And why are *you* so happy?"

"I'm not," I protested. I tried—hard—to wipe the relieved grin off my face. "So what happened?"

"I don't know!" Abbie said through gritted teeth. "He seemed so interested at that bookstore. But just now he acted like he didn't even know me. It was *humiliating*."

It was better than I'd thought! Not only was she not going to ditch me again; she was probably going to insist that we leave the party.

"Ouch," I said. "Tell me *everything*."

"Wait," Abbie said. "Are there any chips left?"

She got up and stomped over to the refreshment table. But before she could load up on junk food and return to me, one of the local girls dragged a folding chair to the center of the dock. She stood on it and waved her lantern—a Chinese-style globe decorated with tissue paper dragonflies.

"Everybody," she screeched. "It's time to light 'em up!"

Whoops and hollers rose up from every corner of the dock. Giggling, everyone scrambled for matchbooks and lighters. I perked up too. With all my sisters' drama, I'd almost forgotten about the lanterns. I'd also failed to notice that the sky had gone black and the streetlights hanging over the dock had come on.

"Alex?" the girl shouted with one hand cupped around her mouth.

All heads swiveled toward a tall boy with an impish grin. He was fiddling with what looked like a fuse box, which was mounted on a pole at the dock entrance.

A moment later the lights went out.

"Whooo!" everyone shouted, except, of course, for me and probably Abbie. She'd disappeared in the darkness. Suddenly blind, I felt a little dizzy and gripped the seat of my chair.

"One!" the girl shouted.

There was a collective clicking noise as lighters sprang to life all over the dock. People laughed and shouted some more, waving their flames over their heads like they were at a stadium concert.

"Two!" This time the whole group chanted the number along with the leader. I gripped my chair a little harder and grinned. It was so exciting, I couldn't help but join in on the final chant, even though I had no lantern to light and nobody to enjoy this with. The other kids' fun was infectious.

"THREE!" we all shouted.

Lantern after lantern came to life!

There was a collective, quiet intake of breath as we absorbed the beauty of the lights.

The leader's buggy globe went bright orange, wobbling high

above the crowd. Fred and Wilma seemed to dance with each other. The giant tree was dazzling, emanating light from every leaf. Even Jason's stupid Darth Vader head looked amazing, with creepy yellow eyes glaring at the crowd.

At once everybody erupted into cheers.

"Whoo!" I joined in. I felt a little goofy and self-conscious jumping and clapping with everybody else, but then I brushed it off. Nobody here knew me. I was invisible to them. And for the moment, rather than being a bummer, that was a gift. I could geek out all I wanted to the perfect summery beauty of this moment without feeling embarrassed.

With my hands clasped I watched the lanterns float over my head. I gasped as I spotted the one shaped like an orange phoenix with wings outstretched, and smiled at the giant mason jar with little "fireflies" twinkling inside.

Somebody started the music back up. A ballad came on, sung by a woman with a sweet high voice, so breathy and wispy that you almost had to strain to hear her. A few couples started dancing, swaying lazily to the music. Everyone looked so pretty, almost ethereal, in the golden glow of the lanterns.

The moment was just . . . lovely. It made me swell up with happiness and feel a yearning pang all at once. It had been that way, ever since Granly had died. Every moment of joy had an ache around its edges. But when I looked at the dancing girls— this one gazing into her guy's eyes, that one whispering into her partner's ear, another laying her head on a boy's shoulder—I realized that the ache might be for something different this time.

And then my gaze shifted to the dock entrance.

I don't know what made me look, except that somehow I knew he was there.

Josh.

He was standing in the little gateway that led from the parking lot to the dock, holding on to the railing with one hand. He was wearing a short-sleeved button-down shirt in a retro checked print. His hair was glossy and neat, and his face had a recently scrubbed shine to it. In the glow of the lanterns, he looked . . . beautiful.

Or maybe he just looked that way because of the sweet, shy smile on his face. The one that seemed to be directed right at me.

I resisted the urge to turn around and make sure there wasn't some other girl behind me, one with straighter hair and a fancy lantern.

I took a halting step forward.

So did Josh.

Several steps and what felt like way too many seconds later, we faced each other.

"Hi," he said.

"Hi," I said. My voice sounded thin and fragile. I felt off balance, like the flickering of all those lantern candles was making my eyes go funny. I cleared my throat and gestured at his hands, which were empty.

"No lantern?" I asked.

"Um, no," Josh said. "It was kind of a last-minute decision. To come here, I mean."

"Oh," I said. It seemed nosy to ask why, so I just said, "They're beautiful, aren't they?"

Josh's eyes widened and he looked confused.

I gestured out to the party.

"The lanterns?" I asked. "Aren't they amazing?"

"Oh, the *lanterns*," Josh said. "Oh, yeah."

He gazed out into the party as if he were noticing the spectacle for the first time. Which was weird. They were kind of hard to miss!

He returned his gaze to me.

"Yeah," he agreed finally. "They're pretty amazing."

I smiled.

And he smiled.

And I started to wonder, even though it seemed crazy, if he had come here . . . just to see me.

A little voice in my head scoffed: *That's impossible. He couldn't have heard Abbie talking about it at Dog Ear, so he didn't know you'd be here. In fact he was probably sure you wouldn't be here, since this is just a local party.*

And yet I had this feeling that if I gave Josh a lantern pop quiz—*Are there any* Star Wars *characters in the crowd? There's one very tall lantern here. Is it a tree or a skyscraper?*—that he would fail miserably.

That's when my smile grew bigger. And, yes, more confident.

I decided I should just come out and ask him. Enough with all the mystery. I would channel Abbie and just put it out there: *You like me, don't you? And you don't know how to say it any more than I do.*

I opened my mouth.

"Josh?"

A petite, sporty-looking girl pressed out of the throng of

partiers. She had chic, close-cropped hair and white short-shorts that made her muscular, dark-skinned legs look amazing. A lantern that looked like a big, pink purse dangled from her bent arm.

"Ohmigod, the workaholic has come out of his cave," the girl squealed.

She placed the hand that wasn't holding a live flame on Josh's arm and squeezed.

"Hi, Tori," Josh said. Now he was back to looking sheepish, and I thought I saw a flush of color creep up his neck.

Wait, he's blushing? What does that mean?

Tori turned to me and lowered her voice, like we were besties sharing a secret.

"He's always like"—she dropped her voice an octave to imitate Josh—"'Can't make it. I have to *work*. *Again!*' Oh, it's so boring!"

"Yeah, well." Josh shrugged lamely.

Tori shot me a sidelong look and let out another one of those conspiratorial laughs. The only thing was, I didn't know what we were conspiring about.

"So, how do you know Josh?" Tori asked bluntly.

"Dog Ear," Josh and I said at the same time, which made for more blushing.

"Oh, of course," Tori said. "Well, I'm the coxswain on his team."

"Coxswain?" I said. I was completely baffled.

"You know, his crew team?" Tori raised her eyebrows.

I nodded slowly. "Oh, right . . . crew."

"Crew is rowing," Josh explained.

"Oh!" I said with a nervous laugh. "Yeah, of course. When in lake country, right?"

Oh my God, could I be more of a dork?

"We row on the river, actually," Josh said. "The coxswain is the person who sits in the front and calls the rhythm."

"Don't forget, I steer, too!" Tori noted proudly. Then she turned to me. "I admit it. I like being able to shout orders at eight guys. They have no choice but to do my bidding."

She cackled, before adding, "The coxswain is usually a girl, because you're not supposed to weigh too much."

Then I swore she gave me one of those body-scanning looks, her eyes traveling from my neck to my ankles and back again. My curvy five feet six inches were radically different from her tiny, muscular bod. Involuntarily I crossed my arms over my chest.

The awkward silence that ensued seemed to be all Tori needed to assure herself that I was no threat to her. I could almost see the to-do list forming in her head.

1. *Wait until Josh ditches the dishrag who doesn't even know rudimentary terms like "coxswain" and "crew."*
2. *Bring Josh his favorite drink (that I just happen to know, being his coxswain and all).*
3. *Pretend to trip so he can help me to my feet and take note that I'm as light as a feather and I smell like watermelon body wash.*
4. *Let the spit-swapping ensue!*

Clearly she was confident enough about my drippiness to leave me alone with her crush.

"Ooh, I see Hazel and Callan," she said, waving wildly at two girls. When they saw Tori with Josh (and apparently overlooked me entirely), they giggled and flashed her a thumbs-up. Subtle!

"See you later, Joshie," Tori said before turning to me. "And nice to meet you . . ."

She looked at me, then back at Josh, waiting for an introduction.

Josh turned even redder. Only then did I realize he'd never asked me my name! And I'd never volunteered it.

"Chelsea," I said, unable to meet Josh's eyes. "Chelsea Silver. I'm here for the summer from LA."

"Awesome! I *love* LA," Tori said brightly. "See you around, Chelsea."

She practically skipped off to her friends, and when she reached them, they collapsed into a fit of giggles.

She couldn't have been more obvious about her intentions for Josh if she'd licked his face.

I snuck a sulky glance at him. I expected him to be gazing after Tori. How could he not? She was one of those bright-eyed, bubbly, anybody's-version-of-pretty types who *commanded* attention.

But instead Josh was looking straight at me. And there seemed to be a new light in *his* eyes.

"So . . . Chelsea Silver," he said.

"So . . . Joshie," I said. "Is that what your friends call you?"

"No!" Josh said, rolling his eyes. "And neither does Tori. I don't know *where* that came from."

Hello? I thought. *From her completely obvious crush on you.*

I wondered if mine was just as obvious.

"Oh, hey!" Josh said as if he were just remembering something. "Can you hold on a minute?"

"Uh—"

I didn't have time to respond before he darted toward the refreshments table.

Okay, I thought, insecurity washing over me. *I guess he's just really hungry. Boys are like that, right?*

That was the thing about living in a house full of women (and one not-exactly-macho accountant). Boys were a complete mystery to me. My main impression from my friends with brothers and/or boyfriends was that boys were *always* hungry. And in those rare, satiated moments when they weren't dreaming about food, they were obsessed with sex.

Which was a step up from middle-school boys, I guess. They'd seemed to devote most of their energy to coming up with new fart or burp jokes.

So when Josh dashed, I didn't know if "Hold on a minute" meant, "I'll be right back" or "Nice talking to you. Off to mingle with other cute girls now. Don't wait up!"

He was taking a long time at the refreshment table, which was pretty much a disaster by then. He poked around the wet napkins, crushed chips, half-empty soft drink bottles, and discarded paper plates.

I scanned the party for my sisters. It was hard to find anybody among the lanterns, but I finally spotted Hannah leaning back against the railing on the other side of the dock. Pressed up *really* close to her was Liam. He had one arm wrapped around her waist, and he seemed to be aiming his lips for her neck.

Hannah laughed and shoved him away—but not very far away. And she didn't seem annoyed that this guy was trying to kiss her in front of fifty strangers.

I was, though. She'd just met the guy! Okay, *re*-met him, but still. Your first kiss with someone new should be at least a *little* private, right?

Abbie clearly agreed with me, because suddenly she appeared at Hannah's side. She gave Liam a quick, insincere smile before she tugged Hannah away.

I watched them tuck their heads together for a quick conference. Surely Abbie wanted to leave.

But it looked like Hannah wanted to stay.

And me?

Well, that depended. I returned my gaze to the refreshment table and felt my heart sink.

Josh wasn't there.

I searched the rest of the party, squinting to try to find him in the sea of lights. At that moment I couldn't remember what he was wearing. All I could picture was his shy, sheepish smile.

Like he was sort of nervous/excited to see me.

Until, maybe, he realized that girls like Tori found him irresistible, and going on a "food run" had become incredibly important.

I ground my teeth in frustration and looked down at my feet. Even in the dim light I could still see my blue shoes and turquoise toenails. They were so bright, they practically glowed. And yet they'd been planted in one spot for most of the night, waiting. Waiting for my sisters, waiting for Josh.

Well, I wasn't going to wait anymore. I started to head over to Abbie and Hannah. I was going to poke my head into their little conference and announce, "That's it. We're leaving!"

And really, really hope they listened to me.

But just as I started across the dock, I heard a voice.

"Chelsea!"

I whipped around to see Josh, standing right where he'd left me. He held two red plastic cups and, in the crook of his arm, a bowl of pretzel rods.

He held one of the cups out.

"I got you something to drink," he said formally.

I smiled tentatively and walked back to him. He'd braved the gross refreshments table to get me a drink. And snacks! Nobody had ever gotten me drinks and snacks at a party before, except maybe my dad. It seemed like such a grown-up thing to do!

"It's Faygo Redpop," Josh said as I took one of the cups. "That was the only one that still had any fizz left."

Okay, *sort* of grown-up.

Josh thrust the bowl at me, and I took a pretzel rod. Not that I was even slightly interested in eating or drinking right then.

"So, I'm on page forty-two," Josh blurted. "What about you?"

"Page . . . ?" I was completely confused.

"Coconut Dreams," Josh said. "Or did you chuck it after the one-page description of Kai's smoldering brown eyes?"

I laughed out loud.

"You're not *actually* reading it," I said. "Are you?"

"Enough to get to that tragic description of the suckling pig at the luau," Josh said. "The writer laid it on a *little* thick, didn't she?"

"Oh my God, yeah," I said. "All that stuff about the singed eyelashes and little charred tail? I think she wanted us to think of the suckling pig as Wilbur and become vegan activists or something."

"Lemme tell you," Josh said, "*Charlotte's Web* is kind of a thing at Dog Ear, and Veronica Gardner is no E. B. White."

"But it's like a car wreck now," I said, and giggled. "I can't look away. Plus, the library's, like, *never* open, and I've read everything else in our cottage."

"You should get that book I showed you," Josh said. He chomped on a pretzel absently. *"Beyond the Beneath."*

"I'm pretty broke," I said. "I'm trying to save up for a new e-reader, but at this point I can barely buy myself a paperback. I guess I should look into getting some babysitting jobs, since we're here for the rest of the summer. I'm waiting until I get desperate enough."

"Oh, so you have no sympathy for suckling pigs *and* you hate children," Josh said with teasing grin.

"I like kids," I protested. "But there's only so much Candy Land and PB&J a girl can take."

"Well, how do you feel about tuna salad?" Josh asked.

"Um," I said, "I guess some kids like it, but—"

"No, I mean you," Josh said. "I happen to know that Mel and Mel's is about to put a 'Help Wanted' sign in their window."

"The coffee shop?" I asked.

The coffee shop that's right next door to the bookstore where you work every day?

"Yeah," Josh said. "Melissa's good friends with my mom. She

mentioned that they were looking for somebody new."

I pictured Mel & Mel's. It was called a coffee shop, but it wasn't the kind that had hissing espresso machines and nutmeg-dusted mochas. The coffee was pretty much regular or decaf, poured in endless refills from a potbellied glass carafe with an orange plastic handle. They sold soup and sandwiches, and for dessert they had one of those rotating pie cases. Abbie, Hannah, and I used to press our noses to that glass case when we were little, watching the towering wedges of lemon meringue and chocolate cream pies twirl slowly by. Choosing our flavors had been agonizing.

The waitresses there were old-school. They wore aprons and tucked pens behind their ears. The older ones had leathery necks and wore too much makeup. The young ones always seemed to have lots of tattoos. They called us "sweetie pie" when they plunked down our pink lemonades on the faux wood-grain table. And when they served you pie, they topped it with a big squirt of fake whipped cream, straight from the can.

"I don't know," I said, shaking my head. "Do you think they'd be looking for someone like me? I've never waited tables before."

"Do you like cats?" Josh asked.

"They're okay," I said.

"Well, *don't* say that to Melissa," Josh said. "Tell her you *love* cats, especially calicos. And before you talk to Melanie, make sure you know the score of the most recent Cubs game."

"O-kay," I said with a laugh. "Anything else I should know?"

"How are you at chopping up celery and pickles?" Josh quizzed me.

"Oh, those are my specialties," I joked.

"They'll love you," Josh said. Then suddenly he seemed to find his fizzy red drink really interesting, because he ducked his head to stare into it.

And if I could have seen better in the late-night darkness, I would have sworn he was blushing.

Shyly I looked away. That's when I saw that Abbie was motioning at me frantically from across the dock. When she saw that she'd caught my eye, she pointed dramatically at Hannah and Liam.

They were full-on making out! Yes, they were in a shadowy part of the dock with no lanterns nearby, but you could still see *everything*—Hannah's fingers in Liam's hair, his arms clasped tightly around her waist, her ankle wrapped around his.

"Oh my God!" I exclaimed.

"What?" Josh said, following my gaze.

"Never mind!" I cried. "It's nothing."

The last thing I wanted Josh to see was my *sister* macking with one of his classmates.

"It's just," I said quickly, "I came here with my sisters and I think they're ready to go."

"Oh, okay," Josh said. I was so focused on Hannah's gross PDA that I couldn't read Josh's tone. Was that disappointment I heard in his voice? Or indifference?

"But thanks for the Mel and Mel's tip," I said. "You know, I think I'm gonna go for it!"

I had only made the decision that very moment. But suddenly I desperately wanted to tie on an apron and start calling people "hon." It sounded kind of fun! More fun, anyway, than changing diapers.

Plus, I couldn't help but wonder if Josh was a regular at Mel & Mel's. It *was* just next door.

The way he smiled at me—we're talking deep dimpling—I kind of thought he might be.

"They open at seven," he said.

July

*T*he morning after the party I left a note to my parents on the kitchen table and headed for Mel & Mel's at six forty-five.

Sparrow Road was eerily quiet, and the sunbeams filtered through the trees at a very unfamiliar angle. I was *never* up this early when I was in Bluepointe. But I told myself, maybe just a little defensively, that my job quest had nothing to do with Josh. Okay, not *much* to do with him.

I'm just being a go-getter, I thought. *Who knows how many people might be lined up for this waitress job?*

I also credited the date—the first day of July.

New month, new job—it's a fresh start. I'm already getting bored with lying around on the beach.

When I arrived at the corner of Main and Althorp, I cast a furtive glance at the not-yet-open Dog Ear, just to make sure nobody was inside. Luckily, it was dark and still, just like most of the other businesses on Main.

The brightly lit coffee shop next door looked sunny and welcoming in comparison. Just as Josh had predicted, there was a HELP WANTED sign taped to the glass door.

I peered through the door. One of the Mels, I think it was Melanie, was setting heavy china mugs out on the tables. She wore her chin-length gray hair tied back with a bandanna. Her apron—layered over jeans and a tank top—was embroidered with a calico cat.

She glanced up and saw me.

"Be right there, sweetie," she called.

"Oh, okay," I yelled back. I stepped back to the sidewalk, feeling awkward and intrusive, but Melanie (Melanie, right?) smiled sweetly as she unlocked the door.

"Well!" she said, planting her fists on her hips. "*Somebody's* really ready for chocolate chip pancakes this morning!"

"Oh, uh, no thanks," I said. "Chocolate chip pancakes really aren't my thing."

I smoothed down the marigold-colored cotton dress I'd chosen. On the plus side, it was very 1960s diner waitress. On the minus, it was horribly wrinkled. I hoped she wouldn't notice.

"Well, maybe you'd like some cinnamon streusel coffee cake?" she offered. "You would not *believe* what the secret ingredient is."

"Actually," I said, pointing back at the HELP WANTED sign, "I'm here because of the job?"

"Oh!" Mel said. She wiped her hands on her apron. "Did you just move to town?"

"Uh-huh," I said. "For the summer, anyway."

"I was kind of hoping for someone longer-term," Mel said skeptically. "What's your experience?"

"Um, I babysit for one family back in California that has four kids," I said. "Those kids can *eat*. Sometimes I feel like a short-order cook."

Melanie bit her lip. "Let me talk to my sister."

She looked over her shoulder and called, "Melanie!"

Oh! This sister wasn't Melanie; she was Melissa. That's right. It was *Melissa* who liked calico cats.

Melissa likes cats, I reminded myself. *Melanie like the Cubs. Melissa—cats. Melanie—Cubs.*

Then my stomach swooped.

I'd just remembered the other tip Josh had given me: *Make sure you know the score of the Cubs game.*

Okay, so I had no experience, I was here only for the summer, and I didn't even know who the Cubs had played last night, much less the score. I had a dim awareness that the Cubs *always* lost. I think I'd heard Granly joke about it.

So I went out on a limb as Melanie—wearing cargo shorts, a sporty-looking T-shirt, and a royal blue baseball cap with a red C on it—came out of the kitchen.

"Hi, I'm Chelsea Silver," I said, giving her a wave. "Shame about the Cubs last night, isn't it?"

"What? That they broke their losing streak?" Melanie crowed. "Three to two, baby!"

She held out her hand to Melissa for a high five. Melissa ignored the hand.

"What?" Melanie said defensively. She crossed her arms over her chest, and I noticed how tan and sinewy they looked. Melanie looked like the kind of person who spent her free time hiking up mountains or biking fifty miles or some other ridiculously out-doorsy activity. "That's a perfectly respectable score."

I laughed a little. "You remind me of me and my sisters."

"*Sisters?*" Melanie said, shooting Melissa a teasing grin. "You have more than one? You must have a strong constitution."

"That's why you should give me a job," I blurted.

The Mels raised their eyebrows at each other. I felt a wave of nervous heat wash over my face. That probably wasn't what Abbie and Hannah had meant when they'd said I should be more confident.

"She's interested in waitressing for the summer," Melissa said to Melanie.

"Just for the summer?" Melanie said skeptically.

I glanced at the cash register at the end of the counter. It was covered with photos of calico cats, each photo sheathed in a yellowed plastic sleeve.

"Oh, are those your cats?" I said desperately. "So cute!"

Melanie ignored that and motioned Melissa over for a tête-à-tête.

I leaned against the counter in defeat. It had only taken about five minutes for me to reveal myself to be a total spaz. An *unqualified* spaz. A spaz posing as a cat-lover.

The front door opened, and a couple with two little kids walked in. Melissa waved at them.

"Just have a seat anywhere," she called with a smile. "I'll be right over."

I eyed the bin of menus mounted on the side of the counter, and shrugged. I had nothing to lose. Why not try to steal a run, as a baseball fan would (maybe?) say.

I grabbed four menus.

Then I glanced at the family as they settled into their seats, and I put two of the menus back, replacing them with kids' menus. I brought them all over to the table.

"Hi there!" I said, way too cheerily. "Can I get you something to drink?"

"I'll have coffee," the dad said. He pointed at his little girl, who looked about three. "And she'll have—Tally! Leave the salt shakers alone! Sorry. She'll have—Tally! What did I say?"

"Tally," I said, bending down to meet her pretty, round blue eyes. "Would you like some milk?"

Tally's face lit up in a shy smile.

"Juice," she said.

I glanced at her mom. She was giving her daughter one of those sappy my-baby's-growing-up smiles, which I guessed meant juice was allowed.

"Apple or orange?" I asked.

"Apple!" Tally cried, clapping her pudgy little hands together.

"Apple!" I said with a nod (and a silent prayer that the Mels had apple juice).

"Thank you!" the mom said. "And I'll have unsweetened iced tea, and, Zeke, you want OJ, right?"

As their son nodded, I said, "Okay. Coffee, iced tea, apple, and orange. Right?"

"Yup!" Zeke said.

The parents beamed some more.

"Check out the menu," I said. "You might want to try the cinnamon streusel coffee cake. You'll never guess what the secret ingredient is."

"Cake!" Tally cried.

"Thanks," the dad said to me before turning to his daughter. "Now, Tally, first eggies, *then* cake . . ."

I felt a surge of pride as I turned to walk briskly away. The surge, of course, was quickly squelched when I remembered that I had just done a bit of guerilla waitressing—and I had no idea what to do next.

The Mels were staring at me. I couldn't tell if they were mad or amused. I think it was a little of both.

"Um . . . they want a coffee, iced tea, apple juice, and OJ," I said. "Do you . . . have apple juice?"

"Lucky for you we do," Melanie said. She glanced at Melissa.

"How about we do a trial for the day," Melissa said. "And we'll see how it goes."

"Okay!" I said. "So do you want me to start now?"

"Well, you already did, didn't you?" Melanie said.

"I guess I did," I said, giving Tally a little wave. She flapped her fingers back at me.

"Melissa usually works the counter, but she can finish up with that table while I get you set up," Melanie said, hustling back toward the kitchen and beckoning me to follow her. "You do know, don't you, that taking that drink order was the easiest thing you're going to do all day?"

"Of course," I said, even though that had never crossed my mind. This was pretty much the most impulsive thing I'd ever done. I was elated and terrified all at once.

An hour later the breakfast rush started to feel more like a breakfast onslaught. And the other two waitresses—Ginny and Andrea—seemed ready to stab me with their Paper Mate pens.

That's when I started wondering which failure the Mels would reference when they told me never to come back to their coffee shop again, even to buy coffee.

Would they mention the slippery streak of ice water I trailed across the linoleum floor at least three times?

Or the moment I served four sides of bacon to the wrong table—a table that happened to be filled with vegetarians?

What about the time I jammed up the cash register, even after Ginny had taken a full five minutes (which apparently was an eternity in waitressland) to show me how to use it?

Or when I filled three pages of my waitress pad with the order of one finicky family because I didn't know any of the shorthand that the other waitresses used to communicate with Melanie in the kitchen?

If none of those gaffes sealed my doom, I was sure it was going to be the plate I dropped—the plate that had been swimming in maple syrup. It almost exploded, spraying syrup in every possible direction.

By the time the rush began to ease up, I could feel big tufts of frizz popping out of my ponytail. My armpits were so damp, I worried I might have dark circles on my dress.

The remaining customers were all in Ginny's and Andrea's sections (I'm sure that was no accident), so I slumped into one of the stools at the counter and gave Melissa a guilty look.

"Turns out," I said, "serving a restaurant full of people is more challenging than babysitting four little kids. Who knew?"

I gave a lame laugh.

Then, slowly, reluctantly, I placed my order pad on the counter and started to untie my apron. Even though the morning had been *so* hard, it had also been kind of fun. A sticky, egg-yolky, spazzy kind of fun. Plus, I'd made almost forty dollars in tips! In three and a half hours! That was way better than babysitting money.

Melissa, who had a stack of receipts piled at her elbow, glanced up from the numbers she was pounding into the cash register.

"What are you doing, sweetie pie?" she said. "Your shift isn't over for two and a half hours."

"But, but . . . I was a disaster!" I said.

"I hate to agree with her, Melissa," Andrea said as she popped a new filter full of grounds into the coffeemaker. "But she kind of was."

She sat next to me at the counter, smiling sympathetically through dark red lipstick. Andrea looked like she was in her early twenties. She had a ton of tattoos and wore Adidas sneakers with tube socks pulled up to the knee. I loved her style, and I marveled at how non-sweaty and pretty she still looked after that brutal shift.

"No offense, Chelsea," she said.

"None taken," I said sadly.

"Oh, Andie," Melissa scolded. "You on your first day, now *that* was a disaster. Remember the way you cried! 'I can't do it, Mel! I can't *do it*! Just let me wash dishes!'"

"You started me on Sunday brunch!" Andrea protested. "Talk about trial by fire! Today's only Monday! A slow Monday, at that."

"That was slow?" I squeaked.

"Moderately," Melissa admitted. Then she looked at me. "Listen, if you'd had any experience, I'd say, yes, this day was a disaster. But for someone on her first day, I'd call you, oh, a mild calamity."

"Is that good?"

Ginny breezed by on her way to a table, with a parade of oval plates stacked along the full length of her arm. She was probably in her fifties, had short salt-and-pepper ringlets, and her eyes looked tired even when she was smiling, as she was now.

"Calamity's not bad," she said encouragingly. "You'll get there. If Andie did, *anybody* can."

"Hey!" Andrea said poutily.

"So . . . do you want me to stay?" I asked Melissa cautiously.

"Well, I'll have to talk about it with Melanie," Melissa said, "but I think you might be a good fit. You are good with the little ones, and we get a lot of those in here."

"I know," I said with a grin. "I was one of those! I've been coming here for forever."

"Oh, now you're making me feel old," Melissa complained with a good-natured smile. "So, what, do your parents have a summer cottage here?"

"My grandma," I said automatically, before catching myself. "I mean, she did. I mean, the cottage is still here but my grandma . . . isn't. She passed away."

"Oh, I'm sorry to hear that," Melissa said. "What was her name?"

"Delia Roth," I said, looking down at the white Formica counter. It blurred a little bit.

"Oh, right, I did know that," Melissa said softly. "I remember Delia coming in here with all those granddaughters. That must have been you and your sisters. I should have recognized you from your—"

"Hair," I said, and sighed, smoothing back the frizzy corkscrews that had pulled out of my ponytail. "I know."

"Well, I'm sorry for your loss, sweetie pie," Melissa said.

I nodded and swallowed hard. "Thanks. It's okay."

I was glad for the distraction when Melanie called through the order window.

"All righty!" she said. "Just got my first lunch order. Turn on the specials board!"

Melissa hopped promptly off the stool behind the cash register and walked over to a glossy black screen propped on an easel next to the pie carousel. Ceremoniously she plugged it in. The specials—written in different colors of neon marker—lit up, glowing brightly.

"Wow, that's fancy!" I said.

"I know!" Melissa said, giving the light board an affectionate pat. "We just got it last season. I think it really sells the specials, don't you?"

"Melissa," said Andrea, propping her chin on her fist, "are they really specials when they're *always* the same?"

"Well," Melissa said, giving Andrea a scolding glance, "only since, you know, the *order*."

I wondered what they were talking about as I scanned the specials on the light board.

SPINACH ARTICHOKE DIP WITH TOAST POINTS . . . $4.99

EGG SALAD–CHICKEN SALAD–TUNA SALAD COMBO
ON BED OF LETTUCE . . . $8.50

PIMENTO CHEESE SANDWICH ON PUMPERNICKEL . . . $6.50

GRILLED ASPARAGUS WITH LEMON AIOLI . . . $3.99

I was starting to see a theme here. A certain ingredient that *all* the specials contained.

Then I remembered something I'd noticed that morning as I'd rushed from the dining room to the kitchen and back again. In my frantic state it had barely registered, but now that I had a moment to think, it finally clicked.

Just inside the swinging doors that led to the kitchen was a tall, chrome shelving unit. The top and bottom shelves were filled with various dinery items—spare salt and pepper shakers, red and yellow squirt bottles, a big glass jar of pickle relish, and several stacks of napkins.

But by far the predominant feature on the shelves, placed square at eye level, was the mayonnaise—jar after mammoth plastic jar of it. The industrial-size mayo containers were stacked three deep and covered two entire shelves.

Suddenly I realized why Josh had thought I had mayo-on-the-face paranoia the first day I met him.

And why he'd asked about my celery-chopping abilities.

"Melissa," I said, "what *is* the secret ingredient in the cinnamon streusel coffee cake?"

Melissa hung her head.

"Let me guess," I said. "Mayonnaise?"

Melissa nodded.

"I had a little ordering snafu," she admitted, looking a little weary. "There was . . . an extra zero."

Andrea shook her head and gave a little snort of laughter.

"The supplier wouldn't take them back," Melissa went on, "and even though the jars are sealed, there *is* an expiration date on them. So . . ."

"When life hands you mayo?" I prompted.

"Make lots and lots of tuna salad," Melissa finished. "And dips and cake and old-fashioned Jell-O molds . . . Well, it's actually kind of interesting how many uses there are for mayonnaise when pressed to the wall. It's great for moisturizing your hair. You can even use it to polish piano keys."

Melanie had wandered out to pour herself a cup of coffee during the lull.

"The only problem," she interjected, "is now we're so sick of mayonnaise, *we* can't eat it. Ugh, I *dream* about mayo. Sometimes I just want to throw it out! But little Miss Waste-Not-Want-Not over there won't let me."

Melissa glared at her sister defensively.

"It's immoral to throw away perfectly good food," she said.

"It's a *condiment*," Melanie said. "It barely counts as food."

"Hey!" I said. "What about donating it to a soup kitchen or shelter? It wouldn't go to waste there."

"Did it!" Ginny said as she swung around the counter to fill a few plastic cups with ice. "We gave 'em so much mayo, they said to please stop. They couldn't take any more."

"Wow," I said. "That's a lot of mayo."

Melanie swung her arm over Melissa's shoulders and looked mock-sorrowful.

"It is our burden to bear," she said. "And our shame."

I laughed out loud.

"Oh!" Melissa scoffed. "It could have happened to anyone."

"Sure it could, sweetie pie," Ginny said. "Don't you listen to Melanie."

Melanie scowled and gave Ginny a fake punch on the arm as Ginny strolled over to a customer sitting at a two-top near the counter.

"What can I get you, sir?" she asked the man.

"I'll have the club sandwich," he replied.

Andrea and I shrieked at the same time, "Want mayo with that?" Then we both laughed so hard that tears streamed down our faces.

The man looked very confused.

"I'm sorry, sir," Ginny said to him, giving us a glare. "I'll get right on that. And while I do, *Chelsea's* going to get you a free iced tea."

I hopped off my stool and hurried to do what Ginny ordered, a big slaphappy grin on my face.

I needed that jolt of lightness to get me through the lunch

rush, which was almost more hectic than the breakfast one. My section was full of people in work clothes, needing to eat fast and run back to their jobs.

I couldn't help but notice that Josh was not one of them. But I didn't have time to think about it. Or about Granly or about anything really, except the constant rhythm of taking orders, delivering food, checking in on customers, then checking them out. There was only, "We don't serve fries, only chips." And, "The soup of the day is spring vegetable." And "Of *course* you can have extra mayo on that."

I realized that maybe that was what I liked most about this job. It was a vacation from my vacation—the one that left me way too much time to brood about . . . everything, especially what might be going on on the other side of that wall that separated Mel & Mel's from Dog Ear.

*M*elissa scheduled me for the two-to-eight p.m. shift the next day, and put me down in the schedule for four afternoon shifts a week.

"We're more of a breakfast and lunch place," she told me, "so you can slow down and learn the ropes a bit."

I got to town at one fifteen the next day. But not because I wanted to get to work early.

I was going to Dog Ear.

At the corner of Main and Althorp, I paused—and hyperventilated a bit. Clutching my stomach, I ducked onto Althorp, which was really more of an alley than a street—skinny, one-way, and mostly stocked with service entrances to the stores on Main.

I smoothed down my poofy A-line skirt, adjusted the straps of my blue camisole, and tried to calm down.

What's the big deal? I asked myself. *I'm just stopping in. I'll talk to Josh, pick out some books, and be on my way.*

What's more, I'd done a mirror check right before I'd left the cottage, so I *knew* there was nothing on my face.

I gave my head a little shake, smoothed down the puff of frizz that the head shake had unleashed, and walked purposefully around the corner.

When I went into Dog Ear, Stella was behind the counter.

"Hi there!" she said, fluttering her fingers at me. "C'mon in. It's Nutter Butters today."

I grinned at her. The prospect of dribbling peanut buttery crumbs into a book that I had just *bought* made me giddy. I decided to look for a book first, and Josh second.

I was headed to the YA section when I got distracted by a chirpy voice coming out of the kids' area. I peeked over the white picket fence at a mom-ish-looking woman perched on a tiny chair. She was reading to a small crowd of toddlers who alternated between listening raptly and pointing at the pictures to shout out things like, "It's a duck!"

"Cute," I whispered to myself.

I was just heading back to the YA section, when I froze.

Between the kids' play area and the YA aisle, there was an aisle filled with picture books. Sitting on the floor of that aisle, shelving a stack of them, was Josh.

He was looking right at me.

"Hi," I stage-whispered. I didn't want to disturb the story hour.

He waved and smiled.

Which made me feel both flustered and floaty. Suddenly the thought of delaying talking to Josh in favor of shopping for books seemed really ridiculous.

After walking down the aisle, I lowered myself to the floor, trying to simultaneously be graceful and not give Josh a glimpse of my underwear. He was holding a copy of *Where the Wild Things Are* but seemed to have forgotten all about it. Instead he just stared at me.

Then we did that thing where he smiled and I smiled back and he smiled harder and so did I, and *boy* was I glad nobody else could see us right then. It comforted me to know that we were *equally* dorky.

"Listen," I said when I finally remembered that I'd actually come here to tell him something. "I was going to buy a book and then thank you. But now I'm thanking you first."

Josh smiled bigger. "You're not broke anymore?"

"No!" I said. "Look at this!"

I opened my purse and pulled out a rolled-up wad of money. It was fifty-two dollars in one-dollar bills—my final tip count from the previous day.

"That's, like, five paperbacks right there," I said.

"So, I guess you got the job?" Josh asked.

"Oh, yeah, I forgot to mention that," I said. "They started me right away. And I'm going back today for the dinner shift! So, uh, that's why I wanted to thank you—for telling me about it and giving me those pointers."

He didn't have to know how badly I'd mangled the whole calico cat/Cubs part of my interview.

"You're welcome," Josh said.

There was a moment of smiley silence, except for the voice of the reader starting a new book: "'One Sunday morning the warm sun came up and—pop!—out of the egg came a tiny and very hungry caterpillar.'"

"So," I said, because we couldn't just sit there grinning at each other for minutes on end (could we?). "I guess we'll be working next door to each other."

That's when Josh's smile faded and his face seemed to go a little pale.

And that look in his eyes—was that panic?

I felt like I'd been slapped in the face. Suddenly Josh and I were right back to the first day we'd met, when he'd started out sweet and flirty, then turned on me. Now he was doing it again. He'd *told* me about the Mel & Mel's job, and yet here he was, freaking out because I'd taken the Mel & Mel's job! Was he realizing he doesn't like me after all? Again?

"I've gotta go," I blurted.

Even though I have half an hour until my shift starts. Which I'm now going to have to kill somewhere else. What am I supposed to do, go buy fifty-two dollars' worth of fudge?

"You're leaving?" Josh said. His voice cracked a little as he said it, and he cringed.

"Yes, I'm leaving," I said frostily.

But my outfit seemed to have another idea. As I tried to get up, I realized I'd sat down on the hem of my skirt. I was pinned down!

I took a deep, long-suffering breath and started yanking my skirt out from under me. Never had my vintage habit so betrayed me! I was totally going to switch to miniskirts after this.

"'On Wednesday,'" the mom read, "'he ate through three plums, but he was still hungry.'"

"Yah!" I grunted, finally freeing myself. I smoothed the poofy skirt down, then planted my hands on the floor to push myself to my feet.

But before I got very far, Josh planted *his* hands on me! On my shoulders anyway. I fell back to the floor.

"Oof!" I grunted, giving him a *WHAT are you doing?* glare.

From the stunned look on his face, it seemed Josh was asking himself the same question.

But then his fingers tightened on my shoulders and he answered the question for both of us by leaning in—and kissing me!

It was just one kiss. By the clock it probably only lasted a few seconds. But in my head (not to mention the *rest* of me) that kiss—Josh kissing *me*—seemed to go on and on. I felt a tingly jolt in my lips. Josh's palms felt incredibly warm on my shoulders, and my arms and legs went rubbery.

No, that wasn't the right word for it. I felt *melty*.

I couldn't believe it.

Whenever I read a romantic book (and I'd read a lot of them), I'd get to the part where she "melted beneath his touch" or "melted into his arms" and roll my eyes.

That's just a goofy thing writers write, I'd told myself. *Nobody really melts when a boy kisses her.*

Now I knew. The melting really did happen—if you kissed the right boy. For the first time in my life, I seemed to be doing just that.

And I was doing it with a chirpy mom reading *The Very Hungry Caterpillar* literally six feet away. Not to mention all those little kids. This was . . . weird!

Also wonderful.

And very, *very* surprising.

That's surely what Josh saw in my face when we finally pulled away from each other. That and a whole lot of hot-and-bothered hair frizz.

"Um . . . ," I said.

"Um . . . ," he said.

"So I gotta . . . ," I said, pointing in the general direction of the door. Kissing Josh seemed to have rendered me half-mute.

Josh only nodded. I guess he was *fully* mute.

As I drifted to my feet, I couldn't help but wonder if that was a good or bad thing. Maybe another girl (my sister, Abbie, for instance) would have come out and *asked* him if it was a good or bad thing. But I didn't. I *couldn't*.

For one thing, there was the half-muteness.

For another, I couldn't look Josh in the eyes. Not after his lips had just been on my lips and he'd just seen my face more close-up than I'd seen it myself. It was so embarrassing!

Also amazing.

I turned and headed out of the picture book aisle, trying not to wobble as I walked. I forgot about book shopping entirely and reported to work twenty minutes early. This earned me completely unintentional brownie points, as well as the privilege of chopping up some celery for Melanie while I waited for my shift to begin.

Once it did, it took a while for my tables to fill up, which was a good thing. I was ridiculously distracted from a job I hadn't even begun to master yet.

Okay, the first question, I thought as I laid napkins and flatware on my tables, *is why! Why did Josh kiss me? Does he really like me? Or maybe kissing me was an accident, somehow. I mean, it doesn't get less sexy than* The Very Hungry Caterpillar.

And besides, I know he regretted telling me to go for the job next door. I could see it in his eyes. So why—Oop! Party of six in my section.

I hurried over to scoop up menus as three middle-aged couples settled themselves into my section's biggest table. I handed the menus out, then managed to get their drink orders correct—even if I did hand the wrong drinks to each customer, down to the very last person.

"I'm sorry!" I said as they laughed and passed their drinks around the table until each one found the person who'd ordered it. "It's only my second day."

"In that case," said one of the customers, a jolly-looking guy with thinning hair and a big grin, just the kind of guy my dad would *love* to regale with one-liners, "I'll have a chef salad with ham instead of turkey. And egg whites only, no yolks. Dressing on the side. And I'd like extra dressing."

"Okaaaay," I said, sticking my tongue in the corner of my mouth as I furiously scribbled the complicated order.

"Now the extra dressing," the man instructed, "I want on the salad. Oh, and I'd like ham instead of turkey."

"Wait a minute," I said, "didn't you just say turkey instead of ham?"

And doesn't a chef salad have both turkey and ham? I wondered frantically.

"Sweetie," said the woman across the table from the man, "he's messing with you! He does this every time we go to a restaurant."

Then she scowled at her husband.

"John!" she scolded. "You're scaring the girl to death."

"All right, then," the man said, grinning at me. "I'll have a burger. With everything."

I squinted at him. "Really?" I said skeptically.

"Really, sweetie," his wife said. "John! Stop!"

He chuckled and crossed his arms over his big belly as if to say, *My work here is done.*

Old people amused themselves in really weird ways.

Then again, young people could be kind of weird too. For instance, some of them planted out-of-the-blue kisses on unsuspecting girls during completely inappropriate children's story hours.

I swooped back to the kiss—to the unexpected yet wonderful kiss and the imprint of Josh's hands on my shoulders that I swore I could still feel—and completely missed the next two orders.

"I'm sorry," I said as John's wife said something about an extra plate. "Can you repeat that?"

I saw the customers exchange a look and shift in their seats.

It's going to be a long afternoon, they telegraphed to each other. *You don't know the half of it, people,* I thought.

*B*y the end of my shift, I was beyond exhausted. If Melissa thought two-to-eight was the easy shift, then she was a super-hero. My feet ached and my arms were sore from lugging heavy trays. I had a greasy spot on my camisole from a salad dressing spill. I was starving, but I also had no desire to even look at food.

I was also just as bewildered by the Kiss as I'd been six hours earlier. In my few minutes of free time that afternoon, I'd sent Emma three urgent *NEED ADVICE* texts, but her phone must have been turned off. Her mean teachers at the Intensive appar-ently loved to snap cell phones in half if they dared to ring during class. The ballet world was so weird.

Of course, everything was seeming weird to me at that moment—customers who left tips entirely in nickels, Melanie making a gross blue and red cake in honor of the Cubs . . . Weird-est of all, of course, was Josh acting all phobic one moment, then planting the best kiss of my life on me the next.

I went to the little office off the kitchen to take off my apron and get ready to leave. I considered calling a couple other friends from back home to get their take on the Kiss, but I was too tired to explain all the backstory to them. Then I thought about talking to Hannah. With her I could speak in sisters' shorthand. Then she'd probably do that thing where she reads between the lines of what I tell her and informs me of what I'm *really* saying. Usually I find that excruciatingly annoying, but in this case I actually kind of craved it.

You've got two sisters who've just been through all this, Hannah and Abbie had told me before the lantern party.

I hated when they were right, but they were right. I decided to talk to Hannah right after I got home.

As I walked through the dining room, waving good-bye to Melissa, I pulled the rubber band out of my messy ponytail and held it between my front teeth. I pushed through the front door backward as I used both hands to smooth my hair back so I could make a new, neater pony.

But as soon as the door *swooshed* closed behind me, I heard the jingle of Dog Ear's door opening and closing as well.

I glanced up. The elastic band fell out of my mouth and my hands dropped to my sides, causing my hair to poof frizzily around my face.

Josh was standing in front of the bookstore.

He looked kind of like he wanted to dive right back inside.

For once I knew we had something in common, because I kind of wanted to do the same thing.

But I also couldn't stop staring at him. At his smooth face, his super-short hair, and his cute orange-and-green sneakers.

"Hi," I said. My voice sounded hesitant and a little raspy after talking over the clatter of dishes all day.

"Hi," Josh said, sounding just as nervous as I felt. Feeling clumsy, I grabbed my hair elastic off the sidewalk. Then Josh pointed behind him. "Are you walking this way?"

I nodded and started down Main. Josh fell into step beside me, and it felt . . . wonderful. He was so close that our arms almost touched, so close that I could feel the warmth radiating off his body.

I guess that was what made me turn off Main and head down

Althorp. Suddenly, instead of wanting to get home as soon as possible to shower, eat a mayo-free dinner, and puzzle out this Josh business with my sister, I wanted this walk—with Josh—to last as long as possible.

When we were a few feet from the end of the block, Josh stopped, turned, and looked down at me. He really was tall. His face looked sweetly sheepish and a little aggravated.

"Listen," he said. "I know you must think I'm crazy. I mean, I haven't exactly been, um, consistent. With you."

I raised my eyebrows.

"I guess it's safe to say," Josh went on, "I've been a little, how do I say this . . . taken aback."

"Taken aback?" I asked. This did *not* sound like a positive thing.

"See?" Josh said, wringing his hands. "I never say the right thing to you. It's like I don't have control over my mouth."

See? I thought. *He all but said it—he* did *kiss me by accident!*

I bit my lip, bracing myself for heartbreak.

"Chelsea," Josh said, "here's the thing. You tried to rescue those books from me. And you think *Coconut Dreams* is as fabulously horrible as I do. And you wear those vintage clothes, and you have that *hair*—"

"I hate my hair," I said, my hand instinctively springing to my head to smooth it down.

"See?" Josh repeated. "I did it again."

He looked down at the ground, suddenly even shyer.

"And then I went and . . . you know," he said. "Earlier."

"Yeah, earlier," I whispered.

"So anyway, about that," Josh said. "I'm sor—"

Josh didn't get to finish what he was saying.

Because I grabbed him by the shoulders and sprang to my tiptoes—and kissed him!

Josh stumbled backward. I started to pull away from the kiss, but he plunged his hand into my messy mane of hair and pulled me closer.

And now I wasn't kissing him and he wasn't kissing me.

We were kissing each other.

My eyes fluttered closed. I let my right hand trail down Josh's arm—which was thin but muscular and so smooth and warm—until my hand found his. Our fingers intertwined.

Josh tilted until his shoulder blades touched the brick wall behind him. I tilted along with him.

And now "melty" took on a different meaning. All the confusion and hurt I'd been feeling? All those mixed signals Josh had given me? They all melted away—canceled out by one perfect kiss after another.

My dad woke me and my sisters up early the next morning.

"I'm commandeering you for the morning," he announced. "Your mother wants some time to herself, and *I* want some time with my wayward daughters."

"Dad," I said, shoving a curl out of my eyes as I slumped out of my bed, "me having a *job* doesn't exactly make me wayward. You and Mom are the ones who make us earn all our own money."

"Well, then I guess I'm only talking about Hannah," Dad said lightly. "Anyway, be in the kitchen in five. No primping!"

I laughed as he hurried down the hall, then I whispered to Abbie, "What does he mean 'Hannah'? What's she been up to?"

"Didn't you know?" Abbie said, throwing off her covers and sitting up in bed. "She had a date with Fasthands last night. She got home after you were asleep."

"Liam?" I said.

"Yes, *Liam*," Abbie grumbled. "When she got home, she was all giggly and floaty. *Very* un-Hannah-like."

"Oh!" I said.

I hurried over to the closet and ducked inside it, ostensibly to throw on some clothes, but also because I had to hide my incredulous grin.

How had this happened? Instead of Hannah and Abbie doing all the dating, it was Hannah and *me* who'd been with boys last night.

That was very un-Chelsea-like, too.

Part of me wanted to dash to Hannah's room and ask her if she felt just like I did—all dreamy and incredulous. I kept wondering if the previous night had really happened. Then I'd touch my lips and remember what *Josh's* lips had felt like and realize, yes, it really had.

"Girls! I've got bagels toasting!"

It was my dad—giving me no time to dish with Hannah about Josh. What *was* this mystery outing? I quickly threw on some knee-length khakis and an A-line top with a swirly, psychedelic pattern on it. I grabbed some heavy-duty bobby pins off the dresser and piled my hair into a sloppy bun on top of my head.

In the kitchen my dad handed each of us a hot bagel wrapped loosely in a paper towel. He grabbed a coffee thermos and a stack of paper cups and shooed us toward the front door.

As we passed through the living room, I saw my mom standing in front of the built-in hutch. It was the centerpiece of the living room, its shelves filled with books, family photos, knick-knacks, and a tiny TV. The bottom of the hutch was all cabinets. Inside of these were so many of the things that made the cottage Granly's. There were decks of mismatched playing cards and lots of battered board games. Photo albums filled an entire shelf. There was an accordion folder full of essays my mom had written in high school and college, and a dried corsage. I'd always loved Granly's sewing basket and the box of super-loud costume jewelry that she'd worn in the sixties and seventies. My sisters and I used them to play dress-up when we were little.

My mom was staring down at those cabinets. Her hands were on her hips and her eyes looked tired, even though she was usually such a morning person.

"Hi, Mom," I said quietly.

She jumped, startled. When she looked in my direction, her eyes were a little unfocused—until they crinkled into a beaming smile.

"Oh! Hi, sweetheart," she said. The perkiness in her voice was set to extra high.

Maybe I should have lingered a moment and given my mom some sympathy as she got ready to sort through Granly's cabinets.

But I just didn't want to go there. Not when a tiny remnant of last night's magic was still lingering inside me.

So I just said, "Well, have a good morning."

"You too," Mom replied. "Enjoy the fishing!"

"Fishing?" I squawked. Then I stomped outside. "Daaaad!"

He knew we hated fishing! He'd totally conned us!

Hannah and Abbie were already settled into their seats, munching their bagels. Dad had started the car. I flounced into the backseat next to Hannah and pointed an accusing finger at our father.

"Do you know where he's taking us?" I said as my dad hurriedly put the car into reverse and skidded out of the driveway. "Fishing!"

"Daaaaaad!" Abbie and Hannah complained.

"Throw me a fish bone, will you?" my dad said, with his dadly chortle. "It's the one father-son kind of thing I ever ask of you."

"Oh, poor Dad," Abbie teased. "You know you love having girls."

"I *would* love it, if you'd just put on a happy fishing face for me," Dad said, pretending to be grouchy about it.

"First of all, I don't know how Americans turned fishing into a male thing," Hannah said. "In most cultures it's the women who gather the fish."

"Second of all," I piped in, "I don't know why boys *or* girls like it. It's *boring*. Only men would define sitting and waiting for some unsuspecting fish to eat your fake bug as a sport."

"A *fashionable* sport," my dad said. He opened the car's center console and pulled out a beat-up tan hat with neon-colored lures all over it.

"Ew, it smells like fish!" Hannah said, waving her hand in front of her nose.

So much for our bagels. We put them aside in disgust, opened the windows, and teased my dad the entire drive to the South Branch Galien River.

I have to admit, it was really fun.

The river was gorgeous, all breezy and glinty in the early-morning sunshine. My sisters and I baited our hooks, plopped them into the water, and lay back on the smooth, warm, weathered wood of the dock.

But after a short while Abbie popped up.

"Daddy," she said, "since you turned us off our bagels, can't you please go get us some Casper's Donuts?"

"Abbie," Dad said, messing with a lure and his line, "I haven't even caught—"

"Toss it in," Abbie said, pointing at Dad's hook. "We'll watch if for you, I promise. Pleeease. Casper's is so close, and those donuts are *so* good."

"Pretty please," I joined in the begging.

"Pretty please with cinnamon and sugar on top?" Hannah added with a grin.

"Ooh, yeah," Abbie said. "Cinnamon sugar cake donuts. Get those!"

Dad frowned at us, then scratched his head beneath his fishy hat.

"If you promise to have a good attitude about this fishing expedition," he said, "I will get you the donuts."

"We promise," Abbie said. "Thanks, Dad."

"Oh, now I'm Dad again," my dad grumbled. "Now that you've gotten what you want."

"Bye, Daddy!" we singsonged together, laughing and waving at him.

He grinned as he drove away. The minute he pulled into the

road, Abbie planted her fists on her hips and glared at Hannah.

"You're so lucky I got rid of him before I ask you this," Abbie said to Hannah. "*What* is that?"

Abbie pointed at Hannah's neck.

Hannah gasped and pulled her loose hair tightly beneath her chin.

"Do you think Dad saw?" she asked.

"Saw what?" I sputtered. "What is it?"

"Oh, you wouldn't understand," Abbie said, brushing me off with a wave. Then she jumped at Hannah and pushed her hair back, exposing a reddish-blue mark on her neck.

"Hey!" Hannah swatted at Abbie's hand. "Stop it!"

"Ew," I said, pointing at the splotch. "What is that?"

"It's a hickey," Abbie said smugly. "Only the tackiest thing a girl could ever come home with."

Hannah looked both mortified and a little proud.

"What, you're the only one allowed to mess around with guys?" she said to Abbie. "It's no big deal."

"I bet that's what he said," Abbie scoffed. "What else does Fasthands say is no big deal?"

"I know what I'm doing," Hannah said. "I *am* older than you, you know."

"Then act like it," Abbie said.

While Hannah glared at Abbie, I jumped in.

"What did you mean, I 'wouldn't understand'?" I demanded. "I know things."

Abbie and Hannah both looked at me like I was a black fly buzzing around their heads.

"What kind of things?" Abbie said in a patronizing tone.

"I kissed a boy just last night!" I blurted.

It wasn't exactly how I'd planned to pass along this momentous information. I'd pictured a much more romantic moment—my sisters and I would be stargazing together or taking a long walk. And then I would blushingly tell them that I was deeply in like with a boy named Josh.

"What! When? Where?" Abbie and Hannah asked.

"After I got off work," I said, sticking my chin out. "On Althorp Street."

"Well, who is this boy?" Hannah said.

"He's . . ." I drifted off as I gazed out at the river. Josh's face was floating before my eyes again, with those dimples and those smiling eyes, and those *lips*.

My eyes refocused when I noticed a skimming motion on the river. I put my hand over my eyes to block the sun.

It was a long, skinny boat, sort of like a canoe, but it was as long and sharp as a needle. The person rowing the boat was bending forward and back, his long oars flashing as they skimmed over the surface. His back was to us, but I could see he was tall and skinny.

And he had very short brown hair.

He was . . .

"Josh!" I exclaimed. "That's him!"

"What?" Hannah said. "*That's* the guy you kissed. In that boat?"

"Oh my God," I whispered. "What do I do?"

Abbie cupped her hands around her mouth and hollered, "Josh!"

Josh was so startled, one of his oars missed the water and hit his canoe or whatever with a *thwack*. He peered over at us.

"Abbie!" I whisper-shrieked. "I hate you so much."

"Chelsea?" Josh called.

"Um, yeah," I yelled. "Hi."

Even when you're yelling across a body of water, it's possible to sound nervous, I noted with a cringe.

"Hi!" Josh said. He was at least fifty feet away, but I could still see his teeth because he was grinning so hard. Then he waved so energetically, he almost tipped himself off his boat.

"Hi!" I yelled back. I was up on my tiptoes, leaning against the rail, my voice catching because I felt so giddy.

"I don't have your number!" Josh yelled.

I inhaled sharply and glanced back at my sisters. They raised their eyebrows, impressed.

"I don't have yours either!" I yelled. Then Josh and I both laughed like idiots. And *then* the current took him so far past the dock that we couldn't yell to each other anymore.

I turned to my sisters, my giddiness quickly replaced by insecurity.

"I'm such a spaz," I said. "But that was good, right? I mean, him wanting my number and me wanting his? That's good?"

"That's great!" Abbie said. "Most boys are all about the arm's length. They'll do anything to *avoid* getting your number. But here yours doesn't just ask for it; he yells for it from the middle of a river!"

I grabbed Abbie and gave her a squeeze.

"Abbie! I love you so much."

Then all three of us squealed and jumped up and down.

"Chelsea has a boyfriend, Chelsea has a boyfriend," my sisters chanted while I covered my mouth with my hand and shrieked.

"Chelsea has a *boyfriend?*"

My dad's voice brought us down to earth with a thud. He was standing behind us, looking kind of disheveled and pathetic with his grease-stained brown paper bag and a quart of milk.

"Milk, Dad?" Abbie said, eyeing the carton. "What are we, ten?"

Dad got a look on his face that seemed to say, *I very much wish you were.*

A year ago I might have agreed with him. I was wearing braces then and had just gotten my first underwire bra. Every time I tried to drink coffee, it gave me the shakes and tasted awful. I was pretty much convinced that growing up meant being physically uncomfortable at all times.

But now my teeth were straight, I liked coffee (albeit with so much cream that you could barely call it beige), and I had (maybe?) a boyfriend!

I still liked milk, though, so I sidled up to my dad, gently took the carton from him, and said, "Milk is perfect for cinnamon sugar donuts. Thanks, Daddy."

He started to smile at me, but then we heard an ominous sound: *Zzzzzzz.*

Dad glanced at his fishing rod propped against the dock railing, and shouted, "Girls!"

The pole was bending dangerously over the railing, and the

line was zipping into the river so fast, the little handle on the reel thingy was a blur.

"Oops. I guess you got a bite, Dad," Abbie said.

"You *guess*?" Dad bellowed. He thrust the food into my hands and rushed over to his rod. "You girls were supposed to keep an eye on it!"

"Chelsea had her eye on something much more interesting," Hannah explained with a glint in her eye.

"Shut up!" I said cheerfully.

"No, you shut up!" she shot back with a grin.

My dad rolled his eyes as he wrestled with his fishing rod and called out, "A little help here? I need my net and my emergency line and a donut, stat!"

Giggling, we got him everything he needed, and he eventually reeled in his fish. It was huge! Well, big enough that Dad didn't have to throw it back the way he usually did.

"I am hunter!" Dad said, beating his chest with one hand while he used the other to hold up the poor dead fish. "Hear me roar! And take my picture, somebody!"

"Ohmigod, Dad," Hannah burst out. "How reactionary can you be?"

Dad faux-scowled at her.

"You know, when we found out you were going to be a girl, everybody congratulated me," he said. "They said, 'Oh, daughters and fathers. She'll think you hung the moon.'"

"And I did think you hung the moon," Hannah shot back, "right up until you killed that fish!"

"Ha-ha!" Dad said. "You'll thank me at dinnertime."

*I*n the car on the way home, I texted Emma:

You awake?

YEAH, YOU?

Duh, I'm texting you! And it's lunchtime out here. How's the intensive?

INTENSE! I'M DOING THE PAS DE DEUX FROM DON Q.

I have no idea what you just said. Guess what? Have news.

WHAT KIND OF NEWS!?!?!?

The boy kind.

?!?!?!?!?!?!

His name is Josh. We kissed! Last night.

DEETS!!!!!!

He works in a bookstore! He's so cute.

I stopped typing for a moment. My deets were true, but they only scratched the surface of what I liked about Josh. All the things I *really* thought of him couldn't possibly fit in a text. Which was, I thought, a very good thing. I had a big, goofy smile on my face as I typed, *How's Ethan?*

GOOD!!!! I THINK . . .

You think?

NO, NO, HE'S GOOD. HE'S JUST, WELL, IT'S NOT LIKE HE'S GOING TO JUST SIT AROUND WAITING FOR ME AFTER MY DAYS AT LAB. HE'S GOT A LIFE TOO.

Deets?

HOW'RE THINGS GOING WITH YOUR FAMILY? IS IT STILL SUPER-SAD?

I frowned at my phone. Could Emma have been more obvious

with her subject change? *Yeah, a little, but it's okay. My dad is working through it by killing small animals.*

WHAT???

We just went fishing.

OH. GROSS.

Know what's not gross anymore? Kissing! You were holding out on me.

ARE YOU KIDDING?!? I TOLD YOU EVERYTHING.

Bunhead, I was being sarcastic!

LATE FOR CLASS! LUV U.

I snapped my phone shut and frowned again. The conversation wasn't nearly as satisfying as it would have been by Emma's backyard pool with ginormous smoothies.

Then again, I reminded myself, *if I was poolside with Emma right now, I wouldn't be here in Bluepointe. With Josh.*

I smiled through the rest of the drive.

When we got home, Mom was in the vegetable garden. She was decked out in a floppy hat and gloves the color of Pepto-Bismol. She was shoveling with such force that she was out of breath, red-faced, and sweaty.

"What are you doing?" I asked. There was a big pile of dead plants and weeds next to her.

"I just couldn't stand this mess of a garden anymore," my mom said. "Something needed to be done!"

"What *are* you going to do with it?" I wondered.

"I don't know . . ." Mom trailed off, gazing at the big patch of bare earth as if she were seeing for the first time what she'd done. "I hadn't gotten that far."

She waved as Abbie and my dad carried our big cooler around the house to the back.

"How was the fishing?" Mom asked as she pulled off her gloves and tossed them to the grass.

"Check it out!" my dad said, flipping open the cooler and pulling out his big fish. It looked dull and stiff and very, very dead.

My mom clapped a hand over her mouth, and her eyes immediately welled up.

"Rachel—" my dad said in a *What did I do?* voice.

My mom shook her head and waved him off.

"I'm fine," she said. "I was just a little surprised, that's all."

"Aren't you excited to have fresh fish for dinner?" Dad asked a little wanly.

"Of course!" Mom said. Her voice was doing that perky thing, but it was choked up, too. "Listen, I'm tired after all this digging. I'm just going to take a little nap."

She almost ran to the house, and by the time we followed her in, Granly's bedroom door was closed.

My dad heaved a big sigh, then tapped on the bedroom door and went inside.

The three of us wandered into the living room. I peeked into the cabinets in the hutch. The jewelry boxes, board games, and photo albums were right where they'd always been—untouched.

Abbie gave her head a little shake and whispered to us, "Beach?"

"Let me get my stuff," Hannah whispered. "I've got some reading to do."

"I'll get some food," I said.

I went to the kitchen hoping I could find something that *wasn't* a baked good with a hole in it. As I fished some peaches out of the fruit bowl, I noticed that my mom had left her laptop open on the kitchen table.

I'd barely looked at a computer since we'd arrived. How funny that, other than texting with Emma and a couple other friends, I'd barely wondered what was going on at home. Maybe the long drive out here had made my "real" home feel far away and unreal. Or maybe it was the fact that when you're in a place like Bluepointe, it's kind of hard to believe a place like LA even exists.

Or maybe it was because I'd been preoccupied with a certain boy. . . .

It was partly guilt that made me log in to Facebook to see if I'd missed any big news. But there wasn't anything that caught my eye.

I took a big bite of peach and clicked on my messages. I scrolled quickly through them, until I got to the last e-mail. It had just arrived a few minutes earlier.

When I saw who it was from, I let out a little shriek.

It was from Josh Black, of Bluepointe, Michigan, born February fourth, the same year as me.

The message said: *Kai's long, shiny locks reminded Nicole of the black keys she'd so loathed during her years of piano lessons. But now she was just itching to touch them.*

I clapped my hand over my mouth so my family couldn't hear me laughing.

I rushed to my room and snatched my copy of *Coconut*

Dreams off my nightstand. Abbie was just snapping the strap of her swimsuit's halter top into place.

"Aren't you gonna change?" she said.

"Go on without me," I said, waving her away. "I'll meet you down there."

"O-kay," she said slowly. "Let me guess—your J-boy?"

I felt a twinge of guilt. I knew what it felt like to be the odd girl out, when everybody else seemed to be in a constant state of swooniness.

"Is that . . . is that okay?" I asked.

"Whatever," Abbie said, fishing her goggles out of her beach bag. "I'm doing my two miles, so I don't have time to hang on the beach anyway."

"Yeah, but . . ."

"Chelsea," Abbie said. She smiled at me. "It's *fine*. I mean it. He seems really sweet."

I smiled, hugged *Coconut Dreams* to my chest, and headed back to the kitchen.

I flipped through the book until I found the perfect passage.

Nicole and Kai danced on the sand, and the gossamer moonbeams danced with them, I typed. *When Nicole placed her slender fingers upon Kai's chest, she felt that his heart beat in time with her own; it beat for her.*

I bit my lip through a grin and hit send.

The chime of his reply came only a couple minutes later.

So, can I go ahead and get that number from you?

My hands shook a little as I typed my number into the reply box.

It only took a minute or two for the phone in the pocket of my khakis to start buzzing.

I felt happier than I had in a very long time. I was sure Josh would be able to tell through the phone when I answered.

But that was okay. I wanted him to.

I flipped the phone open.

"Hi," I said. "It's me."

*T*he funny thing about dating Josh was that it took us a while to go on an actual date.

Our obvious first choice—seeing the fireworks on the Fourth of July—got squelched by a massive thunderstorm.

For days after that we were both scheduled to work. So we did a lot of flitting back and forth between Mel & Mel's and Dog Ear.

He was the first one to sit in my section, for instance, whenever I started my afternoon shift at the coffee shop.

The third time he showed up at precisely two p.m. and settled himself into my section's corner booth, I laughed and said, "Oh, you again?"

"Can I help it if I really, really like pie?" Josh asked. "I get peckish at two p.m."

"You did *not* just use the word 'peckish,'" I said.

"I read it," Josh said, holding up the book he'd brought with him. "It's no *Coconut Dreams*, but . . ."

"Oh!" I said. "Allison Katzinger? I *love* her! But . . . wait a minute! *Leaves of Trees*? I've never heard of that one, and I've read all her books. Or at least I thought I had . . ."

"This is a galley of her book that's about to come out," Josh said. "She's coming here in August and I'm doing the poster, so I thought I'd re—"

"Oh my God!" I said. I sat down across from him and grabbed the table. "Why didn't you tell me you had the new Allison Katzinger? And she's coming here? To Bluepointe?"

"Yeah," Josh said with a shrug. "My mom arranged it. *That's* her favorite part of having a bookstore."

"So, is it good?" I asked Josh. "What am I saying? Of course it's good. But is it devastatingly good? I mean, is it one of her funny ones or one of her tragic ones? I can never decide which kind I love more—"

"Listen," Josh offered, "I'll need it back, but if you want to read it, you could bor—"

Before he could finish his sentence, I'd reached across the table and snatched the book out of his hand.

"Really?" I blurted. "You know I'll read it *so* fast. I can't believe I have to wait six hours to start. I'm sooooo excited."

"I'm beginning to think you just like me for my books," Josh said.

"Just like you like me for my pie," I said. I passed the book back to him and let my fingertips touch his for a quick, thrilling moment before I stood up. "Hold that for me? I'll be right back."

When I returned, I presented him with a slice of lemon meringue.

"Is this what you normally do?" Josh said, giving me a confused smile. "Choose pie flavors for your customers?"

"I know what you were going to order," I said.

At the same time we both said, "Cherry."

"But trust me on this?" I whispered, glancing over my shoulder to make sure neither of the Mels was within earshot. "You want to go with graham cracker crust for the next couple days. Melanie's, erm, tinkering with the fruit pie crust."

"Don't tell me . . . ," Josh groaned.

"Yup," I whispered, "mayonnaise. I'm afraid to try it."

Josh grinned as he took a big bite of his lemon pie.

"Mmm, good choice," he said.

I felt a little zing. I loved that I knew Josh's favorite pie flavor, just like he knew that I took my coffee with five creamers and two sugars (even if he did make fun of me for it).

He'd told me that he loathed his dictator-like high school art teacher and had learned most of his drawing techniques on YouTube.

And I'd told him that I read *Little Women* at least once a year, but still cried every time Beth died.

Sharing things like that with Josh made kissing him even better. Knowing what was going on *inside* his head was what was really making me swoon. This was the part of having a boyfriend I'd never imagined—the best friend part. I'd dreamed about the kissing and the hand-holding. But I'd had no idea that the most mind-blowing part of dating could be the *talking*. Looking into a boy's eyes and understanding what you saw in them. And each day learning a few more of the little quirks and details that made him *him*.

It made me feel different. Changed. Sometimes when I looked in the mirror, I expected to see someone else there. Someone older, with a knowing glint in her eye (and maybe fewer freckles).

As Josh took another bite of pie, I leaned against the table and wondered, "How far do you think she can take this mayo-in-everything scheme? Can you think of anything grosser than mayo pie? I think all the egg fumes are starting to scramble her brain."

"I heard that!"

I gasped and spun around to see Melissa glaring at me with her fists on her hips. Where had she come from?

"Oh, Melissa," I gasped. "I didn't mean—"

"Listen, Melanie's *always* been that crazy," Melissa whispered. "It's not the mayo's fault. And besides, it seems like you've got mayo on the brain too!"

She tipped her head toward the specials board, where I'd scribbled a little paragraph in the empty black space beneath the list of pie flavors.

B. hoped nobody could see the shiny new horns beneath her bangs as she held out the platter. "Deviled egg?" she offered.

I shrugged and laughed.

Melissa grinned back at me.

"Do you know, since you put that up there the other day," she said, "our deviled egg order has tripled? We had to send Andrea to the market for more eggs and paprika! Where'd you get such an idea, honey?"

"Oh, I don't know," I said with a smile and a shrug. "I was just serving someone deviled eggs, and the name struck me as funny. Do you want me to erase it?"

"Are you kidding?" Melissa said. "Don't you dare. *And* stop mooning over that boy and go give menus to that four-top over there. They want two blacks, two decafs."

"You're the best, Melissa," I breathed.

When Josh left, he wrote on his check, *Your Tip* → with the arrow pointing at the Allison Katzinger book.

Of course, I *had* to stop by Dog Ear after my shift to say thank you.

And there just happened to be a wine-and-cheese happening for a local poet when I got there. Josh was working the cash register, so I stayed to chat with him during lulls. We debated Allison Katzinger's funny books versus her tragic ones. I fetched Josh a plateful of artichoke dip and little endive leaves squirted with blue cheese and olives, and we agreed that they were as delicious as they were gross-looking. We had absolutely no privacy all night except for one brief moment, when the tipsy poet knocked over a stack of books with a sweep of her bangled arm, and Josh and I crept under the table to pick them all up.

But somehow it all felt romantic. More romantic than going to a movie or eating dinner in a restaurant with candles on the tables.

I didn't know if this was because I had a warped sense of romance—or because anything I did with Josh seemed romantic, even gathering books off the floor, our fingertips touching as we reached for the same one.

But finally one afternoon a few days after the Fourth of July fireworks got rained out, Josh shook his head.

"Chelsea, look at us," he said.

"What?" I replied. We were at the Pop Guy's cart with E.B., scarfing down frozen treats during a ten-minute break. Josh was wearing shorts and one of his cute plaid shirts. He had a wad of plastic bags poking out of his pocket (kind of a must when you're taking an overweight Labrador for a walk). I was still wearing my waitress apron. My fingers had ballpoint pen and neon marker (and probably mayonnaise) on them.

"You know, people sometimes see each other for longer than ten minutes," Josh said. "Or without a cash register sitting between them. They might even get a little dressed up. It's called a date."

If only I hadn't just taken a big, cold bite of my melting pop just as he'd said that. Then I could have given him a flirty pout and said something clever like, "What took ya so long?"

The truth was, though, that despite all the hanging out we'd been doing—the quick meetings, the texts, and, of course, the kissing—the idea of going on a date had never occurred to me. It seemed so old-fashioned, so formal.

"What, are you going to come pick me up at seven and shake my dad's hand and pin a corsage on my dress?" I laughed.

"Um, that was kind of what I was thinking," Josh said, looking sheepish. "I mean, except for the corsage part. Maybe a sparkler, though? It'd be a better fit for the DFJ."

DFJ meant "Deferred Fourth of July." The rained-out fireworks had been rescheduled, and the town had posted flyers about the event all over Main Street.

"That's datey, right?" Josh said. "A picnic, fireworks, marching band music?"

"I've always found marching band music to be very romantic," I said, laughing.

"Hey, it's better than our usual sound track," Josh said. "The little bell on the cash register."

He reached out with the hand that wasn't sticky with pop drips and brushed my cheek with his fingertips. It sent a jolt through me. I imagined being alone with Josh for an entire evening. "Dreamy" didn't begin to cover it, which was why I thought there must be a catch.

"Aren't your school friends going to be having a party or something?" I said.

"Maybe," Josh said with a shrug. "I'd rather be with you."

"Oh," I whispered. Josh's habit of bluntly saying what was on his mind still made me reel. But in a good way now.

"So . . ."

"So . . . ," I said. I smiled at him, shyly at first, then with giddy excitement. "So, pick me up at seven, I guess!"

*B*y the time I woke up the next morning, there were only a couple hours *left* in the morning. I smiled lazily and stretched.

After our first frenetic weeks in Bluepointe, with all the educational outings and sporty field trips, our family's pendulum seemed to have swung in the other direction. Life had seriously slowed down. And all that togetherness? That had tapered off too. Abbie had decided to train for a triathlon—because that was her warped idea of leisure—so her ninety-minute swim workout had expanded to include a couple hours of running and biking, too.

Each day, Hannah commandeered the swing on the screened-in porch so she could check another line off her to-read list. (I'm pretty sure she snuck in some naps on the porch swing too. It was impossible not to.)

My dad holed up for a few hours in the makeshift office he'd set up in Granly's bedroom. And I did my afternoon shift at the Mels or hung out at Dog Ear or the beach.

My mom's to-do list was to go through Granly's things—her clothes, her mementos, her artwork and wedding china and egg cups . . . the whole life she'd suddenly left behind here.

But somehow something else always seemed to come up.

There was the afternoon of antiquing she'd scheduled with an old high school friend.

"I *have* to see her. It's been years," Mom said as she put on makeup for the first time since we'd arrived in Bluepointe. Abbie and I sat on the bed watching her get ready, the way we used to do when we were little. "It's been years!"

"*Who* is she again?" Abbie said.

"ZiZi Rosbottom," my mom said. "From high school."

"Never heard of her," Abbie said. She turned to me. "You?"

"Nope." I shook my head.

"Yes, you have," my mom protested. "We edited the yearbook together. ZiZi!"

"I think we would remember a name like *ZiZi Rosbottom*," Abbie said.

"Yeah, because Abbie would have made all sorts of disgusting jokes about the fact that her name had the word 'bottom' in it," I agreed.

"Well," Mom said lightly as she breezed out of the bedroom, "maybe that's why I never mentioned her."

She made other excuses to flee the house too. She had to go to three different stores to get the right jars for making blueberry jam—even though blueberries wouldn't be in season until the end of July.

Or she passed a field full of sunflowers en route to the grocery store and had to go back and capture it with the tripod and the good camera.

This morning she was sitting on the living room floor surrounded by mounds of clothing. Most of the items looked so small, they couldn't possibly have been Granly's.

"What is that stuff, Mom?" I asked. I stood in the doorway between the living room and the hallway. I wasn't sure yet if I wanted to go in.

"Your baby clothes!" Mom said. She held up a tiny pink onesie with a duck on the front. "Well, yours and Abbie's and Hannah's. I'd forgotten they were here."

"Why *are* they here?" I asked.

"Oh, Granly and I used to say we were going to make a quilt out of them," Mom said, picking up a fuzzy little blanket and rubbing it between her fingers. "But it seemed like there was always something else to do."

"Oh," I said quietly.

Even as my hands gripped the door frame, I realized my body was tilting backward, poised for flight. I didn't want to think about yet another thing Granly wouldn't get to do. Or see.

Mom didn't seem to want to think about Granly either. She was lost in our pink, ruffly past.

"Oh!" she said, reaching for a hot-pink dress with a ribbon of orange tulle around the hem. "You and Abbie both wore this at your second birthday parties."

"Oh, yeah!" I said. "I remember the pictures."

"This would make the perfect center square for the quilt," Mom said, pawing through the tiny outfits. "And then the colors could get lighter and lighter as I move toward the edges. I can just see it!"

The thing was, I couldn't. Of course, I understood why my mom was nostalgic over baby clothes. She got all misty-eyed every time she thought about our babyhood, to the point that I sometimes felt kind of rotten about having grown up.

"You know, I should just do it," Mom announced. She began laying little dresses and sun hats and bodysuits out on the rug, organizing them in their full range of color, from powder pink to bubble gum pink to shocking pink.

"Ooh," Mom crooned. "I remember bringing you home from the hospital in this. . . ."

She was technically talking to me, but in reality I think she forgot I was even there; *she* might remember me as a baby with no teeth and chubby thighs and a little orange afro, but I didn't.

When I turned to go, she barely noticed.

I stalked through the laundry room and into the backyard. The sun was directly overhead, and the cicadas were grinding away from their invisible perches in the treetops. That sound, combined with too-long grass and the empty, dried-up garden plot, made the yard feel overheated and oppressive.

I found myself pacing back and forth along the stepping stones, my arms folded over my chest.

I should have been glad Mom had decided to do this quilt

thing. I hadn't seen her this happy and excited since we'd arrived in Bluepointe.

But . . . it just felt weird. This summer was supposed to be about Granly, not about *baby* clothes. She was walking down the wrong memory lane!

Not that I should have been complaining. I hated the thought of moving Granly's stuff. I wanted her sewing box and photo albums to stay in the hutch forever.

So I should have been happy that Mom was leaving everything untouched, right?

But I just . . . wasn't.

Because as long as we kept things just as they'd always been, we were in limbo. We were always in the process of saying good-bye to Granly . . . but never finished.

I heaved a deep sigh, then idly bent over the garden to pull a big clump of clover. My mom had done all that work turning over the soil in this garden, and then she'd abandoned that, too. Weeds were quickly creeping back in, and the dirt looked dry and cakey.

I pulled another few weeds, then cocked my head to give the garden a hard look. I went over to the shed and pulled open the squeaky screen door. I found a stiff rake, carried it back to the garden, and slammed it down into the dirt with a satisfying *whumpf*. Dragging the rake through the dirt broke it up, unearthed the baby weeds, and made a nice, straight, flat track of earth.

I could picture a row of tomatoes there.

I dropped the rake and headed back inside.

"Going to town," I called to whomever cared. I dug my phone

and a wad of tip money out of my dresser drawer, then slammed purposefully out the front door.

An hour later I returned with a rusty Radio Flyer wagon full of little plastic pots. Each held a feathery seedling. I'd gotten the plants at the fruit and vegetable stand where we always bought our corn and tomatoes. Mr. Jackson had given me a 75 percent discount because the planting season had pretty much ended.

"I don't know if they'll make it," Mr. Jackson had said to me as he'd helped arrange the seedlings neatly in the wagon. The plants looked even more spindly in his big, meaty hands. "They're pretty leggy—the ones everybody else passed over."

"And I know nothing about gardening," I'd said, biting my lip.

"Well, the good news is these are easy plants," Mr. Jackson had said. "Tomatoes, cucumbers, squash, lettuce . . . I mean, all they want to do is grow."

"Oh!" I'd said. "I forgot one more thing I wanted. Radishes. Do you have any of those?"

By dinnertime my pathetic little plants were in the ground. I'd followed exactly the instructions Mr. Jackson had written for me on a sheet torn off a yellow legal pad, spacing the tomatoes eighteen inches apart and tucking the radishes into two neat rows.

I grinned at my baby garden as I gave it a gentle spray with the hose. Then I pulled off Granly's pink gardening gloves, went inside, and opened the spice cabinet in the kitchen.

"Cayenne pepper," I whispered, finding a big bottle of the orange-red stuff near the back.

Mr. Jackson had sworn by it.

"Just sprinkle it all over the garden after you water each

morning," he'd told me. "Oh, that'll keep all the critters away."

As I dusted my garden with the red hot pepper, I pictured the beautiful basket of plum tomatoes, romaine lettuce, and crunchy pickling cucumbers I'd be pulling out of this garden in August. Not to mention the egg-shaped heirloom radishes.

I thought Granly would be proud of what I'd made of her little garden.

I couldn't help but think about what would be different by the time these little sprouts were ready to harvest (if they made it past the first week).

The summer would be almost over.

I'd be saying more good-byes—to Granly's cottage, to Blue-pointe, to Josh.

But at the moment that seemed as distant and unreal as the idea that these little sprouts could grow into big, succulent vegetables.

So I just shrugged my shoulders, gave the garden one last shake of cayenne, and went inside.

I waited until the morning of the DFJ to tell my family about my date.

Mostly because it took me that long to be able to whisper the words "I have a date" without covering my mouth and giggling like an idiot.

The day of the fireworks started off feeling like any other, except for the fact that my dad was making us banana pecan pancakes instead of working.

When he plopped a trio of them onto my plate, they each had two round ears.

"Dad!" I complained. "I don't eat Mickey Mouse pancakes anymore!"

"Oh, lighten up," Hannah said. "He made them for all of us."

"Even me!" my mom said, coming to sit at the table with her own plate of Mickeys. "I don't know. Somehow they taste better with those little ears."

"Well . . . okay," I grumbled. I poured a puddle of syrup into the space between my mouse ears, and said, "So . . . what are you guys doing tonight?"

Mom and Dad glanced at each other with raised eyebrows.

"What are *we* doing tonight?" Mom said. "Um, watching the fireworks with our three daughters, of course. Why, did you have other plans?"

"Well, yes," I said. "I—I have a date."

Mom and Dad looked at each other again, and their eyebrows went even higher.

"With this boy, Josh?" my mom said.

"Of course with Josh," I said. "We've been together for, like, weeks now."

"Together when?" Dad said. His fork was poised over his own plate, but it wasn't moving.

"Well, that's the thing," I said. "We've only seen each other before and after work. And during, sometimes. So he asked me out for the DFJ. You know, fireworks, picnic, marching band music?"

"Marching band music?" Abbie snorted.

"It's a figure of speech," I growled. I sliced an ear off one of my Mickey Mouse pancakes and shoved it into my mouth.

"How old is Josh?" Dad asked. "If he's your boyfriend now, we need to meet him."

"That's the whole plan!" I said. "He's fifteen, and he's picking me up at seven. You can meet him then."

"Honey," Mom said gently, "we were really looking forward to spending the evening with you girls. I mean, you've been working so much, and Hannah—well, who knows if she'll be with us on the Fourth next year. Right after breakfast your dad and I are going shopping for a really nice dinner on the beach."

"It's not even the real Fourth of July," I complained. "It's just the *Deferred* Fourth of July. Anyway, when did this holiday— whatever it is—suddenly become as important as Thanksgiving? I don't remember you ever caring that much about us being together for it before."

"Well, that was before," Mom said. Her lips went thin, and she dropped her fork to her plate with a clatter. "I'm not going to *order* you to have dinner with us. I'm going to ask you to do the right thing. You could always ask your friend to join us for dessert and the fireworks."

"How about I have dinner with you, and then Josh can come meet you when we're done?" I negotiated. "And then he and I can watch the fireworks by ourselves?"

Once again I watched my parents' eyeballs do their silent summit.

"All right," my mom said after a long moment. "Home by ten thirty."

"You let me stay out until midnight when I go out with Hannah and Abbie," I complained.

"*Because* you are with Hannah and Abbie," my dad said pleasantly. "Don't push it, Chels."

I brooded through the rest of my pancakes, wondering how I was going to tell Josh that my parents were being ridiculously clingy.

I was just putting my syrupy plate in the sink when my phone rang.

"Hi!" I said to Josh, rushing out onto the screened porch and shutting the front door behind me.

"Hi," he said. "Listen, I have something really awkward to tell you."

"O-kay," I said, feeling nervous heat prickle along my hairline.

"My parents have somehow decided that the DFJ might as well be Christmas," Josh said. "And you know, my dad's been in Chicago a lot for work, teaching that seminar at Loyola, but he has four days off in Bluepointe—"

"And they're not letting you ditch dinner?" I interjected gleefully.

Josh cleared his throat.

"Okay, that's not the reaction I was expecting," he said.

"No, it's just that mine got all weird about the DFJ too," I said. "We're in the same boat. I'm free for fireworks, though."

"Fireworks," Josh said. "I'll make it happen."

"Oh, but first you have to meet my parents," I said. "I can text you to let you know where to find us on the beach."

"Okay," Josh said, sounding less assured this time. "I can make that happen too."

"Don't worry," I said. "They're not too scary. And remember I have two older sisters. By the time they get around to doing all the parental requirements on me—you know, making me eat my broccoli, scheduling extra teacher conferences, meeting boyfriends—they've kind of lost their steam."

"Ha," Josh said. "Wonder what my parents' excuse is, then."

I bit my lip.

Josh and I hadn't talked much about his parents. All I knew was that his dad was a philosophy professor, which pretty much meant he thought of life as a series of hypotheticals.

"It's when it gets real," Josh had told me one day during a slow walk home after we'd both gotten off work, "as in a clogged toilet or remembering to go to the Bluepointe Business Association meetings, that he kind of loses interest. I don't think any of his ancient philosophers ever had do stuff like stock bookshelves and break down the boxes."

"Well, what about your mom?" I'd asked him. "I mean, Dog Ear is more her thing, right?"

"Yeah, but you know my mom," Josh said. "She thinks if she makes things charming enough, people will forgive anything, even lack of electricity."

"Maybe she's right," I said. "Dog Ear is the most amazing bookstore I've ever been in. You should feel good that you're helping her make it happen."

"You're right, I should," Josh said. "I wish I were super-passionate about Dog Ear. But like you said, it's my mom's thing.

It's not mine, really. Except now it has to be because it's the family business."

"And you *are* really good at doing all that organizing," I told him.

Josh rolled his eyes.

"Glad I could impress you with my file labels," he said. "I know they're really sexy."

I laughed before I pressed on.

"What about your posters?" I asked. "Josh, they're *really* good. I can't wait to see what you do with the Allison Katzinger."

Josh had smiled in thanks but changed the subject.

Now he did it again.

"So, should I wear a tie or something to meet your folks tonight?" he asked.

"Oh, definitely," I joked. "Bow tie, shined shoes, the works. And bring my mother flowers. Her favorite is the hothouse hyacinth."

"Oh, Nicole," Josh said, the way he always did when we quoted *Coconut Dreams*.

"Oh, Kai." I gave him my standard reply with a giggle in my voice. "See you tonight."

*I*nstead of going to our usual beach that night, we went to the public stretch closest to town, where they'd be setting off the fireworks. My mom insisted we go early so we could stake out enough space for this elaborate picnic she and my dad had planned.

"Can't I meet you there?" I said. "If we go early, it'll still be all hot and muggy out. I don't want to get all sweaty and gross for . . . for later."

Which was kind of ridiculous. Most of the time Josh saw me, I was coming off six hours of hustling around Mel & Mel's. Even though I took time to wash my face, redo my hair, and put on lip gloss before I saw him, I knew it could only help so much. I probably smelled like a combination of dishwasher steam and deviled eggs.

But on a date (okay, half a date) you were supposed to look different. You opened your door, and your guy did a double take because you'd done something different to your hair and put on jewelry. Your heels made you two inches taller. You were supposed to smell like shampoo and perfume, not like the fishy end-of-day wind that comes off Lake Michigan in the heat of the summer.

"Chelsea," Mom said, putting her hands on her hips. I noticed a couple of Band-Aids on her fingers—she kept stabbing herself with pins as she pieced together the baby clothes quilt. "I'm asking for one thing—that we be together for the Deferred Fourth of July. Please? For me?"

"All right," I grumbled.

It wasn't until we set out for the beach late that afternoon that I realized why Mom wanted this family moment so badly. It wasn't because of the (non) holiday.

It was because she'd decided that this would be Gatsby night.

Granly had always insisted that we do Gatsby night at least once every time we visited her. That was just her name for a fancy picnic where the adults drank champagne and the kids had sparkling grape juice in bowl-shaped goblets.

The food was always very fussy: crustless cucumber sand-wiches, slivered carrots and celery with spinach dip, tiny pickles and expensive olives, hearts of palm salad, and baked oysters. It was something we'd always done—like the stack-of-sisters photo on the beach—that I hadn't thought about too much. I'd assumed my mom had kind of taken it for granted too.

But obviously I'd been wrong.

As we all headed toward town that afternoon with a heavy picnic basket, blankets, and another basket full of clinking dishes and champagne glasses, I whispered to Hannah, "Why didn't she just say it was Gatsby night?"

Hannah shrugged.

"It was always kind of spontaneous when Granly did it," she whispered back. "Y'know, like one morning she'd just snap her fingers and announce it, and we'd all spend the day pitting olives and peeling shrimp. Remember?"

I did. I remembered my sisters and me getting giggly and excited about Gatsby nights. We'd put on satiny "dress-up" clothes and steal Granly's pink lipstick and say things like "Ooh la *la*!"

My mom was really different from Granly. Granly had always had a bright manicure, and she wore big rings with chunks of tur-quoise or lapis lazuli in them. When she talked with her hands, they made a *clickety-clack* sound.

My mother's nails were always short and unpainted. The only ring she ever wore was her narrow platinum wedding bad. Her wavy, chin-length hair was as different from Granly's wild red curls as hair could be.

When Granly threw a Gatsby picnic, it was fun, a little dramatic, and most of all effortless.

My mom's Gatsby night came less naturally to her. It took more work.

So when we made it to the beach and laid out our fancy spread—with the votive candles and the tiny silver forks and everything—I think I appreciated it more than I ever had when Granly was alive.

"Now, Chelsea," my mom said, arranging food on my plate while I texted Josh with our location, "I know you usually don't like goat cheese, but just try a little with this pepper jelly. I bet you'll love it."

"Looks yummy," I said.

My mom looked up in surprise.

"Really?" she said, giving me a skeptical smile. "Well, how about some smoked oysters?"

"Eh, let's not push it," I said with a laugh.

I didn't really like the goat cheese either, but I didn't tell my mom that. It didn't matter anyway. I loved the olive tapenade and the artichoke torte and lots of the other fancy stuff she and my dad had made.

And Abbie cracked us up with a story about Estelle, the crazy art gallery owner, who'd had another one of her famous tantrums recently.

People we knew from town started claiming spots around us and saying sweet, funny things about our hoity-toity picnic.

Dad passed around a small bowl of the first blueberries of the season. They were tiny and on the sour side, just the way we all liked them. We nibbled them as we watched the sun go down. It was so fun and the sunset was so mesmerizing that I almost forgot to be nervous about my date.

So of course that was just when Josh showed up.

I didn't realize he was there until I saw him standing at the edge of the picnic blanket, holding a cute little bouquet of daisies and gaping at our fancy china and champagne goblets and candlelight.

"Josh!" I said, quickly swallowing the blueberry in my mouth and hoping desperately that I didn't have any food in my teeth. "You're here!"

I jumped to my feet, smoothing down my yellow halter dress with one hand and tucking the frizz away from my hairline with the other.

As I gave him an awkward we're-in-front-of-my-family hug hello, he whispered, "I didn't think you meant it about the bow tie!"

"I didn't!" I said with a laugh.

He was wearing a white T-shirt with a cool, faded American flag on it, rolled up khakis, and had bare feet. He gave our fancy dishes and silverware a glance, then looked back at me with raised eyebrows.

"Oh, this is just something we do," I scoffed, waving my hand at the Gatsby picnic. "For a laugh. We're not *really* fancy."

"Speak for yourself," Abbie said. She was leaning on one elbow, popping blueberries into her mouth.

"That's my sister Abbie," I told Josh. "And this is Hannah, and, um, my parents."

"I'm Adam," my dad said, standing up to say hello.

"And I'm Rachel," my mother said as she pulled some dessert plates out of our picnic hamper. "We were just about to have dessert if you want to join us."

"Oh, that's okay," Josh said. Then he seemed to remember his daisies and thrust them toward my mom.

"For you," he said bluntly.

My mom and I raised our eyebrows at each other as Josh whispered to me, "I didn't know what the heck a hyacinth was."

"Those are perfect," I said.

Which was true. They were simple and sweet. They were just the kind of not-fancy flowers my mom loved. She smiled as she gave the little bouquet a sniff, then plunked it into her water glass.

It made for an easy, guilt-free exit.

"I'll be home by ten thirty, I promise," I told her, crouching down to say good-bye. "Thanks for the Gatsby night. It was . . ."

I couldn't say it was perfect. Because perfect would have included Granly.

"Well, I really loved it," I said.

And that was the truth.

I guess since I'd forgotten to feel nervous before Josh arrived, all my nerves hit during our walk down the beach. I couldn't think of anything to say as we picked our way around shrieking packs of little kids and college students laughing as they popped the caps off bottles.

I wanted to hold Josh's hand, but the wind was picking up and I needed my hands to hold my skirt down.

Josh was quiet too. He asked a couple polite questions about my parents and my sisters.

Then I asked him how dinner had been with his parents.

"Oh, fine," he said. "Some of those poets who like to come into Dog Ear set up right next to us, and they started improvising."

"Ooh," I groaned. "Improv poetry? That sounds painful."

"Oh, my dad ate it up," Josh said. "He likes that kind of thing. He went to Woodstock, but don't ask him about it unless you want to listen to him go on about it for three hours."

"Woodstock!" I said. "But how— How old—"

"Sixty-six," Josh said, answering the question I couldn't quite bring myself to ask. "He was fifty-one when I was born, and my mom was forty."

"Wow," I said. "I mean, I knew they were, you know, on the older side . . ."

"Yeah." Josh shrugged. "That's why they only had me. But I think that's what they wanted anyway. I mean, my parents have never been the romp-around-with-a-bunch-of-little-kids types."

"Oh," I said.

I hadn't really thought before about how different our lives really were. I'd grown up in a suburban house where there had always been us three kids (and usually a few of our friends) hanging out in our TV room, raiding the fridge, or playing in the backyard.

Meanwhile, Josh had never even *had* a backyard. Before moving to Bluepointe he and his parents had lived in an apartment in

Chicago, and Josh had taken the subway everywhere he needed to go. Now they lived in one of the lofts that overlooked Main Street, just a few steps away from Dog Ear.

It seemed very sophisticated and grown-up.

Maybe that was why Josh had proposed a "real" date, when I'd just been content to hang out wherever we landed. *And* why he felt the kind of responsibility for Dog Ear that never would have occurred to me.

We arrived at a spot where the picnic blankets were sparser and there was an empty patch of sand in front of the dune grass.

"This looks like a good place to see the fireworks," Josh said.

We sat and stared at the darkening sky for a few long moments. For some reason I was at a loss for words again.

"I wonder when they're going to start," was what I finally came up with.

Then I started to feel miserable. Why was I suddenly making small talk? This was *Josh*, with whom everything had been so easy and fun and *right* ever since our first kiss.

Josh reached over and took my hand, but just like my small talk, it felt forced. Like what you're *supposed* to do on a date, instead of what he wanted to do.

"Well . . . ," Josh said, staring out at the horizon just as I was, "this is weird."

"I know!" I said, exhaling with relief and turning to look at him. "Did my family freak you out?"

"No!" Josh said. "I liked them. I mean, from the three minutes or so I spent with them. Your mom seems like such a normal mom."

"What, like June Cleaver?" I said with a laugh.

"No, she just seems, I don't know, comfortable in that mom role," he said. "She seems kind of sad, too."

"Yeah," I said, hanging my head. "My grandma."

"I know," Josh said. His hand tightened around mine. "Listen, do you want to go back? We could watch the fireworks with them, if you want. Or . . . you could be alone with them."

I looked up at Josh's face, searching for what he *really* meant. I wanted to know what he was thinking just from gazing into the depths of his eyes. I wanted to be back on that road that we'd started on, the one where we just *got* each other and being together felt completely natural.

But now Josh felt opaque. I couldn't figure out what he meant by his offer. Was he being selfless? Or was he pushing me away?

"I don't want to go back there," I said.

"Okay," Josh said with a nod.

"No," I said urgently. "I mean back to how things were when we first met, and I liked you and you liked me, but both of us were too scared to say anything about it. And you sent me all those mixed signals . . ."

Josh frowned.

"What mixed signals?"

"You know!" I said. "When we first met. You were all hot and cold. You were sweet, then you were surly. You told me about the job at Mel and Mel's, but then when I got it, I swear your face went *white.*"

"And then I kissed you," Josh said quietly. He looked like he wanted to kiss me right then, but I wasn't having it.

"Yeah!" I said. "You can see how I was a little confused. But then, well . . ."

I grabbed Josh's hand, loving how familiar his long, slim fingers felt and how neatly and automatically they crisscrossed with mine.

"But then I thought we were all figured out. I mean, it's been amazing. Until tonight."

Josh cocked his head and said, "Chelsea, you of all people should know nobody gets 'figured out.' You *never* figure it all out—but you keep trying."

Now I cocked my head at him.

"That's a funny thing for *you* to say," I said.

"Why?"

"Well, I hope this doesn't sound bad," I said, "but I think you've got some issues with, you know, control."

Josh smiled a tiny bit, then took his hand back and leaned into the sand, propping himself up on his elbows. He gave me an *I'm listening* look.

"Well, there's the way you have a folder or drawer or cubby for every little thing at Dog Ear," I said.

"That's true." Josh nodded.

"And you do this sport that's all about precision and timing," I said. "And what about your friends? You skipped that whole lantern-making extravaganza even though I can think of one person—one *girl*—who would have really liked to see you there."

Josh snorted.

"And then there's your hair," I said.

"My *hair?*" Josh said, slapping his hand on top of his head.

"No, no, I love your hair!" I said, getting up on my knees so I could reach over and stroke his sleek, spiky hair. His eyes fluttered closed for a moment. "It's just that it's so different from a lot of boys' hair. It's so close-cropped, it never gets messy, never gets in your eyes. It's very . . . practical."

Josh shook his head slowly as he gazed at me. And in the almost darkness I couldn't quite tell what was going on in his face. Was he mad?

"But attractive," I said with an earnest nod. "Did I mention th—"

I didn't get to finish what I was saying, because Josh was on his knees too, wrapping his arms around me and kissing me hard. He came at me with such force—or maybe just because it was too dark for him to have good depth perception—that we toppled over into the sand. We landed, our arms still tangled up together, on our sides.

This made us burst out laughing. But then, quickly, we were kissing again, our hands buried in each other's hair and our bodies pressed together. When we finally broke apart, we were breathing hard. We lay on our backs for a moment, staring up into the black sky.

Then Josh rolled over so that he was facing me, and I rolled toward him. He put his hand on my cheek.

"I think you *do* have me pegged," he said.

"Oh, I don't know," I said with a coy smile. "I think I've got to do some more investigating."

Josh moved his hand up to my temple. He pulled free a curl

that had poofed out of my ponytail and spiraled it around his finger. Automatically I reached up to tuck it back behind my ear, but he stopped me.

"You like *your* hair under control too," he said. "But I loved it that day you came into Dog Ear with your sisters. It was all loose and wild."

"And *red*," I said with a long-suffering sigh.

"And red," Josh said, but from the way he said it, I could tell he thought it was a good thing.

Also because he started kissing me again.

But then abruptly he stopped and pulled back far enough to look me in the eyes. I wished I could see the pretty, velvety brown of his eyes, but it was too dark to see colors. We'd become black and white, like an old movie.

"You make me want to, I don't know," Josh said with a little self-conscious laugh, "not *lose* control so much as release it."

"That's the nicest thing-that-I-don't-completely-understand that anybody's ever said to me," I teased.

Josh shrugged happily.

"Like I said, that's the whole point," he said. "Not-figuring each other out."

I touched his hair again.

"I'm enjoying not-figuring you out," I said.

"I'm enjoying not-figuring you out too," Josh said. Then he squelched my laugh with another kiss—a kiss so long and deep that it made me feel dizzy, especially in the pitch-dark of our little nest near the dune. I sank into the kissing so deeply that I forgot where we were.

Which is why I was startled when we were interrupted by a huge *Pow!*

Only when I saw bright red sparks tendrilling down through the sky over the lake did I remember.

"The fireworks!" I said.

Josh's hand was on his chest.

"I forgot too!" he said breathlessly.

Pow!

The next one was gold and shimmery. It made a sizzling noise after it exploded.

I sighed and leaned against Josh. He swung his arm around my shoulders, and I snuggled in even closer.

Usually, watching fireworks made me feel tiny, almost consumed by the huge starbursts looming above me. But in Josh's arms I felt different. Safe and not quite as small as before. But way more exhilarated.

"I've changed my mind," I said to Josh during one of those breathless pauses between explosions. "I think I like dates after all."

"Me too," Josh said. "I think we should go on another one"— he paused for another big *Pow*—"as soon as possible."

*A*nd that's why Josh showed up at my house on my very next day off—carrying two giant paddles.

"This one's yours," he said, thrusting one of them at me with a big grin.

"You've got to be kidding," I said, stepping off the front steps into the gravel with my arms crossed. I was wearing my favorite bathing suit, the high-waisted black halter with the white polka dots. It wasn't vintage but looked it. Over that I wore my gauzy, flowy cover-up. "I thought we were going to the lake!"

"We are," Josh said. "Just not Lake Michigan. We're going to Wex Pond. Well, to be specific, we're getting into a boat on Wex Pond. My parents' landlord has a little rowboat there, and he said we can use it whenever we want."

Wex Pond is what Bluepointers called the Albert R. Wechsler Reservoir, because that was a pretty fancy name for what was really just a big bowl of water surrounded by farmland, some crooked trees, and a few docks.

I propped the oar on its end next to me and looked at it dubiously.

"I think you've got the advantage here," I said dryly. "Is this thing gonna give me blisters?"

"How about we just try it," Josh proposed. "I packed us a mayo-free lunch and everything. If you don't like it, we can go back to the beach. I promise."

I couldn't help but smile and nod my consent. It was so easy to be adventurous with Josh. I think I would have even agreed to go fishing with him, even though that would have driven my dad crazy.

"Let me just water the plants," I said, laying the oars down in the gravel and leading him to the backyard.

"Oh, yeah. How's the garden?" Josh asked. He walked over to check it out while I unwound the hose from its reel on the back of the house.

"Wow!" he said.

"I know!" I said, proudly pulling a couple weeds from around the lettuce plants. "I mean, about half of the radishes croaked, and one of my cucumber vines is looking pretty puny, but everything else is getting *huge*."

It was a little embarrassing how proud I was of my garden. The tomato plants got visibly bigger and fluffier every day. The pale-green romaine leaves were looking less delicate and translucent. They stood straight up. And most of the other plants had started sprouting trumpet-shaped yellow flowers.

"Hey, look!" Josh said, bending over to peer closely at the biggest tomato plant.

I crouched next to him to squint at the fuzzy branch. Then I gasped.

One cluster of little yellow blossoms had been replaced by tiny tomatoes! They were as green as Granny Smith apples and just as hard, but they were unmistakably tomatoes. Each had a little cap of pointy leaves that made it look like a gift-wrapped present.

"That was so fast!" I exclaimed. I did a quick inspection of the other plants and shrieked again when I found a collection of little cucumbers, curled under the big, flat leaves like shy caterpillars.

I jumped up and down with my garden hose, accidentally spraying Josh a little bit.

"Sorry!" I said. "I just can't believe I actually grew something. I mean, all I did was stick them in the ground and water them, but still! Pretty cool, huh?"

"Pretty cool," Josh said with a crooked smile and a hint of a tease in his voice.

"Okay, I know it's dorky," I said. "But I don't care. I'm super-proud of my little vegetables, and I will not be inviting you over for salad when they're ready."

"No!" Josh said, rushing over to put his arms around me. "Salad vegetables are the only ones I like. Please?"

"I'll consider it," I said. I finished spraying the soil. The July heat was getting so bad that the dirt caked right back up by late afternoon. I put the hose back and grabbed my jar of cayenne pepper from the windowsill. After giving the plants a quick sprinkle, I led Josh inside.

My mom was at the kitchen table, pinning pink and pinker squares together in a complicated pattern.

"Hi, Josh," she said warmly. Even though I still thought her baby clothes quilt was a little weird, I was happy to hear a normal warmth in her voice again, instead of that forced perkiness that had been there when we'd first arrived in June.

"I'm just going to get my bag from the bedroom," I told Josh, slipping into the hall.

When I got there, Abbie was sitting on the floor with her legs stretched out to the sides. On the rug between them were various piles of papers. They were in all different sizes, colors, and states of wrinkliness, but they all looked old.

"What're those?" I asked lightly as I headed for the closet.

"Granly's letters," Abbie said. "Most of them to and from Grandpa."

I froze at the closet door and turned to stare at my sister.

"Wh-what?" I stammered. "Why are you looking at them?"

"Listen," Abbie said brusquely as she slapped one of the letters into a pile, then scooped up another from a box sitting at her hip. "Mom has abdicated. We both know this quilt project of hers is not about getting all nostalgic about us as babies. It's about *avoiding* thinking about Granly!"

"Well," I murmured, "I think it's a little of both. . . ."

"Whatever," Abbie said. "You have a date with Josh, Hannah is off getting hickeys or whatever with Fasthands. And *I'm* here. So I might as well go through Granly's things myself. I mean, isn't that the point of us being here all summer?"

I felt terrible.

"Listen," I said, sinking to the floor just outside her circle of paper piles. "You shouldn't have to do that by yourself. Do you want me to say something to Mom? Or I could—"

Abbie held up her hand to stop me.

"You know what?" she said. Her face and voice softened. "I actually kind of like it."

She picked up the letter that she'd just slapped down, and smoothed it out on her leg, as if apologizing to it for the rough treatment. Then she read from it. With her head bowed and her hair spilling forward, I couldn't see her face, but her voice sounded a little different—slower and more lilting. Less like Abbie and more like Granly.

"'Dear Artie,'" Abbie read. That's what everyone had called Grandpa, though his real name had been Arthur. "'It feels funny to be so looking forward to the summer when *last* summer was so beastly. But my New Year's resolution was to look forward, not back, and I have been better at keeping at that than I have been at studying for my statistics exam. I really don't believe stats have anything to do with library science, and no (boring) thing you can say will convince me otherwise. By the way, you did catch what I said about last summer, didn't you, Artie? Now what, or whom, do you think is the reason for *that*?'"

As Abbie read, I put my hand over my mouth without realizing it. I could just *hear* my grandmother saying those words, even if they were in my sister's voice.

But then again I couldn't. Because that had been a Granly I never knew, the Granly who was young, writing a love letter to her boyfriend when she was supposed to be studying. And that "beastly" summer. What was *that* about?

"You know what I think she's talking about? That summer?" Abbie said as if she'd seen the question in my eyes. "I think they broke up."

"But we never heard about that!" I whispered, glancing at the door.

"Well, obviously it all worked out in the end," Abbie said with a laugh. "It's funny, isn't it, how someone's story can change? Maybe when Granly wrote that letter, *that* was their story, that they had come close to saying good-bye to each other forever."

"Which would have meant no Mom," I whispered, shaking my head in wonder. "No us."

"Yeah, and once they were married, who knows if they ever thought about it again. Maybe when your big picture is in place, all those bumps in the road along the way get sort of smoothed over."

I thought about that.

"Do you ever feel like," I asked, "right now, it's nothing but bumps?"

"Oh, yeah," Abbie said, nodding in recognition. "Why do you think I love to swim so much? There're no bumps in water."

Abbie replaced Granly's letter in its pile and smoothed it out carefully.

"Anyway, I think you should read these letters . . . sometime. Mom, too. When you're ready."

I picked another letter up, holding the dry, crackly-feeling paper between my thumb and forefinger.

"I . . . I might be ready."

Abbie shook her head.

"I know you're not," she said. "But that's okay. I am. I don't know why I am, but I am. So I'm going to get them all *organized* for you in little folders, which I know Hannah will approve of, and we can take them home with us. And when you're ready— they will be too."

I teetered over the piles of paper to give Abbie a thank-you hug.

"Aren't *we* huggy," Abbie said, pushing me away with a grin. "You're clearly getting some action."

"Shut up!" I whispered, glancing again at the bedroom door as I got to my feet. "You're so gross."

"Maybe," she said. "But I also know what I'm talking about."

I laughed as I checked myself in the mirror. I'd worn my hair half-down as a concession to Josh, with only the front sections pulled back into a big tortoiseshell clip. But there was nothing I could do about my freckles, other than smear them with tons of sunscreen and hope no more popped out after my day in the sun. I grabbed my bag, blew my sister a kiss, and met Josh out front.

$\mathcal{B}$ y the time we arrived at Wex Pond, which was about a two-mile walk from Sparrow Road, we were both hot and sweaty.

Josh led me to the end of one of the rickety, rocking docks. There, bouncing against the timbers, was a shabby once-white rowboat that looked barely big enough for the two of us. The interior of the boat was blackened with dirt and a little puddle of water. There was one seat in the center that hardly looked big enough for two backsides.

"Isn't it great?" Josh said, jumping easily into the boat and holding out his hands so I could hand him the oars and our bags.

"Um, do you want an honest answer?" I said as I shuffled my feet out of their flip-flops.

"Of course not," Josh said with a smile. He got a sly look in his eyes as he pulled a nylon picnic blanket out of his bag. He spread it out on the bottom of the boat. Then he produced a little pillow and tucked it into the back of the boat (or maybe it was the front, I couldn't quite tell).

"I was lying about you having to row," Josh said. "You get to sit there while I row you around. You can pretend you're Daisy Buchanan."

My mouth dropped open. "Seriously?"

"Well, you like playing Gatsby, don't you?" Josh held out a hand to help me climb into the boat. "And, conveniently, my English class read that book this year. If I get tired of rowing, I'll peel you a grape."

I burst out laughing.

"I'm not *that* much of a princess, you know," I said. "I'm a waitress! And I'm pretty good with a garden rake."

"All the more reason you deserve to relax," Josh said. "If you want something to do, think of another installment for *Diablo and the Mels.* The same bit's been on the specials board for the past three days."

"No pressure or anything," I said as I sank into the little waterproof nest he'd made me. "Besides, it's a good bit, right? 'B. smites that low tipper.' I should leave it up longer as a cautionary tale."

Josh laughed, which made me smile—it always did. And he was right. Even though I could feel the cold of the puddle beneath the blanket, and it smelled kind of moldy down there, lounging while he rowed me around the pond *did* make me feel kind of like a princess.

My perch also gave me a great view of Josh's arms flexing as he leaned forward and back, pulling at the oars.

"Do you need me to be your coxswain," I said. I imitated Tori's cute, squeaky voice and pointed. "A little to the right, *Joshie.*"

"Har-har," Josh said, a little out of breath with the rowing. "By the way, you don't say 'right'; you say 'starboard.'"

"Oh," I said. I watched him take a few more pulls on the oars.

"What do you like about rowing?" I asked.

Josh cocked his head to think for a moment.

"I like the efficiency of it," he said. "One stroke can take you a whole boat-length down the river. And I like how a whole row of guys can all be communicating with each other, matching each other's rhythm, putting extra muscle into it, sprinting for the win, all without saying a word."

I nodded slowly, imagining the steady, strong back-and-forth motion of a queue of boys, all with shaggy hair fluttering in the breeze, save one.

That communication without words but through breath and rhythm and some sort of telepathy . . . it fascinated me.

Sometimes I felt that Josh and I had that kind of silent way of speaking to each other, with our eyes and our gestures.

And of course with kissing.

Everything seemed to make me think about kissing lately. But I didn't want *Josh* to know that (even though I had a feeling that he felt much the same way). So I grabbed my bag and rooted around in it until I found *Someone New*, an Allison Katzinger novel that I was rereading after finding my own left-behind copy on Granly's bookshelf.

"You brought a book?" Josh squawked.

"Of course," I said, blinking at him. "What, you don't have one?"

"Do you just bring a book with you everywhere you go?" Josh said. He looked like he was trying to decide if this was maddening or cute.

"Um, pretty much, yeah," I said. "I mean, if I still had my e-reader, I might not have brought it onto a *boat*. Then again, I probably would have. That's kind of why I don't have an e-reader anymore."

I sighed, remembering my little electronic tablet fondly.

"Anyway, I thought you wanted me to relax," I said, giving his leg a nudge with bare toes.

"That *is* what I said, isn't it?" Josh said. He angled the oars so they backchurned the water, slowing the boat down. He kept on working the oars until we'd pretty much stopped.

Then he grinned at me.

"Wouldn't want you to get seasick."

"Oh, really?" I said. "Well, fine!"

I tossed my book back into my bag, pulled myself up, and plopped down on the seat next to him. Grabbing the oar out of his right hand, I said, "Teach me to row."

"Yeah?" Josh said, squinting at me.

"Yeah! You make it sound so magical. I want to try it."

"Okay," Josh instructed, "flatten your oar while you're pulling back, then turn it just as you hit the water, like you're scooping ice cream. I'll count, and you go with that rhythm, okay?"

I nodded.

But every time Josh brought his paddle forward, mine seemed to go backward. And vice versa.

And then somehow I was paddling twice as fast as he was, but when he sped up, I slowed down.

The upshot was that our rowboat was spinning around in circles, and I was laughing so hard, I couldn't row anymore.

"I hate to say this," Josh gasped between laughs, "but I think you have no future as a coxswain."

"*Now* do I get to read my book?" I joked. I stood up to turn around so I could settle back into my nice waterproof nest.

But the boat was still twirling a bit. So Josh, trying to be helpful, dug an oar into the water to stop it.

Which tossed me off balance, and well, you can guess what happened next.

Splash!

It took Josh about two seconds to jump in after me.

"Are you okay?" he cried.

My feet found the bottom of the pond, and I stood up. The water only reached my shoulders.

"I think I'll make it!" I replied, laughing as I wiped water off my face. "I'm not even ruining any clothes."

I reached down and peeled my soaked cover-up over my head and tossed it into the boat.

"But thanks for coming to my rescue," I said, giving Josh a light kiss on the lips.

"Anytime," Josh said, giving me a bigger kiss in return.

I turned to float on my back. My fingertips grazed his torso as I fluttered my hand to keep myself balanced.

"It's so peaceful in here," I said. "So different from the big lake. I could stay out here forever."

Josh said something, but with my ears underwater, it was garbled. I splashed myself back to a standing position.

"What was that?" I asked.

Josh looked down at the water for a moment, pensive, "I said 'I wish you would.'"

My easy smirk faded.

"When do you leave again?" Josh asked.

Automatically I waved my hand—a *Not for forever* gesture. Because that's how this summer had seemed for so long—like an endless stretch of days, each longer and hotter and lazier than the last. The ending felt so distant, I'd stopped believing it would ever arrive.

But now that Josh had asked me to think in terms of the calendar, my eyes widened.

"We leave the third week of August," I said. "We've got to give Hannah time to get home and pack and fly back out for school in September."

Josh looked down at the water. Our hands flittered back and forth beneath the surface, keeping us upright.

"That's about a month away," he said.

"A month," I said. My voice sounded craggy suddenly.

"Well, that's better than weeks," Josh said, and I could tell he was adding brightness to his words, the way my mom perked up faded fabric in her quilt by edging it with sunshine-yellow thread.

"*Much* better than days," I added.

It didn't feel quite real that these rowboat, beach, and blueberry days . . . were going to end. That my life was going to go back to slamming locker doors, and spiral-bound notebooks, and babysitting, instead of slinging mayonnaise and reading nothing but novels. And being with Josh.

It didn't seem real, and yet, when Josh pulled me to him, there was a new urgency in the way we kissed.

I let my hands linger on his bare shoulders, trying to memorize all his curves and angles.

He lifted a hand to smooth back my hair and sent water trickling down my face. It felt like tears.

I let my feet leave the soft, loamy mud at the bottom of the pond so that I was afloat, held in place only by Josh's arm around my waist.

And we kissed as if we had all day. If we pretended the day was endless, then a month was nothing to fear.

Suddenly signs of summer ending were everywhere. The days were getting hotter, but they were also getting shorter.

My dad started working less as his clients got ready to make the "great migration" to their August vacations. And Hannah started taking long afternoon naps, as if she wanted to cram in as much sleep as she could before she started pulling all-nighters at U of C.

Finally, on a day when she knew I wasn't working at the Mels, my mom pulled the stack of tin buckets out of the hall closet.

The buckets meant blueberry picking. And blueberry picking meant—inescapably—that it was the last week in July.

This was the week we always went picking when we were in Bluepointe, because it fell right before the berry season peaked and the orchards got crowded. Late July was also when the berries were still small and tart. None of us could stand a super-ripe, sweet, squishy blueberry. It must have been genetic.

"Mom," I said as she clanked the stack of buckets onto the kitchen table. "Is it okay if I invite Josh to go picking with us? I'm working the next few days, and I'd really like to hang out with him."

My mom frowned and glanced at the other end of the table, which had pretty much been permanently overtaken by her baby quilt.

"I don't know, honey," she said. "We've always gone with just us."

I followed her gaze to the quilt top. It was really starting to take shape, with cone-shaped swatches of fabric making a shell-like spiral in the center, framed by small squares. It was amazing, but I knew I didn't see in it what my mother saw. She looked at it and was carried back to the powdery smell of our baby heads, and the satin feeling of our baby skin, our fuzzy never-cut hair, and our mouths that looked like little rosebuds.

I just saw a bunch of cute old onesies.

"Listen," I said, "if you want, I won't invite him. But . . . everything's different this summer anyway."

Mom's eyes got glassy for the first time in a while—at least that I'd seen. I felt guilty.

But I also wanted her to say yes.

She nodded slowly and said, "See if he wants to come. Tell Hannah she can ask Liam, too, if she wants."

Abbie had just walked into the kitchen to pull a snack out of the fridge when Mom made that proposal. She snorted.

"I can guarantee Fast—I mean Liam—doesn't want to go on a family berry-picking outing with us," Abbie said. "He prefers to see Hannah alone. At night. Where nobody can see anybody's *necks*."

"Abbie!" I growled, looking shiftily at Mom.

My mom rolled her eyes.

"Do you think I didn't see that hickey on Hannah's neck?" she asked us. "And did you think I didn't already have a discussion with her about it? Please. Always remember"—she looked straight at me then, and her eyes did *not* look glassy anymore. Instead they were her steely *Don't mess with me, I'm a teacher* eyes—"there's not much about you girls that I don't know."

I think she did know how I felt about Josh—which was why she'd said he could come blueberry picking with us. I flashed a grateful smile and trotted toward my room to start getting ready while I called him.

Before I could finish dialing, though, my phone rang! I didn't even check to see if it was Josh.

"Hiiiii," I crooned into the phone.

"Chelsea? You sound weird."

"Emma!" I blurted with a laugh. "Um, I thought you were—"

"Josh?" Emma said. "Wow. So things are good, huh?"

I could tell by the flat tone of her voice that she had not called me—at six a.m. California time!—to dish about my boyfriend.

"What's wrong?" I asked, flicking on my closet light and stepping inside. I pulled out a dress I'd been thinking would be perfect for blueberry picking—very 1940s housedress, but in a cute way—and tossed it onto my bed.

"Nothing!" Emma replied quickly. "Tell me about Josh."

"Well—"

"It's just that— Oh, Chelsea! I'm totally wrecking things!"

"With Ethan?" I said. I pulled out a pair of red-and-white pedal pushers and tossed those onto the bed too. "What are you talking about?"

"I don't know!" she said. "I just love him so much. And I don't have a lot of time, what with the intensive and rehearsals for *Don Q* on top of that."

"So, you're dying because you don't have time to see him?" I said.

"When I have the time, he doesn't," Emma said. "And when I don't have the time, he does! Supposedly. I'm starting to think he's just making that up. I think I'm getting on his nerves. But I can't help it. I think about him all the time. I can't sleep! I almost want to quit the Intensive so I can have time for him. Maybe that would help?"

"Emma, no!" I gasped, dropping the tank top I was holding. "What are you talking about? That's crazy!"

"I know, but love makes you do crazy things," Emma said. "*You* know."

"I guess?" I said, even though I wasn't sure I *did* know what she was talking about.

"Okay, like, how do you handle it when you want to call Josh for the third time that day?" Emma asked.

"Um, I don't think that's happened," I said. I sat on the edge of the bed and frowned in thought. "But I guess I would just . . . call him?"

"And what would he do?"

"Well, if he was working, he'd probably let it go and call me back later?" I said. I wasn't really sure what she was driving at.

"See?" Emma said. "Ethan, too! Doesn't that make you crazy?"

"No," I said. I was starting to feel weird. Was it *supposed* to make me crazy? "Listen, Josh and I talk every night before we go to bed. So, I know I'll talk to him then."

"You dooooo?" Emma said yearningly. "That's soooo romantic."

And she was right. It was. But it was also what Josh and I had done since the day after our first kiss. We'd just fallen into that sweet pattern, and I'd already gotten used to it. I hadn't known it was so revolutionary. To me—to us, I was pretty sure—it was just the natural thing to do.

I wondered if I was truly crazy about Josh if I wasn't feeling *crazy* about Josh. Being with him made me feel kind of floaty and giddy. And I had noticed that everything seemed a little more intense since I'd started dating him. Like my dad's bad jokes started to seem funny, and kittens or cute commercials on TV made me go all crumple-faced and sappy. And food tasted really delicious.

But did I feel crazy or desperate the way Emma did? I didn't think so.

I guess it helped that when I called Josh after hanging up with Emma, he sounded so happy to hear my voice. And when I invited him to go berry picking, he dropped what he was doing to say yes. (He literally did! I heard a big stack of books hit the counter with a thud!)

I couldn't stop smiling as I hung up the phone and plucked the 1940s frock off the pile on the bed.

If Emma had it right, being with Josh was supposed to make me act either cagey or crazy. And falling for Josh was supposed to make me feel lost.

But instead I felt found. And if that meant I was doing this relationship thing wrong, I decided not to care.

*N*ot surprisingly, my family always went to the same blueberry farm: Chloe and Ken's U-Pick Farm and Art Gallery.

"Oh, yeah," Josh said when we told him where we were

going. "I know them. Did you know they're selling free-range eggs now?"

My dad clapped his hands and laughed.

"Of course they are!" he said. "And I bet they're miserable about it."

"Totally miserable!" Josh said with a grin.

Ken and Chloe desperately wanted to be brilliant starving artists who made a meager living with their blueberry farm. Instead they were wildly successful blueberry farmers who made really bad art. Chloe worked with clay—wobbly vases that looked like she'd caught them in midair just as they'd careened off her potter's wheel, or little animals with drunken, hooded eyes and buck teeth. Ken was always carving up wood. He made sculptures and woodcuts, all of them splintery and angry.

It seemed like the more frustrated Chloe and Ken got as artists, the more their farm thrived, just to spite them.

Sure enough, when we pulled off the flat, dusty dirt highway, their rows of bushes were fluffy and heavy with berries. Cute little white hens clucked and pecked around the bushes. Up on a hill just behind the rows of blueberry bushes, several rows of boxy hives were swarming with so many honeybees, you could see the clouds of them from the driveway.

When we got out of the car, we were met by Ken, looking long-faced in paint-smeared overalls.

"The place looks good, Ken," my dad said. "Won't you *please* take my card. You need an accountant to manage all this money you're making!"

Ken winced. My dad had said that as if it were a *good* thing.

"We started raising these chickens," he said morosely. "People *really* like the eggs. And, well, the chickens fertilize the berries, so *they're* doing really well. And the bees are making so much honey, we had to add fifteen more hives."

Ken hung his head and sighed.

"Oh!" Mom said. She had her perky voice on, and she was pointing at a tall, crooked log planted vertically in the ground. "Ken, I see you're doing something new. Um, is that a totem pole?"

"Chainsaw carving!" Ken said, perking up. "Let me tell you about it. . . ."

My sisters and I looked at each other in alarm.

Run away! Abbie mouthed.

I grabbed Josh by one hand and a stack of buckets in another, and the four of us dashed into the nearest thicket of bushes, all of us snorting with laughter.

"Quick," I whispered, "before we get sucked into the vortex of bad art."

We headed for the back of the orchard, twice almost tripping over lazy chickens.

"I think we're safe," Hannah said with a laugh. She plucked a few berries from a bush and dropped them into her pail.

"Kerplink, kerplank, kerplunk," she said.

"Ah, *Blueberries for Sal*!" Josh said. "That's a big favorite at the kids' story hours at Dog Ear."

Of course, thinking about the children's story hour at Dog Ear made me remember our weird, wonderful first kiss. And *that* made me want to kiss him right then.

I gave Josh a shy glance and caught him giving *me* a shy glance. His Adam's apple was bobbing up and down, and I could tell he was thinking the same thing.

"You know," I said to my sisters, "these berries look too big and squishy. I think Josh and I are going to try a couple rows over."

"Oh, yeah," Abbie said, nodding vigorously. "The kissing will be much better over there."

"Abbie!" I squawked.

"Oh, did I say 'kissing'?" she said with a mock gasp. "I meant 'berries.' The *berries* will be much better over there."

"You're awful," I told her before ducking through a couple of bushes with Josh to get to the next row. We kept pushing through until we couldn't hear Abbie giggling anymore.

Josh grinned at me when we emerged from the last row of bushes.

"She's awful," I repeated.

"Oh, yeah, awful," Josh said, smiling as he bent over to kiss me.

And kiss me and kiss me until—*clang*—I dropped my bucket into the dirt and we broke apart, laughing.

"Your sister's right, though," Josh said. "The kissing *is* much better over here."

"I hate it when she's right," I said with a grin.

I scooped up my bucket and added, "Come on. We have to pick a *lot* or they'll know what we were up to."

"They know anyway," Josh said. He snaked his arm around my waist and kissed the top of my head, which for some reason made me feel just as melty as when he kissed me on the lips.

"Kerplink, kerplank, kerplunk," I reminded him, twisting away so I could start picking berries.

"All right, all right," he murmured.

But he still stood so close to me that every time he reached for a branch, his arm brushed mine.

Or he would bend for some low-hanging berries, and his fingertips would graze my leg.

Or he would find my version of the perfect blueberry—just tender enough that it wasn't lip-puckeringly sour, but nowhere near as ripe as many people like them—and pop it into my mouth.

It took a while for our berries to stop *kerplink*ing against the bottoms of our buckets. And when we'd finally filled them and headed back to the car, my family had been waiting so long that they'd actually gotten roped into buying some of Chloe's bad pottery.

"Look, Chelsea," Mom said, her voice so perky that it had gone up a whole octave. Chloe was there too, wearing overalls that exactly matched Ken's. Chloe was beaming proudly. "Aren't they, uh, cute?" Mom said.

She was holding two little ceramic chickens, made of rough-looking red clay with plenty of visible fingerprints. They had bulgy eyes with big, bluish lids half-closed over them. Their beaks looked sort of smushed-in. One was a rooster, the other a hen.

"We're calling them Josh and Chelsea," Hannah said with a glare.

I turned to Josh.

"You know we're totally getting sterilizing duty for this."

*S*terilizing the jars is the worst part of making jam. You have to hand wash every jar in steaming hot water, then submerge them in boiling water for at least twenty minutes. We always used Granly's roasting pan, balanced over the stove's two back burners, to boil the jars, while two pots of sugared blueberries frothed away on the front two. You had to plunge your arm through the sticky blueberry steam to fish out the clean jars with a pair of wobbly metal tongs, timing it so they were still freshly scalded when the blueberries reached the right temperature and you could pour them into the jars—bubbling and spitting and flecking your clothes with tiny purple dots.

Sure enough, when we got home with our buckets of berries, my mom pointed Josh and me to the sink, where two dozen Ball mason jars were waiting to be scrubbed.

"Here," Hannah said, placing Chloe's clay chickens on the windowsill above the sink. "They can keep you company."

She placed them beak to beak so it looked like they were kissing.

"Now *you're* awful," I said, rolling my eyes at her. I gave Josh a sheepish glance. His face was definitely a little pink, but maybe that was just from the sun and the steam, because he refused to inch away from his spot right next to me at the double sink. He stood so close that my hip nestled comfortably against his leg, and every time he handed me a soapy jar to rinse, our forearms brushed against each other. I noticed the downy hair on his arm had gone blond, and his skin was a bit more golden than it had been when we'd first met. That was back when he'd spent most of his time at Dog Ear, back before he'd had a reason to escape to berry patches and Wex Pond.

Just when the kitchen started to feel oppressive, with the windows steamed up and the air smelling syrupy, my mom put one of Granly's Beatles CDs into the little countertop stereo. Abbie and Hannah started dancing each other around the kitchen, dripping blueberry syrup onto the floor and laughing hysterically. Josh and I bumped hips (or my hip and his leg) and clinked jars together like they were cymbals.

I thought of those stacks of paper that Abbie had made on our bedroom floor, and I knew—this was one of those days that I needed to write down. Maybe on a scrap of paper that nobody ever saw. Maybe in a letter to Josh. It didn't matter. All that mattered was that my pen on paper preserve this moment, so I could know it had really happened when I was back in LA.

That it hadn't been a dream.

The dreamy feeling didn't go away after Josh headed home for dinner—a jar of still-warm blueberry preserves in each hand. Hannah and I crawled around the kitchen with hot soapy rags, scrubbing at the worst of the jam drips, while my mom got ready to go over the whole floor with Granly's old string mop.

Meanwhile Abbie scrubbed pots in the sink. She kept making new sticky splashes on the floor, and we laughed and screeched at her.

Finally cleanup was done, and the only sounds we heard were the jars of jam settling on the kitchen table. The cooling, and some law of physics that Hannah could probably teach us, sucked the mason jar caps downward. Eventually they would all have slight scoops to them, which meant they were safely sealed. As this happened, the jar tops made little *pings* and *pops* and *squeaks*. It gave the strangely cozy illusion that the jam jars were alive. Which I guess was why I winced a little bit when my dad arrived home from a long walk and excitedly popped open one of the jars so he could spread some of the new jam on toast.

While my dad munched and he and my mom chatted, the rest of us drifted away from the kitchen. I went to get my book off my nightstand, and Hannah headed out to the screened porch, dialing her phone. Abbie flopped onto the living room couch and clicked on the TV.

That's when we were all summoned to the living room by a loud whoop.

"What is it?" I yelled, dashing in, my book still open in my hand.

"Look!" Abbie said, grinning and pointing at the TV screen. "Next up: *Till Death Do Us Part?*"

"No. Way!" I screamed.

"What happened?" Hannah said, her hand pressed to her phone to block out our noise.

"Lifetime movie!" Abbie and I shouted at her.

"It's one we've never seen, and it's just starting," I said, flopping down onto the couch with Abbie. I crossed my fingers, closed my eyes, and chanted, "Please let it star Jennifer Love Hewitt!"

"Either her or Valerie Bertinelli," my mom chimed in, flopping down next to me.

Hannah murmured into her phone, "I'll have to call you back, okay? It's kind of important." Then she sank onto the floor in front of the couch and said, "I want Meredith Baxter. She does crazy really well. I think her eyes are a little off their track."

We watched hungrily as the movie started, with melodramatic swells of violins. As the opening credits flashed past in a blocky font that screamed "low-budget" we realized there were no famous B-list actors in the cast. Or even C- or D-list actors. They were total unknowns.

Or maybe Canadians.

That meant the production values were going to be wretched, the acting awful, and the screenplay riddled with melodrama and awkward catchphrases.

"Ooh, it's going to be *so* bad!" I squealed, clapping my hands.

"Honey," my mom called to the kitchen. "Could you make us some popcorn? And is there any wine left from last night?"

"And *please* tell me we have marshmallows," Abbie called.

The marshmallows weren't for eating, of course. They were for tossing at the TV screen during bad lines.

It turned out *Till Death Do Us Part?* was about bigamy, true love, murder, and reconstructive surgery, not necessarily in that order. I knew we had a winner when wife number one raged at her husband, "John, I supported you through law school so you could study jurisprudence, not mess around with some woman named Prudence!"

When wife number two started lacing John's scrambled eggs with arsenic, Hannah and I screamed, "*Flowers in the Attic*!" at the exact same time. We high-fived each other before throwing our last marshmallows at the screen.

We lost Mom when wife number one got killed off. She left

with Dad to pick up a pizza for dinner. But my sisters and I stayed until the bitter end, when—*duh duh DUH*—there was a shocking appearance from wife number THREE.

We turned down the volume during the final credits but couldn't bear to turn it off.

"Best bad movie *ever*," I said, collapsing into the couch cushions and hugging myself. "When are they gonna be back with that pizza? I'm starving! I hope Dad got extra mushrooms."

Abbie and Hannah glanced at each other over my head and exchanged some secret signals.

"What?" I said. "What have you guys been saying about me *now*?"

"She's showing all the signs," Hannah said to Abbie.

"Of what?" I said, alarmed.

"'Of a force stronger than the law, and more brutal than the laws of *nature*,'" Abbie cried, quoting the movie while shaking her fists at the heavens.

I laughed—until I realized what she meant. Then I swallowed my laughter with a quick gulp.

Hannah gave me a smile that was a little wistful as she said, "Does all food taste incredibly delicious? And does all music seem like it's really about you?"

"Do you suddenly think Josh is a completely unique name," Abbie asked, "even though it's really just another one of those blend-together J-boy names?"

"No it's not!" I said automatically. "It's *so* much better than John or Jim or Jason."

"See!" Abbie said, pointing at me.

I sank back into the couch, feeling floaty and on the verge of elated. Were my sisters right? Was I in love with Josh? How could I know for sure? It wasn't like there was some lever inside you that switched from *like* to *love* one day with an audible click.

It made me feel a little feverish to think about it, so of course I lobbed the issue back to Hannah.

"Well, what about you?" I said. "What's going on with Liam?"

"Liam?" Hannah said, blinking rapidly as if she didn't know who I was talking about.

"Yes, Liam, the boy who likes to give you hickeys?" I demanded.

"Oh my God," Hannah groaned. "It was *one* hickey, you guys! Grow up!"

"We will if you will," Abbie said with a little glower.

"What do you mean by that?" Hannah said.

"I mean, are you really finding it *fun* to hang out with someone who's so . . . blond?"

"Whoa," I said, swinging around to look at Abbie. I was always sensitive to hair-color pigeonholing. "Stereotype much?"

"It's a figure of speech," Abbie said, jutting out her chin. "I just mean Hannah deserves someone less generic. More like . . ."

Just before I could say *Josh*, Hannah whispered, "Elias."

I bit my lip and shot Abbie a look. Looking regretful, she put a hand on Hannah's shoulder.

"I didn't mean to—"

"Listen, Eliases don't come along every day," Hannah said. "But in the absence of one, I think I'm allowed to have some fun."

She pointed accusingly at Abbie.

"You do it all the time!" she said. "You date like it's a sport, just like swimming, but with more contact."

"Yeah," Abbie agreed. "But you're not me."

That, of course, was an understatement. Sometimes I didn't understand how the three of us could be so very different—yet understand each other so well.

Hannah shrugged, grabbed the empty popcorn bowl off the coffee table, and headed for the kitchen, stomping on a couple marshmallows as she went. Which was another way of admitting that Abbie was right. Not that Abbie seemed to enjoy it. She flounced off the couch and headed to our room, stepping on more marshmallows.

I could just picture what Granly would say if she saw us smushing marshmallows into her Persian rug. I slid to the floor (which was easy enough because I was feeling a little weak and rubbery) and crawled around, picking up the flattened marshmallows. I scooped them into the skirt of my cute sepia-colored blueberry-picking dress.

Then I just sat still for a moment and tried to gather my thoughts. I heard a tinny *ping* come from the kitchen as another jar of jam sealed itself closed. That was followed by the soft *thwack* of one of Hannah's textbooks hitting the kitchen table, then flipping open.

I found that the only thoughts I had to gather were ones of Josh, of the way his fingertips felt grazing my cheek, of the dimples that seemed to always go deeper whenever I was around. I pictured the black ink smudge he always had on his middle finger after he'd been working on his Allison Katzinger book launch poster. I could almost smell him, a smell that was warm and clean with a hint of vanilla (maybe from all the cookies floating around Dog Ear).

And then my phone rang, and I knew it was him, and I also knew—with a sudden, breathtaking certainty—that I *was* in love.

I loved Josh's too-long arms and the little cowlick in his left eyebrow. I loved the way he slouched over his coffee cup, and I loved his cherry pie rut. I even loved the way he read books so differently from the way I read them—all businesslike and analytical, always thinking about whether they would sell or sit on the shelf.

But my feelings for Josh went deeper than the details. I just loved . . . him. The him beneath the surface, the him that maybe only I really knew.

I dashed to find my phone, which was on its way to vibrating off the kitchen counter. It felt a little sticky when I scooped it up. I fumbled as I snapped it open, and grinned when I saw Josh's number on the screen and knew that I'd been right.

"Hi," I said, not able to catch my breath somehow. I headed back toward the living room and waited for him to ask what had made me so out of breath.

Would I tell him? *How* do you tell someone something like that?

So, guess what? I just realized that I love you.

I shuddered and shook my head. Then I shrugged and smiled to myself.

The one thing I did know about being with Josh was that there *would* be a time and a way to tell him how I felt, and when it arrived, it would feel natural and sweet and right.

"So, was your mom excited about the jam?" I asked Josh. "Tell her not to put it out in Dog Ear. It'll get gobbled up in a few hours. We worked too hard for that, right? Kerplink, ker-plunk . . ."

My voice trailed off. The silence on Josh's end of the line was . . . too silent.

Something was wrong.

"Josh?"

When Josh finally spoke, it came in a rush.

"While I was gone," he said, "my parents were looking at the book delivery schedule. They found my order for the Allison Katzinger books . . . which I never sent out."

"Oh, um, is that bad?" I asked haltingly. "Her reading is in less than two weeks, right?"

"Yes, it's bad," Josh said quickly. "We were supposed to have a hundred of her books here for her signing, and now we probably won't be able to get any, not in time anyway. And it was my fault. I messed up."

"Josh," I began, "you shouldn't have to—"

"But I do, Chelsea." I didn't like the way he cut me off, or the way my name sounded when he said it. "I do have to do these things. My dad's always in Chicago, and my mom—well, she's not handling it, is she? She just doesn't get it. So it's up to me or the store goes under and everything changes and it's all because of *me*."

"Okay, okay," I said, trying to make my voice soothing. "I think—"

Josh cut me off again.

"Listen, I know you want to make me feel better," he said. "But me feeling better isn't going to solve this problem. You know what will? Me doing my job. I need to focus—to *re*focus on what matters. Dog Ear."

"But . . . ," I whispered, "don't I matter too? To you? Because you—"

"You . . . you know you do. But I need to focus."

"You already said that," I said, hating that my voice sounded tear-choked. "So what are you saying? You want to see each other less?"

There was an awful silence on the other end of the phone.

"Oh," I whispered. "We won't see each other . . . at all."

Josh sighed deeply.

"I can't think of another way," he said.

I tried to make my voice go as cold as his.

"Or you won't think of another way," I said.

"Chelsea—"

"No, I get it," I said. "I'll let you go."

"Chelsea, this . . . isn't what I want," Josh protested. "It's what I have to do."

"Sure, Josh," I snapped. "You do what you have to do."

Then I clapped my phone closed. I looked around. I didn't remember coming back into the living room, but there I was. I stared at my reflection in the mirror hanging above the mantel. My hair was a frizzy, tangled mess, but that wasn't unusual. It was my face that I didn't recognize.

Well, actually, I did.

I remembered looking into the bathroom mirror in LA right

after my dad told me about Granly's stroke, and seeing that same version of me in the mirror—pale, confused, blindsided, and very, very upset.

I'd known I would have to say good-bye to Josh. But it wasn't supposed to be like this! What had just happened?

The front door swung open, and I jumped.

"Hi, sweetie!" my mom said, her face lighting up at the sight of me. My dad was behind her, holding two large pizza boxes. "We got your favorite—extra mushrooms!"

I don't know why *that* was what finally made me crumple to the floor and start crying.

"I want to go home," I sobbed as my mom knelt down next to me, wrapping her arms around my shoulders.

"I don't understand," she said, her voice immediately thick with empathetic tears.

I shook my head slowly, closing my eyes and feeling a fresh river of tears roll down my cheeks.

"Neither do I."

August

*I*t's strange what will drag you out of bed the morning after your heart's been broken.

Food won't do it, even if your dad is making bacon and blueberry pancakes. Even if he has deferred to the fact that his daughter's soul is crushed and he has promised to skip the mouse ears.

Needing something to read won't do it. I couldn't read through the tears in my eyes anyway. The words blurred, or worse—were replaced by images of Josh's face. Either way the pages got wet and splotchy, and I ended up reading the same sentence about six hundred times.

Having to pee? Okay, that made me get up, but it doesn't count if you make it quick and jump directly back into bed.

Being scheduled to work also wouldn't rouse me. If I called in sick that afternoon, I decided, it wouldn't even be a lie. I *was* sick. Heartsick, headsick, and actually a little queasy and headachy, although maybe that was due to lack of food.

So what *did* make me crawl out of bed at around eleven in the morning?

My garden.

My first impression of this first day of August, other than the fact that it was a dismal, awful, oh-the-humanity kind of day (for me anyway) was that it was hot. Not cheery, sunshiny, let's-go-to-the-beach hot. No, this was a ruthless white heat, a wilting, joy-sapping, punishing heat. A garden-destroying heat.

My plants needed me.

Ever since mid-July the garden had required daily watering. If I skipped even one morning, I noticed the plants began to wilt. The stems sagged and the leaves curled inward as if to protect themselves from the sun's glare. The half-red tomatoes would wrinkle, and the cucumbers would take on a dusty cast.

When that happened, I'd feel as guilty as if I'd neglected a pet.

What's more, the garden was on the verge of being edible. The tomatoes were looking plumper and redder each day. The cucumbers had outgrown their gherkin infancy and had grown into stout little pre-pickles. And my squash were getting so pot-bellied, my dad promised to use them the next time he made shish kebabs on the grill.

How lame would it be to let the garden shrivel up now, just because my heart was a raisin?

Maybe it was Granly's ghost who made me roll out of bed and slump to the backyard to unreel the hose. Maybe it was just stubbornness or force of habit. Either way, I did it. I didn't bother to change out of my nightshirt or put on flip-flops before I plodded outside.

I felt like I was watching myself from a distance as I uncoiled the hose and started spraying my plants. I got no satisfaction from watching the dry, dusty dirt become wet, squishy, and nourishing. Nor from the spiky yellow-green scent that sprang off the tomatoes when I watered them. I didn't even feel happy when my spray uncovered a whole new trove of baby cukes, some of them still wearing their shriveled yellow blossoms.

I cared enough to keep the garden alive, but the daily joy it had given me all month? That was gone.

I was numb.

I finished watering and turned off the spigot. Then I leaned against the house and tried to think of something, anything, I wanted to do for the rest of the day.

Beaching it with my sisters would be awful. They'd be all careful and sweet around me, and it would break my heart further.

If I spent time with either one of my parents, I knew I would just curl up into a ball and cry.

Then I thought about Mel & Mel's, and the clatter of dishes *whooshing* out of the Hobart, of filter baskets being slammed into the geriatric coffeemaker, and the constant scrape of chairs on the floor and fork tines on china. I realized that *that* was where I wanted to go. It was the only even remotely tolerable place I could imagine spending this awful day.

But what about Josh on the other side of the brick wall?

I was *almost* certain he wouldn't come into Mel & Mel's. Even if he'd become a cold workaholic robot, he wouldn't be *that* cruel, would he?

Or maybe he'd stay away simply for the time it would save. After all, girlfriend drama or, say, eating would cut into his busy schedule.

Now, I knew, Josh would do *anything* to avoid that.

*B*y the time I left for work, I *thought* I'd pulled myself together. I'd put on makeup. (Well, except for mascara. The last thing I needed was telltale black streaks trailing down my cheeks.)

I'd pulled my hair into its usual ponytail but refrained from twisting it into an angsty bun.

I even decided against my first impulse outfit—a dour black T-shirt and dull, army green cargo shorts—and forced myself to wear a butter-yellow tank top and some stretchy denim shorts.

I looked almost presentable. Certainly not like someone who'd realized she was giddy-in-love just minutes before being brutally dumped.

I even felt a little hopeful as I walked my roundabout Dog Ear–avoiding route to Mel & Mel's. Nobody there had to know what had happened. I could immerse myself in the rhythm of greeting/serving/clearing. The white noise of the coffee shop clatter would cancel out the turmoil in my head. My body would propel itself through what had become routine motions, and the exhaustion I felt at the end of the day would be welcome.

Maybe I'd leave work somehow feeling a little better.

Maybe I would even sleep that night.

But I only had to step through Mel & Mel's door for my whole suffer-in-silence plan to crash down around me.

"Oh, Chelsea!" Andrea cried when she saw me. She'd been en route to the kitchen with a tray full of dishes, but she immediately put it down on a table and rushed over. "What happened?"

"What?" I said, my voice squeaky. "What are you talking about?"

"Well, clearly something's really wrong," Andrea said. "It's all over your face."

"But I put on makeup!" I protested while Andrea guided me to a stool at the counter. Melissa popped up from behind it like a gopher sniffing for trouble.

"Let me get you a drink, hon," she said. She made me my favorite—iced tea and lemonade. "Now spill."

"It's nothing," I said, shaking my head and pushing away the icy drink. It was already beading up with condensation in the steamy heat.

"Drink up," Melissa said in a harsh Big Mama voice. It was so different from the firm sweetness of my own mother's voice, but somehow it was just as effective.

"Okay," I said. I took a huge, delicious swallow. It was so cold and sweet, it made my teeth hurt, but it was also delicious. I could have put a straw into a pitcher of it and drunk the whole thing right there. It was the first thing I'd tasted that day that hadn't made me want to gag.

Finally I plunked my glass back onto the counter, wiped my mouth with the back of my hand, and announced, "Josh broke up with me. He said he needs to focus on the store."

"What?" Andrea cried, putting both hands to her face in shock.

"Well!" Melissa said. "I can't believe it! I mean, I can because he's a *boy* and *they* do crazy things all the time, but . . . *Josh*? That boy is in love with you. We could all see it. Am I right, Al?"

Al Thayer had just walked in and was heading to his usual

table in my section, but when Melissa spoke to him, he wheeled right around and came to join us at the counter. He hopped onto the stool next to mine, which was pretty impressive, considering that Mr. Thayer was pushing eighty. He was also my favorite regular, so it gave me a tiny lift to see him.

"How's my favorite little waitress?" he said, tweaking my ponytail.

"A, that's kind of sexist, Mr. Thayer," Andrea said, crossing her arms over her chest. "And B, I thought *I* was your favorite little waitress."

"Did I ever say, Andie," Mr. Thayer said, his white eyebrows crunching into a bushy line over his big nose, "that you weren't *also* my favorite? You can have more than one, you know."

"No you can't," Andrea and I said at the same time, which made her laugh and made me *almost* smile.

"Well, *I* can," Mr. Thayer said. "Besides, did *you* ever write me into a serial, Andrea?"

He glanced at the specials board, where the latest installment of *Diablo and the Mels* was still glowing beneath the list of pie flavors.

B. didn't like Thayer. She of all people (or whatever) didn't trust a man who ate his eggs with hot sauce. That was her *thing.*

"I expect B. and me to have a grand battle, my dear," Mr. Thayer said. "Make it happen."

I tried to laugh, but all that came out was a pathetic little honk.

"So, what's the problem?" Mr. Thayer asked.

"Josh," Melissa, Andrea, and I said at once.

"I thought as much," Mr. Thayer said. "What happened?"

"He's choosing career over love," Andrea said dramatically. "Men!"

"I don't think you can call Dog Ear Josh's career," I said wanly. "I mean, he hasn't even graduated from high school!"

"He's a good boy," Mr. Thayer said. I felt my eyes well up. My tongue went so thick in my mouth that I couldn't talk, but I nodded. Because I couldn't help agreeing with Mr. Thayer. Even though I was hating Josh for choosing his parents over me, I also loved him for it. He *was* a good boy.

"But," Mr. Thayer went on, "being good doesn't mean you're always right. And being a boy, a young man—well, that's a trial-by-error time if there ever was one."

"So you think he made a mistake?" I choked out. I didn't know why this filled me with such hope. I guessed it was because Mr. Thayer was old. And a man. So he knew more about this honor and manhood thing than I did.

"If he did," Mr. Thayer said, "I don't think Josh will be too proud to admit it. He's a good boy. And I am thirsty. Can I have one of those Arnold Palmers, young lady?"

He pointed at my almost-empty glass. I hopped off my stool, nodding hard and flicking the moisture from beneath my eyes at the same time.

Soon after, a summer swim team came in, celebrating a win and wanting massive amounts of food. After that there was the dinner rush. So, just as I'd hoped, I didn't have time to think.

Which wasn't to say I forgot about Josh. He was always there in the back of my mind.

The fact was, he'd been in that spot, hovering in my consciousness, ever since I'd met him. First he lodged in my head as a curiosity, then as a delight. Now he was a wound, a fresh paper cut that wouldn't stop stinging.

When my shift was almost over, and my section was down to one table—a couple nursing cold drinks—I slumped against the counter and breathed a long, tired sigh.

But I followed it up with a little smile. I'd been right to come in today. I put my elbows on the counter and propped my chin on my fists.

"Do you know what, Melissa?" I said to Mel as she did her nightly receipt tally. "I've made a decision. When I go back to LA, I'm not taking any more babysitting jobs. I'm going to wait tables."

"Put me down as a reference, sweetie," Melissa muttered without looking up from her receipts. But a moment later she stopped herself and looked at me.

"You know, I almost forgot you were from LA!" she said. "You seem so . . . Bluepointe. And you never talk about your life back home."

I bit my lip and glanced at the Dog Ear wall. I hadn't been thinking about my life back home either. I glanced at the little calico cat calendar that Melissa kept tacked up next to the cash register. I quickly added up the days we had left in Bluepointe.

Twenty-one.

Twenty-one days that Josh and I could have been spending together. It wasn't much. On the other hand, you could cram a whole lot of fun—and a whole lot of love—into twenty-one days if you wanted to.

"Too bad he doesn't want to," I muttered to myself, shaking my head.

But then I frowned and replayed (for, oh, about the fortieth time) the things that Josh had said to me the previous night.

"This isn't what I want; it's what I have to do."

I bowed my head, scrunching my fingers into my hair. *How could Josh think that this was right?* He meant well, but if his mom *knew* what he'd done—

I lifted my head abruptly.

Of *course*, Stella didn't know. That was the whole point. Josh's mom was sweet, but kind of clueless. I would have bet she had no idea how much Josh was doing—and sacrificing—for Dog Ear.

I hopped off the stool and untied my apron at the same time. As I hurried toward the kitchen to hang up my stuff, I called to Andrea.

"Can you do me a favor and check out my last table? Please?"

Andrea looked at me in confusion.

"There's something I've gotta do," I said. "Now. Before I lose my nerve."

Andrea glanced over her shoulder at the Dog Ear wall, then looked back at me and nodded excitedly.

"Only if you promise to come back after and tell me everything that happened," she said.

"I hope there's something to tell," I said with a nervous grin. "Thanks, Andie."

I darted into the bathroom and dabbed at my shiny face with a damp paper towel. I rubbed at the circles under my eyes, until

I remembered that I wasn't wearing mascara and those circles weren't going anywhere. I took out my hair elastic and cringed as my curls—which looked even brighter after two months in the sun—sprang out in a Medusa-like puff. I pulled the front bits back and let the rest of my hair coil around my shoulders.

Then I gave myself a last, hard look in the mirror, stalked out of Mel & Mel's, and went next door.

Every other time that I'd walked into Dog Ear, I'd felt elation swell up inside me. It wasn't just about Josh, either, though that had been the biggest part of it. I just loved the place, with its pretty yellow walls and goofy rainbow review cards, the picket fence and Josh's broody posters. I loved that there was always some kid running around with a book in one hand and a yo-yo in the other, and of course I loved the couch and the snacks.

Maybe that's why my eyes teared up the moment I walked in. Because I was afraid of losing Dog Ear in addition to Josh.

As the door jingled closed behind me, E.B. ambled over. He pushed his big, blocky head beneath my hand for an ear scratch. I whispered hello to him and nervously scanned the store for Josh.

I didn't see him, but I was sure he was there. Somehow I could feel him there, the same way I knew it was him whenever he called me.

Isobel was at the cash register. I gave her a little wave and walked toward the stacks. E.B. shuffled along behind me until he realized that I wasn't heading toward the lounge—where there was a basket of Triscuits and a can of spray cheese on the coffee table. He gave a little snort and trotted away.

I couldn't quite believe where I finally found Josh. He was sitting on the floor in the children's aisle, the exact same spot where we'd had our first kiss.

For some reason this gave me hope. Maybe we could somehow go back in time, to the improbable perfection of that kiss and . . .

I stopped there, because even if time travel were possible, I wasn't sure how it would fix things.

Josh looked up at me, his eyes wide and startled. They weren't nearly as cold as his voice had been on the phone the night before. They also had gray shadows that exactly matched the ones under my eyes.

But once Josh got over the shock of seeing me, he clenched his jaw and frowned.

"Chelsea, I—"

I shook my head and gave him a stern *Let me talk* look. Then I knelt before him, glad that I was wearing pants today instead of one of the poofy skirts that could make a quick exit difficult.

"Have you ever told them?" I asked Josh. He went a little pale and cringed. Once upon a time I might have been offended. But now that I knew Josh, I knew what that expression meant. He didn't want to get rid of me. He wanted me to stay—and keep talking.

"What do you mean?" Josh asked me.

"Your parents," I said impatiently. "Do they even know how you feel? Do they know that you grind your teeth every time you have to change the receipt tape or update the store's website?

That *they're* living this owning-a-bookstore dream because *you're* the one with your feet on the ground?"

"Of course they know," Josh said. Now he sounded impatient with me. "How could they not?"

"You're a good son," I said with a shrug. "Maybe they just assume this is your dream too."

"That's the thing," Josh said. He grabbed a book off the shelf and held it up. "This isn't a dream. This is a store. A business. It's like this . . . *beast* that needs to be fed. And if we don't keep up with the feedings, the store goes under, my parents lose piles of money, and where does that leave them?"

"And you?" I added. "You know, you're allowed to put yourself into that equation too."

I pulled the picture book gently from Josh's hands and laid it on the floor. I knew not to shelve it out of order and create more work for him.

"I think if your mom is anything like mine," I said, "she would prefer that you did think of yourself, at least a little bit."

"What do you mean?" Josh said.

"I mean, you should talk to your parents," I said, getting to my feet. "Tell them what's been going on with you, Josh. Tell them—"

I looked down sharply, trying to contain the tears that had suddenly welled up in my eyes.

"Tell them everything," I said. "And tell them what *you* want, for once. I think they might surprise you."

Then I turned to leave. I wanted to take a last, lingering look at Josh's face, but I knew if I did, I would burst into tears. I didn't want that, and not just because it would have been mortifying. I also didn't want to manipulate Josh into coming back to me. I wanted him to do it because being with me made him happy. I wanted it for him as much as for myself.

I guess if I wanted a confirmation that I really did love Josh, then that was it—even if it was too late.

I went straight to bed after I got home. Despite my head's best efforts to keep me awake with a looping tally of anxieties, my exhausted body dragged me into sleep.

And when I woke up, it wasn't quite as hard to get myself out of bed. There was a tiny kernel of hope that maybe I'd gotten through to Josh. And maybe I'd hear from him.

Even if I didn't, at least I'd tried. I'd done *something*. I'd gotten my say. It wasn't exactly cheering, but it made me feel a little better about this whole breakup thing.

I had to water again. The sun was as searing as ever, even at nine thirty in the morning. I had breakfast with my sisters first. They were quietly watchful but didn't crowd me with a *How're you doing?* inquisition. I showered and threw on a blue sundress. It was the one dress I had that happened to have pockets, which meant I could keep my phone on me at all times. You know, just in case. Then I headed into the backyard.

As soon as I stepped off the laundry room steps, I knew something was wrong.

My mom was standing in front of the garden with one hand covering her mouth. She saw me and took a halting step toward me.

"I just got back from a walk," she said. "I thought I'd check to see if there were any tomatoes ripe enough for lunch, and . . . Oh, honey, I'm sorry."

I shook my head in confusion as I walked toward her, but as soon as I got a look at the garden, I knew what she was talking about.

It had been decimated.

The ground beneath the tomato plant was littered with half-gnawed fruit, including lots of green tomatoes. The lettuce leaves were riddled with rodenty bite marks, and two of the cucumber vines had been torn out of the ground altogether. As for the radishes, it was like they'd never even been there.

I slapped both hands on top of my head.

"Yesterday," I croaked, "when I watered, I forgot the cayenne pepper!"

I couldn't believe how quickly my garden had been destroyed. It was like the animals were getting back at me for my spicy repellant.

"I'm sure it was deer," my mom said. "They can tear a garden to pieces just like that."

I thought of Granly, sitting at the kitchen table, watching beautiful forest animals sample her veggies, loving how delicately the deer tiptoed through the plants.

I dropped to my knees at the edge of the garden, not caring if I got dirt on my pale blue dress. I began yanking the stringy remains of my lettuce plants out of the earth. I tossed them into a messy pile at my side.

And it was only when my mom crouched down to put her arms around me that I realized I was sobbing.

"I wanted it to be different!" I said through angry tears.

222

"Different? What do you mean?" Mom asked.

"From Granly's garden," I cried. "Hers got all eaten up, but mine was supposed to be different. It was almost there!"

"Wait, look!" my mom pointed at the one cucumber plant that was left intact. Then she stepped into the garden and said, "And there's a lot of squash still here, and I found three lettuce plants that they missed."

"Okay," I said quietly, wondering why I wasn't comforted at all.

Mom picked her way back through the messy thatch of plants. She handed me a big, unscathed squash, its yellow skin waxy and perfect.

"Thanks," I muttered, swiping away my tears. Only when she sat next to me did I realize she was crying too.

"I'm sorry, Chelsea," she sighed. "About . . . everything."

I nodded sadly. Then we sat there in silence but for the occasional sniffle and, of course, the hot-day hum of the cicadas.

"Why do you think it was so important to you," Mom wondered, "that your garden turn out differently from Granly's?"

I shrugged.

"I guess," I said, feeling guilt wash over me, "I kind of wanted to . . . move on? To not always be stuck in this place where it feels like we have to do all these things that she did, but without her. I guess I just want to get to that place where she's not here but life goes on and . . . and it's bearable."

It felt kind of terrible to utter all these things out loud, especially to my mom. But it also felt kind of wonderful to say them, like something that had been clamped down on me had suddenly released its grip.

Mom sighed.

"It *has* become more bearable, hasn't it?" she said. "I think being here has made it so."

I blinked. It was true. Living in the cottage with Granly's furniture and her photo albums, and even her egg cups, had gotten a little easier.

"But not to the point where you can go through Granly's stuff," I pointed out.

"It's funny. I was just pondering that on my walk," Mom said. "I was thinking that maybe I *am* ready, and I think it's because I'm getting to the end of my quilt."

"It's going to be really pretty," I said. "The quilt."

Mom nodded absentmindedly.

"You know," she said, "I was doing some pattern research online, and I found this article about mourning quilts."

"Morning quilts?" I said. "Like for cold mornings?"

"No, the other kind of mourning," my mom said. "An Appalachian woman, when she suffered a loss, would make a quilt. All that piecing and batting and hand-stitching—it's so absorbing. It doesn't make your pain go away, but it gets you through it. Making the quilt both distracts you and makes you focus on the person you lost. The work carries you through the days. It is true, you know, that cliché about time. It does heal all wounds.

"The funny thing about the mourning quilt is, once it was finished, it was just another quilt to throw on the bed," Mom went on. "It wasn't made into a shrine to hang on the wall or put in a chest. They didn't have that luxury. And besides, the mourning quilt was about the process, not the product."

"Has it been that way for you?" I asked.

"I think so," Mom said, nodding thoughtfully. "I think I've been mourning more than just Granly. I've been sewing up these baby clothes, and sometimes I just can't *believe* you ever wore them. You're all so grown-up. And Hannah's leaving—"

Mom's voice caught, and she shook her head apologetically while I wrapped my arms around her and squeezed.

"I'm not graduating for ages," I reminded her. "I can't even drive yet! You've got me trapped."

Mom laughed and squeezed me back.

"You know that's not what I want," she said

I nodded. I *did* know. And if it was hard to feel exactly lucky right then, what with my phone still silent in my pocket, I did feel grateful.

"Mom?"

My mom and I turned to see Abbie hesitating at the back door. She was holding a big storage bin—the plastic kind with the locking lid. And she had a funny look on her face.

"I found this in the back of Granly's closet," she said as Mom and I stood up and walked over to her. "I thought it was gonna be clothes, but look . . ."

Mom and I peered into the bin. Inside there was a neat stack of cardboard boxes. They were closed loosely, without tape, and on each one Granly had written a name.

Our names.

My mom inhaled sharply, then shook her head.

"She told me about those boxes," she whispered. "Such a long time ago. I'd forgotten."

"What are they?" I asked as my mom took the bin from Abbie and carried it to the kitchen table.

"Adam?" my mom called down the hall. "Hannah? Can you come in here?"

Then she turned to me to answer my question.

"These are the things Granly wanted each of us to have after she died," Mom said bluntly. "During one of our visits here, just before she was taking that trip to Scandinavia, she sat me down and told me where the key to her safe deposit box was and where all her passwords were and things like that. And she told me about this box of things she'd set aside for us. I didn't pay much attention because she was so young. I told her she'd be around for forever."

Mom's voice wobbled but she pressed on.

"When she died," Mom said, "I did remember about the bank vault and the passwords, but somehow I forgot about this."

My dad came into the kitchen, with Hannah right behind him.

"What are those?" Hannah asked, peeking into the bin.

My mom pulled out the box with Hannah's name on it.

"Presents!" Mom said. Tears were streaming down her cheeks, but she was smiling through them.

Granly hadn't written my name on my box in careful calligraphy or anything precious like that. It was just a quick scrawl with a Sharpie. But it still brought me to tears to see her handwriting.

As each of my family members opened their boxes and silently read the notes Granly had written to them, the whole kitchen filled with sniffles. Even my dad's eyes brimmed as he held up a men's watch with a satiny ivory face and gold Roman numerals.

"It's Grandpa's watch," he said, immediately buckling the worn leather band onto his wrist.

Abbie pulled two framed works of art out of her box. They were two of the red Conté nudes that Granly had loved to collect. Both female figures were in motion—their muscular bodies leaping through the air, their hair flying out behind them.

"I remember these!" Abbie said, wiping at her cheek with the back of her hand. "I always loved them."

"She gave me Grandpa's passport holder," Hannah cried, holding up a brown leather wallet embossed with Grandpa's name in gold.

Mom was the only one who wasn't surprised by her gift.

"I always told her I wanted this," she said, lifting a string of pearls out of her box. The clasp looked like a blossom—a cluster of gold petals. "She used to wear these pearls every Saturday night when she'd go on dates with Grandpa."

I was the last one to open my box. Inside I found a thin stack of familiar leather-bound notebooks. Granly's journals. Flipping one open, I saw more of Granly's handwriting—some of it in ink, some of it in smudgy pencil—pages and pages of it.

Two more of the journals were filled up, but the fourth was blank.

I opened the card that Granly had written to me.

For my Chelsea, who's a writer (too). Enough with those scraps of paper! With all my love, Granly.

227

I opened my mouth to speak, then closed it again. I was speechless.

Chelsea, who's a writer?

Where had Granly gotten that idea? I was a *reader*. And yeah, I wrote stuff down on those scraps of paper. But that didn't count.

Did it?

Timidly I opened the first of Granly's notebooks again.

Daddy and Mother want to go to the South Shore for all of June, and I think I'll just die if I have to go with.

My eyebrows shot upward. That was a pretty good beginning. And a familiar one.

I couldn't wait to read more.

*F*or the rest of the morning our cottage was very quiet. We all drifted apart, each of us deep in thought, each of us saying our own thank-yous to Granly's ghost.

But eventually I stopped reading Granly's journals—which were part diary, part very funny short-story collection. I didn't want to tear through them. I wanted to make them last.

Besides, I was starving.

When I wandered into the kitchen, I found Abbie peering into the fridge.

"I think I'm officially sick of blueberries," she said, closing the door with a curled lip.

"Better not be," I said. "The blueberry festival's next week, you know."

"Oh, yeah," Abbie said. "I almost forgot about that crazy festival."

"You wouldn't have if you worked on Main Street," I said. "Every electrical pole is plastered with flyers. Mel's got three different kinds of blueberry pie on the menu. And at Dog Ear—"

I'd been about to tell Abbie about the cute blueberry-themed window display Stella had made for the bookshop. But I decided to just let that one go.

"Were you and Josh going to go together," Abbie asked quietly. "To the festival?"

I shrugged.

"We hadn't talked about it yet," I said.

But I was sure we would have gone to the festival together. Ever since the DFJ, Josh and I had just known—without having to say it—that we'd share all the summer's big events. All its little ones too.

Before I could explain that to Abbie, I heard a knock at the front door. A loud, urgent knock.

"Who is that?" I said in alarm.

Abbie and I jumped up and headed to the door. Nobody ever knocked on Granly's door. Sparrow Road was too remote for salesmen, and anybody who knew us would have just opened the unlocked door and called, "Anybody home?"

Abbie opened the door a crack and peeked outside. Then she turned toward me, flashed me a huge grin, and opened the door wide.

Standing on the screened porch, looking red-cheeked, breathless, and pretty terrified (but also really, really cute) was Josh.

His bike lay on its side in the drive behind him, its front wheel still spinning. I watched that wheel twirl around and around and wondered if my eyes were doing the exact same thing.

"Chelsea," Josh huffed, "can I talk to you?"

I couldn't quite form words, so I just nodded and stepped outside. The moment Abbie closed the door, Josh spoke in a rush.

"I did it," he announced. He flopped triumphantly onto the smushy couch. I sat—way more tentatively—next to him.

"You did . . . what?"

"I did what you told me to do," Josh said, breaking into an elated smile. "I talked to my parents. Both of 'em."

"Well, what did you say?"

"I asked them to step it up at the bookstore," he said. "Because it was their choice to buy Dog Ear, not mine. That I was doing all this stuff to keep the store afloat for *them*, but that it wasn't making *me* very happy. In fact, I told them, I've given up a lot for Dog Ear. And I was pretty okay with that until . . . well, until I lost you."

Josh looked so earnest and serious, I *had* to touch him, just to make sure this was really happening. I reached over and rested my fingertips lightly on the back of his hand.

Josh heaved a shuddering sigh and closed his eyes.

"What did they say?" I asked him.

Josh gave a little laugh.

"You were right," he said, looking at me shyly. "They had no idea. And they were pretty mad at me for keeping it a secret all this time. Then my mom promised to do more practical stuff, though she might need a little training."

My smile felt tremulous.

"Does this training," I broached, "have to happen within, say, the next twenty days?"

Josh leaned in, his face so close to mine that it made me feel dizzy in the best way.

"Not a chance," he breathed.

I closed my eyes and felt his arms wrap around me, so tightly that I gasped. And then he was kissing me. It was the perfect kiss—full of apology and relief and passion.

In an instant I felt like I'd rewound the past two days and landed right back in that moment when my cell phone had rung and I'd just *known* how I felt about Josh. I was feeling it all again.

It turned out I wasn't the only one.

"Chelsea," Josh murmured when the kiss finally ended. "Can you forgive me for being an idiot?"

"Well, you were being an honorable idiot," I whispered with a little laugh.

"Is that a yes?" Josh asked, twining a lock of my hair around his finger.

I grinned and leaned in until my forehead was touching his. I rested my hands on the back of his neck and whispered, "Yes."

"Good, because you know what?" Josh said.

"What?"

"I'm in love with you, Chelsea. I think I have been since the first time I ever saw you, when you tried to rescue that book from my X-Acto knife."

Tears sprang to my eyes, but they couldn't have felt more different from the ones I'd been crying for the past two days.

"What a coincidence," I said. "That's when I fell in love with you, too."

Josh covered my mouth with his. We didn't say anything else—nothing else needed to be said—for a long, long time.

When you see the boy you love through a crowd, he can look completely familiar and be a complete surprise, all at once.

I thought I knew everything there was to know about Josh's face. I knew that his left eye got a little more squinty than the right one when he smiled. And that his chin was square, rather than pointed, if you really looked at it. I'd watched the sun turn his hair the color of milky caramel over the course of the summer. It had also gotten long enough to actually look tousled. I knew that the back of Josh's neck flushed when he got overheated after rowing or, say, rushing over to my house a week earlier to tell me that he loved me.

But when I spotted him in the middle of a throng of people at the Blueberry Dreams Festival, I didn't recognize him for an instant. Was that him? Was that boy, so tan and tall and *gorgeous*, Josh? *My* Josh?

Suddenly he saw me, and I could swear I saw him blink too—before he smiled an incredulous, giddy smile.

We wove our way through the people crowding the Blue-pointe town square. Every adult seemed to be sipping a tall, purple cocktail, and every little kid was sweating inside a puffy blueberry costume. Everybody in between, like me, wore face paint, their cheeks dotted with berries. Or they had on funny blueberry bean-ies, with tufts of green leaves on the crowns instead of propellers.

Josh and I had just seen each other that morning at the beach, but we hugged as if it had been days.

"You look really pretty," Josh said, putting a hand on my still-damp-from-the-shower hair.

"So do you," I said. I laughed before kissing him lightly on the lips. "Should we do a walk around?"

The square was lined with tents in which people were hawking blueberry honey, blueberry syrup, blueberry baked goods, and of course, a whole lot of blueberry art.

We ambled along lazily, our hands clasped, checking out the ceramic blueberry bowls and purple paintings. Only when we got to Chloe and Ken's tent did we *have* to stop.

They were both sitting in the back of their tent looking miserable. Their space was fronted by two folding tables. One was *full* of ceramic animals, wobbly bowls, and rough-hewn wood sculptures. The other table was almost empty. That's where Chloe and Ken had set out their blueberries, eggs, and honey. They had all clearly been snapped up by shoppers.

Josh met my eyes. He cringed, feeling Chloe and Ken's pain.

Then he pulled out his wallet and reached for something in the center of the table.

It was a small chunk of wood that Ken had carved into a little rowboat. It looked craggy and splintery, but it was also the exact same shape as the shabby little boat that Josh and I had floated into Wex Pond.

"Would you take ten dollars for this, Ken?" Josh asked. "It's really awesome."

I've never seen a man's face go from dour to lit-up that fast.

"Absolutely," Ken said, jumping up to take Josh's money. "Would you like some blueberry jam to go with that? Gratis!"

"Oh, no," I said. "We're good, really. We're *awash* in blueberry jam."

Ken shrugged and turned to give his wife a happy kiss on the cheek. As Josh and I walked away, he handed the little rowboat to me.

"You could put the kissing chickens in it," he said, "and put them in the bathtub."

I laughed.

"It's the most romantic present I ever got," I said, kissing *him* on the cheek. "Also the ugliest, but that's okay!"

"You just don't appreciate good art," he said.

"Oh, I think I do," I said with confidence.

I thought about the poster Josh had shown me the day before, the one he'd finally finished for Allison Katzinger's book party. It was dreamy and shadowy and layered with one beautiful image after another. It was perfect. And luckily, it wouldn't be wasted. After Josh's big talk with his parents, Stella had spent an entire afternoon making calls. She'd managed to round up more than a hundred copies of *Leaves of Trees* for the party.

Josh and I approached the Dog Ear tent, where lots of books and big piles of blue Dog Ear T-shirts and baseball caps had been transplanted for the day. E.B. was stationed out front, panting smilingly at the passersby.

I put a hand on Josh's arm.

"Maybe we should go the other way," I suggested. "You know

if you go in there, you're gonna start working. You won't be able to help yourself."

Josh didn't answer. He just quietly watched what was happening in the tent.

His dad was stationed at the front table, working the cash box. His gray hair was hidden under a Dog Ear baseball cap and he was chatting amiably with one customer after another. He didn't look like he was talking about philosophy or academia or anything very serious. He also looked like he was having a ball.

Meanwhile, Stella was hand-selling in the back of the tent, chatting up various books. She pointed one teenage girl to Josh's Allison Katzinger poster. Clearly she was urging her to come to the book party.

"They're kicking butt in there!" I said.

"I know!" Josh replied, staring in awe. "But how . . ."

"I told you they'd surprise you," I said. "Parents sometimes do."

I craned my neck to see if my parents were still where I'd left them a few minutes earlier, talking to some of their friends. They were. In fact, my dad had just told one of his awful jokes. I could tell by the way my mom was rolling her eyes and the way the other couple were shaking their heads as they laughed.

"Aaaand," I added, "sometimes they don't."

"Josh?"

At the sound of a girl's surprised voice, Josh and I turned. A sweet-faced girl with a blueberry beanie was trotting toward us.

"Hi!" she gushed, giving Josh a quick hug. "How's your summer been?"

Josh smiled and slipped his arm around my waist.

"Really good," he said. "Chelsea, this is Aubrey. We go to the same school."

"Oh my God, you guys are *cute* together," Aubrey said.

"Um, thanks," I said with a shy smile. "Hey, didn't I see you at the lantern party? You had that pretty lantern with the dog."

"Yeah!" Aubrey said. "That was me. And *this* guy has been AWOL ever since!"

She gave Josh a poke in the ribs.

"I guess we have you to blame for that, Chelsea?" she said.

"Well, I—"

"Actually," Josh said, looking down at me with an easy smile, "I just got an e-mail about a post-festival party at the dock. I was gonna ask you if you wanted to go."

"Really?" Aubrey and I said at the same time.

Josh held up his hands defensively.

"Hey, I'm not *that* antisocial," he said.

Aubrey and I looked at each other with matching one-eyebrow-lifted looks of skepticism, which made us both dissolve into laughter.

"Well, maybe I'm feeling a little *more* social these days," Josh said, giving my hair a quick stroke. "For some reason."

"We'll be there," I told Aubrey quietly. Then I shot a quick look at Josh. He seemed a little different, suddenly. More confident, more comfortable in his skin.

Was it all because of . . . me?

"Awesome," Aubrey said, breaking into my thoughts with her bubbly response. Then she cocked her head like a dog listening for a distant whistle. "Music's starting. Let's go!"

She pushed through the crowd toward the gazebo, where a band was indeed setting up. It was a quartet of hipster dudes with lots of facial hair and old-timey instruments—an accordion, banjo, and fiddle.

"Ooh," I said, fluffing up my purple poodle skirt. "My kind of band!"

A crowd gathered before the gazebo steps. Josh and I made our way toward its center. As soon as the band started up with a twangy rockabilly tune, everyone around us started dancing.

Josh looked at me with a touch of panic in his eyes.

"I'm a terrible dancer," he admitted.

"Me too," I said.

Then I started wiggling my hips around and pumping my hands in the air. Josh threw his head back and laughed, then shrugged and joined me.

Did we find each other's rhythm and start twirling around as a beautiful unit, our love making us effortlessly graceful, perfectly synchronized?

Not even close. We were even more awkward dancing together than we were on our own. We were the absolute antithesis of Emma and Ethan.

And I was beyond fine with that.

At the end of the song, we fell into each other's arms laughing. We pushed our way out of the crowd, and Josh said, "Let's find the Pop Guy. I'm dying of thirst."

We were headed to his rainbow umbrella when we were intercepted by Abbie and . . . Hannah! Hannah's eyes were red-rimmed, and one of the spaghetti straps on her tank top was ripped. She was using her hand to hold her top up.

"What's going on?" I said. "I thought you were with Liam."

"She was," Abbie said fiercely, "but she's not anymore!"

It didn't take me long to figure out who was behind Hannah's torn strap.

"Hannah?" I said, my voice thin and scared. "Are you okay?"

Hannah nodded quickly.

"I am, I promise," she said. "But I won't be seeing Liam any-more."

Abbie whispered into my ear so Josh wouldn't hear, "He might not be walking for the rest of the day either. He got the big ol' knee from Hannah!"

My mouth dropped open.

"You didn't," I gasped.

"I did," Hannah said, glancing down at her broken strap. "He deserved it."

I turned to Josh regretfully.

"I think I need a little sister time," I said.

Josh nodded quickly.

"No problem," he said, giving me a quick, sweet kiss. "I'll see you."

Hannah seemed a little shaky, so we went to sit on a bench that was hidden behind a cluster of tents.

"I'm getting you some blueberry lemonade," Abbie declared. "Back in a minute."

Hannah pulled her knees up to her chin and wrapped her free arm around her shins.

"I'm such an idiot," she said, shaking her head.

I hated to agree, but . . .

"Why *were* you hanging out with that guy?" I said.

"I don't know. It felt nice to get all that attention," she said. "It's been kind of a lonely year, you know."

"But why did you want *Liam's* attention," I asked. "I mean, he's cute and preppy and all, but he's not exactly a brilliant conversationalist."

"Yeah." Hannah shrugged. "He's just, you know, kind of normal. Average."

"Hannah," I said, "you've never made a C in your life. You need above-average."

Hannah leaned her head back and groaned.

"So I've been told for forever," she said. "I'm kind of over it! Or let's just say I felt like taking a little break from my pigeonhole. Studious, serious, smart Hannah, you know?

The thing was, I *didn't* know.

"I always thought it would be cool to have a *place*," I said. "Like, an identity. Abbie's an athlete, and you're this pre-premed whiz. You know, you're *defined*."

"But if you're not, you can do anything!" Hannah pointed out. "You've got freedom!"

As she said this, Abbie returned and handed Hannah a plastic cup of purple-tinted lemonade. She sat down on the bench so that Hannah was sandwiched between us.

"Is that what you want?" she asked Hannah. "Freedom? Do

you regret choosing such an intense school? Because you could always transfer to UCLA."

She rested her head on Hannah's shoulder.

"Please?" she added.

Hannah tipped her head to rest on Abbie's.

"I'm going to miss you, too," she said. "But no, U of C *is* what I want. Liam proved that to me. I mean, besides being *way* too handsy, the guy was a *bore*. Have you ever met somebody who's never heard of the Human Genome Project? I didn't think that was even *possible*."

Abbie and I rolled our eyes at each other.

"Yeah, she's ready for U of C," I said.

Hannah shook her head in disbelief.

"It is coming up really soon, though," she said. "I'm kind of terrified."

I was too. Unlike Hannah, I'd never known a world without my two sisters in it every day.

So many endings were looming. This summer in Bluepointe. Hannah.

Josh.

But then my eye wandered across the square to the Dog Ear tent. It was still spilling over with people, many of them immobilized because they were so absorbed in their books. I thought about the blank journal Granly had left me.

I'd already filled a few pages. And it had started me thinking—maybe this summer wasn't just about endings and goodbyes. Maybe it was a beginning as well.

*C*hoosing my outfit for the Allison Katzinger party required major strategy. I knew that she was super-stylish from the pictures she sometimes posted on her blog. She always wore big colorful jewelry and cute little dresses. She had a huge collection of funky glasses, not to mention rotating choices of hair colors.

I didn't want to just look pretty when I met one of my favorite authors. I wanted to look memorable.

(Well, to say I'd be *meeting* Allison Katzinger was a stretch. What I'd really be doing was waiting in line for half an hour before I got to stand in front of her for ten seconds. She'd read my name off a sticky note and inscribe my book before giving me a quick smile. Then Isobel or Stella would usher me away so the next person in line could have his or her ten seconds. But still, even ten seconds with Allison Katzinger called for a killer outfit.)

The other problem was that for six hours before Allison's party, I'd be at Mel & Mel's, slinging supper. So my outfit also needed to be mayonnaise-proof.

That was why I might have gone a little overboard with the patterns. Nothing would show up on a tropically flowered skirt with gray, yellow, and purple in it, right? To tone the skirt down, I went with a simple gray tank top, but then *that* needed jazzing up, so I threw on one of Granly's chunky costume necklaces and stuck some glinty chopsticks into my bun.

And *then* I felt so overdone that I wanted to change completely, but it was too late.

Luckily, I didn't have time to be nervous/excited about the party, because we were slammed at Mel & Mel's. I hustled for two hours straight, serving a group of office workers who'd come in after playing in some goofy kickball tournament.

I was just rushing a giant order of artichoke dip to the kick-ballers when Ginny swept over and lifted my tray out of my hands.

"I'll take that, hon!" she said. "You're on break."

"Break?" I squawked. "What are you talking about?"

Melissa scooched up next to me, untied my apron, and looped it around her own waist.

"We're covering for you, Chels," she said. "No arguments. Josh has it all arranged."

She nodded at the coffee shop door. I spun around and saw Josh peeking through the glass. As always, I felt my face light up at the sight of him.

"Josh!" I said as he opened the door. "What's going on? I'm going to see you in just a few hours at the par—"

I choked on my next word. Because walking in behind Josh was Allison Katzinger!

She looked much smaller than I'd imagined. She was wearing a fabulous silky wrap dress and a chunky necklace just like mine. Her hair was a warm blond, and her glasses frames were red.

As soon as she walked into the coffee shop, with these long, purposeful strides and a big wide-mouthed grin, I realized she was bigger than she seemed in her pictures too. Personality just radiated off her.

She hustled right up to me and gave me a hug.

Allison Katzinger. Hugged. Me!

"Hi!" I blurted. "Um, hi! Wow, it's really nice to meet you."

I gave Josh a hurried *What the heck is going on?* look, so he explained, "Allison is here for a late lunch."

"Oh, sure," I said, nodding quickly. "Okay. Let me get you a menu."

"No," Josh said. "A late lunch . . . with you. *And* me. And my mom's going to join us soon. She's just finishing up some work at the store."

I gaped at him.

"There are so many awesome things in that sentence, I don't even know which to respond to first," I breathed.

"Well, let's choose lunch, shall we?" Allison said. She rubbed her hands together hungrily. "I hear you've got a lot of mayonnaise here. I'm Southern, so I speak mayo fluently. Lay it on me."

I laughed loudly—because Allison was funny, but also because I was crazy nervous. I smoothed back my hair and adjusted my skirt as Melissa led us ceremoniously to the best four-top in the house.

"You look fabulous," Josh whispered into my ear as I sat down.

I shot him a grateful look.

Then I stared across the table at Allison Katzinger and wondered what I could possibly think of to say to her.

Luckily, she had that covered.

"So," she said, after ordering a pimento cheese sandwich and a sweet iced tea from Melissa, "Josh tells me you're a writer."

"I am not!" I gasped. "I mean, I jot stuff down here and there."

"What else is writing but a lot of jotting?" Allison said. "With a narrative arc and subplots and lots of dialogue and drama and . . . I'm exhausted just thinking about it. Why do I do this again?"

"Because of people like me?" I suggested. "Who love to read your books?"

Allison grinned and nodded.

"That's definitely the happy by-product, yes," she said. "But believe it or not, I don't think about you readers when I'm writing. I write because, well, I have no choice. The stories are in me, and I *have* to get them down. Just like I have to read myself to sleep every night."

"I do too!" I said. "I'm always falling asleep with the reading light on."

"I hear ya!" Allison said in her twangy Southern accent. "LED bulbs. That's the solution."

Then she asked, "What are you reading now?"

"Well . . ." I was little embarrassed because it seemed so fawning. "You! I'm rereading *Apples and Oranges.* I love it."

"Oh, so you like the star-crossed lovers thing?" Allison said. "Is that you two?"

She looked at Josh, then me.

"You definitely seem to have everyone's stamp of approval," Allison observed. She nodded at Melissa, who was grinning at us like a doting aunt.

"Yeah, there's no feud or anything," I said. "It's just, well, I live in California, and Josh is here. I head home in less than a week."

"Ah." Allison nodded. "Well, that's where writing really comes in handy. And an imagination. And an open mind."

Josh and I looked at each other. I didn't know *exactly* what

Allison was talking about, but I had a feeling I should file it away. For later.

Allison adjusted her (vintage!) cat-eye glasses as she peered at the specials board.

"Do you want a piece of pie?" I said, twisting in my seat to see what flavors were left on the board.

"No, I'm looking at that paragraph there at the bottom," Allison said. She read it out loud, which made it sound kind of . . . cool!

"'B. wondered if this was the moment of her destruction. Thayer had discovered the one chink in her armor. Since she was technically an arachnid, that was no mean feat. But he didn't have to be so smug about it! What Thayer didn't know was that B. had almost a dozen lives to spare, and she was tiring of this one anyway.'"

"It's a serial," I said with a shrug. "If you haven't read the rest of it . . ."

"It's your basic hellhound arrives in a small town, gets a job as a waitress, wreaks havoc, and smites the regulars sort of story," Josh provided for her.

Allison looked impressed.

"You've got a voice," she told me. "You've definitely got a voice. Let me ask you this. If you could never write another word . . ."

She paused, waiting for me to fill in the blank.

"Um, I'm having trouble picturing that scenario," I said. "I really don't know what I'd do!"

"Yup." Allison nodded at Josh and picked up her pimento

cheese sandwich. "She's a writer. Oh, she's got it bad."

I felt both proud and terrified as Allison pronounced this about me, like it was a diagnosis. Was it even possible that *I* could someday be like *her*?

I twisted in my seat and took another look at the little passage I'd written about B., the hellhound in an apron.

It was just a paragraph.

But maybe it really was, as Allison said, more than that. It was my voice and no one else's. It was my imagination.

It was, perhaps, the start of something I'd never dared to dream about.

*B*ut first there had to be an ending.

I tried not to dwell on the days ticking away. If anything, the fact that I was leaving very, *very* soon made every minute I had with Josh that much better. I forced myself to enjoy every kiss, every call, every lazy morning lolling together in a boat or on the beach with a cooler full of sodas and a book.

Had it been my fourteenth summer, I'm not sure I would have been able to keep smiling and savoring like that. But this summer I knew not to waste the time we had. I knew to celebrate but not cling. I think that knowledge was another gift I got from Granly, one that hadn't come in a box.

And besides, saying good-bye to Josh might not be good-bye forever. My parents, after shipping home several boxes of letters, photos, and other Granly relics, had decided to keep the cottage.

"At least while Hannah's in school in Chicago," Dad told us, giving Hannah a squeeze. "It'll give us an excuse to come visit her more often!"

"Oh, great," Hannah mock-moaned.

I didn't ask if we would come back to Bluepointe next summer. I didn't want to plan for that or think that far ahead. Because if it didn't happen . . .

Whatever happened with Josh, I realized, wouldn't change the singular miracle that was this summer—the summer I fell in love for the first time. The summer I learned to live without Granly. And the summer when (maybe, just maybe) I first looked in the mirror and saw a writer looking back.

It was even the summer that I started to feel a glimmer of affection for my red curls. After all, I found out on my last night with Josh, it was the hair that had first hooked him.

We'd decided to make our last date a non-date, since that's what we did best. We packed a picnic and took an endless walk on the beach, holding hands and talking—talking fast, as if we could fit it all in. Of course that was impossible. I couldn't imagine an end to the things Josh and I wanted to talk about.

We kept sneaking looks at each other's faces—memorizing.

And of course we kissed. We lay in the sand between tufts of dune grass, the sun pulling away inch by inch, as if drawing a blanket of shadows over us.

It was here that Josh wrapped a handful of my hair around his fingers and groaned.

"I remember the first time I saw this hair of yours," he said.

"It's one of the reasons I acted so freaked out. I'd never seen anything so beautiful."

I started to reach for my automatic I-hate-my-hair response, but then I stopped myself. Because I didn't. Not anymore. How could I hate Granly's legacy? How could I hate something that Josh adored?

"That's why I wanted you to buy this book," Josh said. He reached into the bag that contained our romantic picnic dinner, which we hadn't had the appetite to eat yet. The book he pulled out was wrapped in classic Dog Ear style—plain brown paper with a whimsical tuft of bright ribbons and a stamped image of E.B. with his tongue lolling out.

I opened the wrapper to find *Beyond the Beneath*, the book with the mysterious red-headed mermaid on the cover.

"Oh, I *wanted* this," I breathed, thanking him with a long kiss.

"The whole time we were talking that first day, all I could think about was this book," Josh said. "And that you *had* to read it."

"And then I rejected it," I said with a horrified laugh.

"You were so stubborn," Josh said.

"I was also broke!" I reminded him, kissing the corner of his mouth. "Now, thanks to you, I'm less so."

"Broke or stubborn?" Josh asked.

"Both," I said. I ran my fingers through his hair, loving how every-which-way it was now that it had grown out some.

"You know, I've saved up enough tip money to get myself a new e-reader," I said.

"Are you going to?" Josh asked. He ran a fingertip over my collarbone, making me shiver.

I shook my head.

"I don't think so," I said. "You know, I really like bookstores. Well, one in particular."

Josh smiled—a little wanly.

"It's not going to be the same without you, Chelsea," he said.

"That's a good thing, isn't it?" I asked.

He nodded as he leaned in to kiss me again. And again and again. I only pulled away when I just had to get one more word in. Two tears spilled down my cheeks, but I smiled through them.

"I won't ever be the same either," I told Josh.

It was true. Josh was my first love. Even if I never saw him again, that—he—would always be a part of me.

ACKNOWLEDGMENTS

Many thanks . . .

To Jennifer Klonsky for another whirlwind summer.

To all the friends who shared the south shore of Lake Michigan with me, particularly the Berkelhamer family and "the BC."

To Little Shop of Stories in Decatur, Georgia—the bookstore that inspired Dog Ear.

To my parents, for all the child care and cheerleading.

To my sweet daughters, for understanding when mom is fiction-addled.

And most of all to Paul. Thank you for being there with me every step of the way and for clearing the way for me to write.

*Want more
sweet summer romance?
Here's an excerpt from*

Sixteenth Summer,

also by Michelle Dalton.

The first time you lay eyes on someone who is going to become *someone* to you—*your* someone—you're supposed to feel the earth shift beneath your feet, right? Sparks will course through your fingertips and there'll definitely be fireworks. There are *always* fireworks.

But it doesn't really happen that way. It's messier than that—and much better.

Trust me, I know. I know how it feels to have a *someone*. To be in love.

But the day after my sophomore year ended, I didn't know *anything*. At least, that's the way it feels now.

Let me clarify that. It's not like I was a complete numbskull. I'd just gotten a report card full of A's. And one B-minus. (What can I say. Geometry is my sworn enemy.)

And I knew just about everything there was to know about Dune Island. That's the little sliver of sand, sea oats, and sno-cones off the coast of Georgia where I've lived for my entire sixteen-year existence.

I knew, for instance, where to get the spiciest low-country boil (The Swamp) and the sweetest oysters (Fiddlehead). Finding the most life-changing ice-cream cone was an easy one. You went to The Scoop, which just happened to be owned by my parents.

While the "shoobees" who invaded the island every summer tiptoed around our famously delicate dunes (in their spotless, still-sporting-the-price-tag rubber shoes), I knew how to pick my way through the long, fuzzy grass without crushing a single blade.

And I definitely knew every boy in my high school. Most of us had known one another since we were all at the Little Sea Turtle Play School on the north end of the island. Which is to say, I'd seen most of them cry, throw up blue modeling clay, or stick Cheetos up their noses.

It's hard to fall for a guy once you've seen him with a nostril full of snack food, even if he was only three at the time.

And here's one other thing I knew as I pedaled my bike to the beach on that first night of my sixteenth summer. Or at least, I *thought* I knew. I knew exactly what to expect of the season. It was going to be just like the summer before it, and the summer before that.

I'd spend my mornings on the North Peninsula, where tourists rarely venture. Probably because the sole retail establishment there is Angelo's BeachMart. Angelo's looks so salt-torn and shacky, you'd never know they make these incredible gourmet po'boys at a counter in the back. It's also about the only place on Dune Island where you *can't* find any fudge or commemorative T-shirts.

Then I'd ride my bike south to the boardwalk and spend my afternoon coning up ice cream and shaving ice for sno-cones at The Scoop.

Every night after dinner, Sam, Caroline, and I would call around to find out where everyone was hanging that night. We'd all land at the beach, the deck behind The Swamp, Angelo's parking lot, or one of the other hideouts we'd claimed over the years.

Home by eleven.

Rinse salt water out of hair.

Repeat.

This was why I was trying hard not to yawn as I pedaled down Highway 80. I was headed for the bonfire on the South Shore.

That's right, the *annual* bonfire that kicked off the Dune Island summer, year after year after year.

One thing that kept me alert was the caravan of summer people driving their groaning vans and SUVs just a little too weavily down the highway. I don't know if it was the blazing, so-gorgeous-it-hurt sunset that was distracting them or my gold beach cruiser with the giant bundle of sticks bungeed to the basket. Either way, I was relieved when I swooped off the road and onto the boardwalk.

I tapped my kickstand down and had just started to unhook my pack of firewood when I heard Caroline's throaty voice coming at me from down the boardwalk. I turned with a smile.

But when I saw that Caroline was with Sam—and they were holding hands—I couldn't help but feel shocked for a moment.

In the next instant, of course, I remembered—this was our new normal. Sam and Caroline were no longer just my best friends. They were each other's soul mate.

As of two Saturdays earlier, that was.

I don't know why I was still weirded out by the fact that Sam and Caroline had gotten together that night. Or why I cringed whenever they gazed into each other's eyes or held hands. (Thankfully, I hadn't seen them kissing. Yet.)

Because the Sam-and-Caroline thing? It was really no surprise at all. There'd always been this *thing* between them ever since Sam moved to the island at age eight and settled into my and Caroline's friendship as easily as a scoop of ice cream nests in a cone.

We even joked about it. When Sam made fun of Caroline's raspy voice and she teased him about his gangly height; when she goosed him in the ribs and he pulled her long, white-blond ponytail, I'd roll my eyes and say, "Guys! Get a room."

Both of them would recoil in horror.

"Oh gross, Anna!" Caroline would say, sputtering and laughing all at once.

Inevitably, Sam would respond with another ponytail tug, Caroline would retaliate with a tickle, and the whole song and dance of denial would start all over again.

But now it had actually happened. Sam and Caroline had become a Couple. And I was realizing that I'd kind of *liked* the denial.

Now I felt like I was hovering outside a magical bubble—a shiny, blissed-out world that I just didn't get. Sam and Caroline were inside the bubble. Together.

Soon after they'd first kissed, both of them had assured me that nothing would change in our friendship, which, of course, had changed everything.

Still, Sam and Caroline were sweetly worried about my third-wheel self. And they were clearly giddy over their fresh-hatched love. So I was trying to be supportive. Which meant quickly hoisting my smile back up at the sight of them looking all cute and coupley on the boardwalk.

I eyed their empty hands (the ones that weren't clasped tightly together, that was) and raised one eyebrow.

"Don't tell me you didn't bring firewood," I complained. "I hate being the only one who did her homework."

"Naw," Sam said in his slow surfer-boy drawl. "We already piled it on the beach. The fire's going to be huge this year!"

"We were collecting wood all afternoon," Caroline said sunnily.

I couldn't help it, my smile faded a bit.

I guess this is how it's going to be, I thought. Sam and Caroline collecting firewood is now Sam and Caroline On a Date—third wheel not invited.

Caroline caught my disappointment. Of course she did. Ever since The Kiss, she'd been giving me lots of long, searching looks to make sure I was okay with everything. I was starting to feel like a fish in a bowl.

"We would have called you," she stammered, "but didn't you have sib duty today?"

She was right. I did have to go to my little sister's end-of-the-year ballet recital.

So why did I feel this little twinge of hurt? I'd had countless sleepovers with Caroline that didn't, obviously, include Sam. And Sam and I had a regular ritual of going to The Swamp for giant buckets of crawfish that were strictly boycotted by Caroline. The girl pretty much lived on fruit, nuts and seeds, and supersweet iced tea.

But ever since Sam and Caroline had gotten together, a kernel of insecurity had been burrowing into the back of my head. All I wanted to do was shake it off. But like an especially stubborn sandbur, it wasn't budging.

This is stupid, I scolded myself. *All that matters is that Sam and Caroline still love me and I love them.*

Just not, the whiny voice in my head couldn't help adding, *the mysterious way they love each other.*

I sighed the tiniest of sighs. But then my friends released each other's hands and Sam plucked the firewood bundle out of my arms. He hopped lightly from the boardwalk onto the sand and headed south. Caroline hooked her arm through mine and we followed him. I ordered myself to stop obsessing and just be normal; just be with my friends.

"Cyrus is already *so* drunk," Caroline said with a hearty laugh and an eye roll. "We have a pool going on how early he's going to pass out in the dune grass."

I pulled back in alarm.

"There's beer here?" I asked. "That's, um, not good."

The bonfire was not more than a quarter mile down the beach from The Scoop, where my mom was working the post-dinner rush. And when you make the most to-die-for ice cream on a small island, everybody's your best friend. Which meant, if there was a keg at this party, it would take approximately seventeen seconds for the information to get to my mom.

Luckily, Caroline shook her head.

"No, the party's dry," she assured me. "Cyrus raided his dad's beer cooler before he got here. What an idiot."

Down the beach, just about everybody from our tiny high school was tossing sticks and bits of driftwood onto a steadily growing pyramid. By now, the sun had been swallowed up by the horizon, leaving an indigo sky with brushstrokes of fire around its edges. Against the deep blue glow, my friends looked like Chinese shadow puppets. All I could see were the shapes of skinny, shirtless boys loping about and girls with long hair fanning out as they spun to music that played, distant and tinny, from a small speaker.

But even in silhouette I could recognize many of the people. I spotted Eve Sachman's sproingy halo of curls and Jackson Tate's hammy football player's arms. It was easy to spot impossibly tall Sam. He tossed my firewood on top of the pyre, then waved off the laughter that erupted when most of the sticks tumbled right back down into the sand.

I laughed too, and expected the same from Caroline. She was one of those girls who laughed—no, *guffawed*—constantly.

But now she was silent. So silent, I could swear she was holding her breath. And even in the dusky light, I could see that her heart-shaped face was lit up. Her eyes literally danced and her lips seemed to be wavering between a pucker and a secret smile.

I looked away quickly and gazed at the waves. The moon was getting brighter now, its reflection shimmering in each wave as it curled and crashed. I zoned out for a moment on the sizzle of the surf and the ocean's calming inhale and exhale.

But before I could get really zen, I felt an *umph* in my middle, and then I was airborne.

Landon Smith had thrown his arms around my waist, scooped me up, and was now running toward the waves.

If I hadn't been so busy kicking and screaming, I would have shaken my head and sighed.

This is what happens when you're five feet one inch with, as my grandma puts it, "the bones of a sparrow." People are always patting you on the head, marveling at your size 5 feet, and hoisting you up in the air. My mom, who is all of five feet two and a half, says I might grow a little more, but I'm not betting on it.

Landon stopped short of tossing me full-on into the surf. He just plunked me knee-deep into the waves. Since I was wearing short denim cutoffs and (of course) no shoes, this was a bit of an anticlimax. I looked around awkwardly. Was I supposed to shriek and slap at Landon in that cute, flirty way that so many girls do? I hoped not, because that wasn't going to happen. After a lifetime of tininess, I was allergic to being cute.

I'm not saying I cut my hair with a bowl or anything. I'd actually taken a little extra care with my look for the bonfire. Over my favorite dark cutoffs, I was wearing a white camisole with a spray of fluttery gauze flowers at the neckline. I'd blown out my long, blond-streaked brown hair instead of letting it go wavy and wild the way I usually did. I'd put dark brown mascara on my sun-bleached lashes. And instead of my plain old gold hoop earrings, I was wearing delicate aqua glass dangles that brightened up my slate-blue eyes. (Or so my sister Sophie had told me. She's fourteen and reads fashion sites like some people read the Bible, searching for the answers to all of life's problems.)

While Landon laughed and galloped doggily back onto the dry sand, I said, "Har, har."

But instead of sounding light and breezy, as I'd intended, it came out hard and humorless. Maybe because I was just realizing that Landon's shoulder had gouged me beneath the ribs, leaving a throbbing, bruised feeling. And because everyone was staring at me, their smiles fading just a bit.

I felt heat rush to my face. I wanted to turn back toward the ocean, to breathe in the cloudy, dark blue scent of it and let salt mist my cheeks.

But that would only make everyone think I was *really* annoyed, or worse, fighting back tears.

Which I *wasn't*.

What I was feeling was tired. Not literally. That afternoon I'd downed half a pint of my latest invention, dark chocolate ice cream with espresso beans and creamless Oreo cookies. (I *might* have eaten the cream from the cookies as well.) My brain was buzzing with caffeine and sugar.

But my soul? It was sighing at the prospect of another familiar bonfire. Another same old summer. A whole new round of nothing new.

Except for this restlessness, I thought with a frown.

That *was* new. I was almost sure I hadn't felt this way the previous summer. I remembered being giddy about getting my learner's permit. I dreamed up my very first ice cream flavors, and some of them were even pretty tasty. I graduated from an A cup to a B cup. (I'm pretty sure all growth in that area has halted as well.) And I was thrilled to have three months to bum around with Sam and Caroline. The things we'd always done—hunting for ghost crabs and digging up clams with our toes, eating shaved ice until our lips turned blue, seeing how many people could nap in one hammock at once—had still felt fresh.

But this summer already felt like day-old bread.

I shook my head again and remembered one of those first ice cream flavors: Rummy Bread Pudding.

If I'd turned stale bread into magic once, I could do it again, right?

It was this bit of inner chipperness that finally made me laugh out loud.

Because me channeling Mary Poppins was about as realistic as Caroline singing opera. And life was not ice cream.

Who was I kidding? Nothing was going to change. Not for the next three months, anyway. On Dune Island, summer was the only season that mattered, and this summer, just like all the others, I wasn't going anywhere.

After the bonfire was lit, I rallied, of course. It's hard to be too moody when people are skewering anything from turkey legs to Twinkies and roasting them on a fire the size of a truck.

I'd already toasted up a large handful of marshmallows and was contemplating the wisdom of a fire-roasted Snickers bar when Caroline trotted up to me. Sam was right behind her, of course. Since Caroline didn't like anything that tasted of smoke, she was just drinking this year's Official Bonfire Cocktail: a blueberry-pomegranate slushie garnished with burgundy cherries.

"This was a terrible idea," Caroline said, taking a giant sip of her drink. "Everybody's teeth are turning purple. But *mmmm*, it's so yummy, I can't stop."

She slurped noisily on her straw.

"Real attractive, Caroline," Sam joked. But from the uncharacteristic lilt in his monotone, I could tell he wasn't joking. He really *was* swooning.

Caroline responded by taking another slurp of her slushie, this one so loud it almost drowned out the crackling of the fire.

I threw back my head and laughed.

And then—because what did I care if I had purple teeth in this crowd?—I reached for her plastic cup to steal a sip of the slushie.

"Get your own, Anna!" Caroline teased. Holding her cup above her head, she shuffled backward in the sand, then turned and darted into the surf.

Laughing again, I ran after her, kicking a spray of water at her back. Caroline scurried back up to Sam, still cackling. She threw her free arm around Sam's waist and nestled against him. He slung a long arm around her shoulders. It was such a smooth, natural motion, you'd think they'd been snuggling like that all their lives.

I didn't want them to know that their PDA was making me regret all those marshmallows, so I grinned, waved—and turned my gaze away.

And that's when I saw him.

Will.

Of course, I didn't know his name yet.

At that moment, actually, I didn't know much of anything.

I suddenly forgot about SamAndCaroline. And the too-sweet marshmallow taste in my mouth. And the fact that you don't—you just don't—openly stare at a boy only fifteen yards away, letting long seconds, maybe even minutes, pass while you feast your eyes upon him.

But I couldn't help it. It was like I forgot I had a body. There was no swiping away the long strands of hair that had blown into my face. I didn't worry about what to do with my hands. I didn't cock my hip, scuff my feet in the sand, or make any of my other standard nervous motions.

There were just my eyes and this boy.

His hands were stuffed deep into the pockets of well-worn khakis, which were carelessly rolled up to expose his nicely muscled calves.

His hair—I'm pretty sure it was a chocolaty brown, though it was hard to tell in the shadowy night light—had perfect waves that fluttered in the breeze.

His skin looked a bit pale; hungry for sun. Obviously, he was a summer guy, though (thank God) he wasn't wearing shoes on the beach. And he didn't have that "isn't this all so quaint?" vibe that some vacationers exuded.

Instead, he simply looked comfortable in his skin, washed-out though it might have been. He shot a casual glance at the party milling around the bonfire, then looked down at his feet. He did that thing you do when you're a summer person getting your first delicious taste of the beach. He dug his toes into the sand, kicked a bit at the surf, then crouched down and let the water fizz through his fingers.

He stared at his glistening hand for a moment, as if he was thinking hard about something. Then he looked up—and straight at me.

I wish I could say that I smiled at him. Or gave him a look that struck the perfect balance between curious and cool.

But since I was still floating somewhere outside my body, it's entirely possible that my mouth dropped open and I just kept on *staring* at him.

It's not that he had the face of a god or anything. At first glance, I didn't even think of him as beautiful.

But the squinty softness of his big, dark eyes, the strong angle of his jaw, a nose that stopped just short of being too thin, that swoop of tousled hair, and the bit of melancholy around his mouth—it all made me feel something like déjà vu.

It was like his was the face I'd always been looking for. It was foreign *and* familiar, both in the best way.

Looking at this boy's face made me feel, not that famous jolt of electricity, but something more like an expansion. Like this oh-so-finite Dune Island beach, which I knew so well, had suddenly turned huge. Endless. Full of possibility.

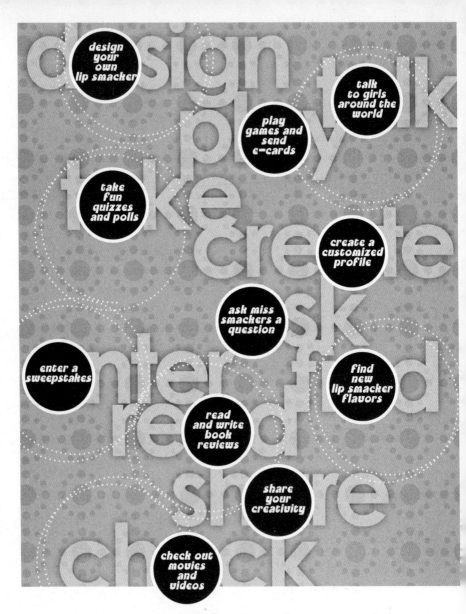

Jammed full of surprises!

LiP SMACKER®
LOUNGE

VISIT US AT WWW.LIPSMACKERLOUNGE.COM!